Playing the Game

Books by M.Q. Barber:

Playing the Game

Crossing the Lines

Healing the Wounds

Playing the Game
A Neighborly Affection Novel

M.Q. Barber

LYRICAL PRESS
Kensington Publishing Corp.
www.kensingtonbooks.com

LYRICAL PRESS BOOKS are published by

Kensington Publishing Corp.
119 West 40th Street
New York, NY 10018

All Kensington titles, imprints, and distributed lines are available at special quantity discounts for bulk purchases for sales promotion, premiums, fund-raising, and educational or institutional use.

Special book excerpts or customized printings can also be created to fit specific needs. For details, write or phone the office of the Kensington Special Sales Manager: Kensington Publishing Corp., 119 West 40th Street, New York, NY 10018. Attn. Special Sales Department. Phone: 1-800-221-2647.

ISBN-13: 978-1-61650-787-9
ISBN-10: 1-61650-787-X

First edition: October 2013

10 9 8 7 6 5 4 3 2 1

Printed in the United States of America

Also available in an electronic edition:

eISBN-13: 978-1-61650-490-8
eISBN-10: 1-61650-490-0

*For all of the encouraging voices that pushed
me to believe in myself, but especially for Dee, who
read every word along the way.*

Playing the Game

Chapter 1

Three flights separated Alice's apartment from the ground floor, but she didn't notice a single step Friday morning. She raced the daylight, as if getting to work sooner would make it end sooner, too. Warp time to deposit her at the dinner with friends she'd anticipated for days. With Henry at the helm, dinner couldn't be less than divine.

She emerged from the stairwell with a growing grin for the man crossing the lobby with sketchbook in hand. A suit and tie, sans coat, though it wasn't eight yet and he didn't have an office to go to. Did he not own jeans?

"Morning, Henry."

"And a good morning to you, Alice. What a beautiful vision for the end of my walk."

She shook her head. He could charm a thief out of robbing him and call it common courtesy. "Out people-watching?"

"Yes, the sunrise first—the sky offered up lovely hues this morning—and then the early morning joggers. Exercise for them, and an exercise in the movement of light and shadow for me. Now it's time to see if Jay has slept through his alarm. Are you off to work, my dear?"

"Got it in one. What gave me away, the basic black pantsuit or the overloaded satchel?" She twirled, knowing he wouldn't take her flirtation as an invitation. Henry had whatever he had with Jay. *The safest sexy guys I know.*

"Simply the time of day and knowledge of your schedule," Henry demurred, his gaze flicking over her form. "Though you do look quite striking in basic black. Have you any plans for the evening?"

He managed to look innocent asking. As if he hadn't left a note on her door a week ago asking for the pleasure of her company.

She lowered her voice to a faux-secretive whisper. "Yeah, with my crazy neighbors. Can you believe this guy? He not only remembers the first anniversary of my move-in date, but he offers to cook dinner to celebrate."

"He sounds like quite the catch." He waggled his eyebrows. "The sort of gentleman who might also remember you often neglect to eat breakfast."

He held out a brown paper bag with a folded-over top.

"You got me breakfast?" She took the bag and peered inside. Apple fritter. Her mouth watered. "My favorite. Careful, or I'll start thinking you're in love with me."

"Oh? And if I declared my undying devotion?" He clasped his sketchpad against his chest. "Here in the lobby, at this very moment? I suppose I could get down on one knee."

She snorted and adopted an airy tone. "Don't be absurd. I insist you don't wrinkle your trousers for me, good sir. Why, it's entirely undignified." She broke off a piece of fritter and took a bite. *Yum.* "Besides, I dumped the last guy who tried that romance crap on me."

"I suppose that would make declaring my love inadvisable." He released a heavy, mocking sigh. "The fritter, however, is acceptable?"

"Delicious." She reached for another bite. "And real. Love's fake. The convenient excuse people give for making stupid decisions. I have a strict no-love policy."

"Ah. Is that why Jay and I haven't seen beaus knocking at your door in months?"

"It's not like I have a no-sex policy. I just keep things short. Simple. Well defined." She popped the fritter piece in her mouth. Chewed. Swallowed. "A couple of months, max. After that, you have to worry about moving in together. Awkward proposals about moving across the country to stay together. Pretty soon, you've been married for years and forgotten how to be your own person."

She wasn't going to end up in that situation and call it love. The word was a four-letter excuse, a chemical reaction tricking the brain into thinking it wanted something it didn't. The way Mom thought she wanted to watch Dad pop pills and forget they'd ever been a happy family. The way her college boyfriend had thought she'd finish her degree at a different school once he graduated.

"Not me," she said. "I avoid love altogether. Thanks for the pastry, though. That, I'm happy to accept."

"You're quite welcome, Alice. Have a lovely day. We'll see you at dinner."

"Seven sharp. I'll be there." She darted outside, waving over her shoulder.

Henry was a nice guy. A good friend. Definitely fuckable. So was his roommate. Boyfriend. Whatever Jay was. She sighed.

That chest. Mmm. Thank God for finding this apartment.

Her old place had screamed slum in a shithole neighborhood waiting on urban revival. The charming atmosphere had kept her tense every night from subway stop to front door. She'd split the rent with three near strangers and squirreled money away.

Leases lurched from August to August in a college town like Boston, and moving day meant a mad scramble for scarce resources. Her roommate's quasi boyfriend coughed up his van with conditions. Fuck if she'd pay the blowjob fee for failing to get the van back on time and undamaged.

The hungry parking meter, though, sucked down quarter after quarter. The faster she got everything upstairs, the less money she'd spend. A few cars puttered past at school-zone speeds, and even fewer pedestrians meandered by on Saturday strolls.

A guy on a bike turned the corner down the block. He rode slow, lazy maybe, or cooling down after a workout.

She pulled open the van, its innards packed to the roof, and hoisted a box in both arms.

"Soonest started, soonest finished," she muttered, hustling toward her new home from the closest parking spot she'd found, about three buildings down.

The grinding *whirr* of backpedaling heralded the cyclist on the far side of the parked cars lining the street. She looked away, passed four more cars and glanced left. The cyclist had kept pace as she approached her door.

"Something I can help you with?"

"Looks the other way around to me." He hopped off the bike, hefted it over one arm and joined her on the sidewalk. "Moving in?"

She wasn't above ogling bike boy's tight shorts and the sweat-wicking shirt hugging his biceps. Telling a strange man where she lived and inviting him up, however, contradicted common sense no matter how much his body reminded her she hadn't gotten laid in months.

She yanked open the outer door and resettled the box as it rocked in her arms. Stepping into the mailbox vestibule, she fumbled for the keychain dangling from her belt loop.

"Here, let me."

Alice stepped back against the bank of mailboxes, about to go off on this arrogant ass who thought he'd follow her in and charm his way into feeling her up. Until he produced his own key and unlocked the inner door.

"We can prop that open, you know, so moving won't be such a hassle."

She envied his athletic grace as he balanced the bike over one shoulder and held the door.

"Thanks. That's, umm, I'll do that."

He nodded. She stared.

"Ladies first."

Oops. He'd been waiting on her.

"I mean, I can hold the door all day. I don't have any plans, and my muscles are totally up to it. I don't want you to doubt that, but eventually somebody's gonna need to open their mailbox."

"Sorry, I was . . . yeah. How about I go in now?" She hurried past, catching a whiff of clean male sweat. How far had he ridden this morning?

The stairs beckoned, back and to the right.

The door clicked closed, and footsteps on the stairs echoed her own. They followed her down the hallway toward her studio, where she'd left the door cracked. She pinned bike boy with an over-the-shoulder stare.

"I'm giving off stalker vibe, right? Sorry. I'm across the hall. Jay. I'd offer to shake hands, but, well, bike." He jostled the bike on his right shoulder. "And you've got—" He gestured at her with the other hand. "Whatever's in the box, so . . ."

"Alice," she said. "Ignore me, I'm paranoid. But I should get going. I have to finish moving before the van's owner decides I owe him an overage charge." She repressed a shudder. No way in hell was she paying the on-your-knees fees. "Nice meeting you, though."

"Of course." He grinned and winked. "It's always nice meeting me. People tell me that all the time."

He slipped past her toward the door on the other side of the hall and disappeared inside.

She used the box to push the door open wide. Cute guy, but full of himself. She wasn't looking right now anyway. No harm in *looking*, though, right?

She set the box in the center of the tiny space. One down, two dozen to go. Plus the furniture, though hers consisted of a futon, a battered trunk, and a floor lamp.

Leaving the door open, she tromped downstairs, pacing herself so she wouldn't run out of steam. At least moving out hadn't required navigating stairs. A search of the lobby floor turned up a cracked brick to prop the inner door.

Her stomach growled as she scooped another box from the van and made for the door. She bobbled the box against her left arm, stretching out her right hand. She hadn't found the handle yet when the door opened.

"Okay there, Alice? I thought we were gonna prop this puppy open." Jay, bikeless, still wore riding clothes.

Wait, we? He wanted to help? Either he was hard up or she looked like the most pathetic, desperate girl in town. Even friends demanded bribes to tote boxes. This guy had known her all of five minutes.

"Yeah, I haven't grabbed anything for this door yet. But you don't—I mean, I'm fine. I've got everything handled."

"Okay. Sure." He nodded. "You should get out of the sun. That fair skin's already pinking up."

She slid past him, her leg brushing his, her shoulder grazing his chest. They'd be neighbors for the next year at the least. Would this Jay be a nice guy or a creep? She crossed her fingers and hoped for the former.

"Thanks for holding the door."

He shrugged. "I was on my way out."

"Oh! Okay." God, she'd assumed he was offering to help. Fuck it. He hadn't seemed offended, and worrying would be a waste of time. "See you around."

"Yep, I'm sure you will. I'm hard to miss."

She shook her head, trying not to encourage his egotistical comedy antics, and climbed the stairs once more. The place mimicked a free gym with all the stair-mastering she could handle and then some.

She set the second box beside the first, two brown cubes in a bare white room. The August heat made the room stuffy. She unsnapped the latches on the windows and raised the lower panes. The view showcased the alley where a handful of residents paid exorbitant fees for unmetered parking, but the breeze satisfied.

A knock came from behind her, three firm raps, and an unfamiliar male voice followed.

"Alice?"

A man stood in her doorway. Mid-thirties, maybe a little older, neatly trimmed light brown hair, smartly dressed in dark gray slacks and a pale blue button-down shirt. Oddly out-of-place sandals.

"Can I help you?"

"My apologies. You must, of course, be Alice, quite as Jay described you. I'm Henry. I share the apartment across the hall with Jay. I thought I might introduce myself and invite you over for a snack. Lunch, if you'd prefer. Moving is draining work. I try to avoid it myself."

"What, moving or work?" *Wonder if this Henry knows he's living with a serial flirt.*

He raised an eyebrow. "Touche. Both, in fact. But you won't tempt me into a doorway discussion, neighbor. I insist we get acquainted properly over a meal."

He was without a doubt the most formal man she'd ever met. He wasn't even crossing the line of the door. Weird, but sweet. Timid? Courteous? Fuck. She didn't want a bad start with her neighbors.

"I'd love to, but I'm in the middle of the whole moving thing, and I need to get it done first. I have to return the van today."

"Oh? I don't see how that's a problem. Have you run into Jay? He was supposed to—"

"Stand aside, coming through!" Jay's voice rang through the hallway at full volume.

Henry stepped back.

"Really, Jay?" Henry wore a small smile as he shook his head.

Jay came through the door with two boxes piled in his arms and set them beside the others.

"You're not wearing a shirt," she blurted, too busy ogling his chest to censor herself.

He was well muscled, for sure. Firm. Lean and very, very firm. Willpower alone kept her eyes, but not her thoughts, above his waist.

"Yes, Jay, by all means, explain how you lost your shirt between here and the curb. I'm dying to know, and I'd wager our new neighbor is as well."

Henry returned to the doorway, standing with ridiculously perfect posture. Would asking if he'd taken ballet be rude?

Jay flashed her a smile. "Wadded up as a doorstop." He turned toward Henry. "We had one stop for two doors, so—you know how much I love math. Back in a minute with more. Shouldn't you be putting lunch on the table? I'm absolutely killing this move. Forty-five minutes, an hour, tops."

He disappeared before Alice wrapped her head around the idea.

She scurried to the door and popped her head out. No dice.

"Wait, he's—I should—I can move my stuff myself."

"Of course you can."

Wow. She gripped the doorframe as Henry spoke inches from her ear. His smooth voice made her want to drink it in.

"You appear quite fit. But you'll remove a source of ridiculous male pride if you don't allow Jay to complete the lion's share of the task. Did you pack the vehicle yourself?"

She laughed, stepping back to put space between them.

"If you knew my old roommates, you wouldn't have to ask. I woke up at eight to load the van, and at that hour, on a Saturday? They have three states: asleep, hungover or still drunk. Today I had two sleepers and one angry hangover victim telling me to can the noise."

"Not one lifted a finger?"

She shook her head. After two years with her roommates, she'd probably interacted with them less than she had with her new neighbors in the first twenty minutes.

"Well, then, you see? You've already accomplished more than half of the work. Jay will simply do the rest."

"He doesn't even know me. I should—"

"Nonsense." Henry gestured her into the hall. "You've worked all morning. You ought to sit down and have a drink. Water? Lemonade? Iced tea?"

She glanced toward the staircase and then in the other direction, past his welcoming arm. She didn't know this guy, not either of these guys, and she was going to saunter into their apartment like some horror-movie idiot opening the basement door?

"I can bring the food to you, if you prefer. I would hate for our new neighbor to feel herself a fly walking into my parlor."

"Why, are you a spider?" She winced at the unintentional flirtation in her tone.

"I wouldn't think so, no, but then wouldn't I tell you the same thing if I were?" He raised an eyebrow. His lips twitched.

"You've got the charming part down well enough."

It *was* nearly lunchtime. She didn't want to carry boxes all afternoon. Was it too damsel-in-distress to give the job to a cute neighbor? It wasn't as if she'd coerced him. She hadn't been in distress or pretended to be. Jay was thoughtful, or something.

She narrowed her eyes at Henry. "I guess I'll have to trust this isn't a trap and you guys don't kill undesirable neighbors on their first day in the building."

"Oh, no, not the first day. We prefer to let them settle in first. Today, you're perfectly safe. Though whoever called you undesirable was quite mistaken." He frowned and waved a hand. "I apologize for how such a statement could be misconstrued. It appears Jay's habits are rubbing off on me."

Considering her ex-roommates' habits, neighbors with a predilection for charm held incomparable appeal. Especially if they were single.

"He does seem to be a flirt," she agreed.

"When he wants to be," Henry said. "But now we've been standing in the doorway entirely too long, and I haven't—"

"Seriously?" Jay's voice boomed from the stairs. "I'm back with two more boxes—told you I was killing it—and you haven't gotten Alice a drink? You're slipping, Henry. She might die of thirst."

Alice stepped into the hall, following Henry out of Jay's way. "I'm not dying of thirst. But if you're determined to show off your macho skills, I'll go have that lemonade. I've never played Southern belle before. I think I need a veranda and a fan."

"An excellent suggestion." Henry's arm moved as though he intended to sweep it against her back and carry her along with him, but stopped short.

She itched with the desire to lean back and find out how his touch felt.

"Jay, when you've finished, join us for lunch on the roof deck."

"Aye-aye, Cap'n." Jay winked at Alice, lowering his voice to a faux-whisper as he approached her door. "Consider it payment for moving the boxes. Keep Henry company while he waxes melodic about lettuce or something. Please. You'll be doing me a favor."

She glanced at Henry's expression, a sort of resigned fondness, as though Jay had said something expected. Hiding her smile, she matched Jay's tone. "What an astonishing coincidence. He said the same thing about you when he asked me to please find enough boxes to occupy you all afternoon."

Jay's face blanked for a moment before he laughed. He kept laughing, deposited the boxes beside the others and bent over with his hands on his knees, whooping for breath.

"It wasn't that funny," Alice muttered, but Henry, too, seemed to struggle not to chuckle.

Jay straightened. "Five minutes and she's got your number, Henry. You better watch out, or she'll have all of your secrets out of you before lunch is served."

She smiled the small, cautious smile of the unsure. She'd definitely missed the joke here.

Henry spoke up beside her, "Mmm. I see the two of you will be dangerous together. Jay, to the boxes. Alice, this way, please."

She let Henry guide her into his apartment. He left the door open behind them. A deliberate attempt to put her at ease? Whatever his reason, it worked.

She scanned the apartment twice. Blinked hard. Either her neighbors made serious cash, or they were up to their eyeballs in debt. The other floors squeezed in four or five apartments, but this one held her studio and their palace. She was paying twelve hundred a month for less than a quarter the space.

Maybe Jay was a wealthy millionaire playboy and Henry his faithful lunch-making butler. *I live next door to Batman.* She stifled a giggle.

Jay's bike hung on hooks near the door. A hall led left, to bedrooms, probably. Henry gestured her to the right. The foyer opened up into a living room, dining room and kitchen, all in a row, the three together larger than her entire apartment.

"You neglected to place a drink order earlier, Alice. Shall I repeat the choices?"

"No, lemonade sounds great. It's warm out there." Not in the men's apartment, though. Nine windows brought in the breeze and the view. Mature trees shaded smaller homes in neighboring blocks. "Are you sure Jay won't get sunstroke after all the biking and box-carrying and stair-climbing?"

Henry gestured her to a bar-height seat at the kitchen island. She sat while he fetched and poured. Homemade lemonade, judging by the slices floating in it.

"He'll be fine, I'm certain, though you're kind to worry for him."

She drained half the glass, embarrassed by her own eagerness. "Guess I was thirstier than I thought. That's good lemonade."

"You share Jay's sweet tooth, I expect."

Henry stood across the counter from her. One of his hands rested on the black granite speckled with blue-and-white glints like stars, as though she stared into the night sky and might tumble into space. Would his hand catch her?

"Now, before I begin preparing lunch, is there anything I ought to know about your preferences? Vegetarian? Vegan? Allergies?"

She shook off her odd thoughts. "No, no and no. But I should go move my stuff. Jay shouldn't have to go to all that trouble for me."

Henry tipped his head, lips pursed as he studied her. He raised his right hand, index finger extended, and though he'd moved slowly, she was surprised when his finger lay against her lips as if he were shushing a child. A gesture that might've seemed offensive or patronizing didn't. Henry shook his head and removed his finger.

"The proper tool for the proper job, my dear. Your fortuitous arrival provides an opportunity for Jay to work off his abundance of excess energy."

"Moving is hard work. Nobody has that much extra energy."

The sound of bouncing feet on hardwood called her a liar, and she waited for Jay's latest witty or flirtatious contribution.

"What, not on the roof yet? You're slacking, Henry. And I lost my audience."

Alice twisted in the chair to look over her shoulder.

Jay made ridiculous puppy-dog eyes at her. "You didn't see me carry that last load. Three boxes. I should start a moving company."

"Perhaps, Jay. Though Alice has questioned your ability to complete the task. I believe she feels your stamina is lacking."

Her cheeks heated. She whipped her head around to face Henry. "That's not—I didn't—thanks *a lot*, Henry."

"You're quite welcome, Alice." His expression didn't flicker.

"Ludicrous," Jay said. "I have so much stamina it's oozing out of my pores."

"Best get a mop, then. The custodial staff shouldn't be forced to deal with your overeager excretions."

"Pfft. Going now. I better see actual food in progress when I come back. Hardworking boys need their meat, Henry. I deserve it, don't I?"

"I'm certain I'll find something to pay proper tribute to your excellent efforts as an aspiring moving business mogul."

Jay's footsteps faded and Henry began pulling dishes from various places around the kitchen.

"Is he always so . . ." What was the diplomatic way to ask if a man was a half-trained puppy who needed frequent pats on the head?

"Eager for praise?" Henry glanced up and smiled. "Always. It's his most endearing trait."

Alice sipped her lemonade while Henry bustled around the kitchen, their conversation punctuated by Jay's cheerful interruptions and progress reports.

Henry did, indeed, wax melodic, though not about lettuce. He extolled the desirable qualities of fresh mozzarella, its softness, moisture content, spreadability. He detailed varieties of heirloom tomatoes and grades of olive oil.

By the time he set a Caprese salad in front of her and invited her to help herself, she'd had a thorough education in every step of its preparation. She'd never enjoyed being in the kitchen quite so much as she had with Henry.

She was eating a slice of tomato slathered with semisoft cheese and sprinkled with fresh-chopped basil when Jay slung his body into the seat beside her. Bare-chested still, he'd draped his shirt over his left shoulder.

He sat eight or nine inches from her, and the overwhelming scent of pure male taunted her. The woodsy smell of his deodorant or bodywash. The deeper note of his sweat daring her to lick his neck and taste the salt of his skin. *Fuck. Rein it in, Alice.*

"That's one load done." Jay wiped his face with his shirt. "It is seriously hot out. Sahara Desert hot."

Henry looked up from trimming steaks for shish kebabs. He glanced at the window, and she followed his gaze. A small digital thermometer clung to the glass.

"Yes, eighty-three degrees. An inferno."

She couldn't tell from his even tone whether Henry was serious or subtly mocking Jay, but she suspected he had a dry sense of humor. She loaded her voice with her best rural twang. "Y'all cain't hardly be jawin' on this here spell o' cold weather. Shucks, it ain't even hit a hunnerd yet."

Both men turned startled faces to her. She picked up another slice of tomato and bit down.

Henry showed a raised eyebrow and a hint of a smile.

Jay nudged her with his elbow. "Well?"

She swallowed.

"South Dakota. And no, we don't all sound like that."

She popped the rest of the slice in her mouth.

Jay reached past her to snag the plate and a tomato slice of his own. "You wanna have lunch before we pick up the rest?"

Alice finished chewing. "The rest?"

"Yeah, you know, the rest." One hand, thankfully not the one holding a tomato slice, waved vaguely. "More boxes? Table, chairs, dresser? Whatever. I can run over with you and help load. It'll go faster." He popped the entire slice into his mouth.

"There isn't any more. I need to take the van back, is all."

Jay stared.

She turned her attention to the appetizer, took her time choosing a third slice.

"Oh. New plan, then. We all have lunch, and Henry follows you with the car while you drop off the moving van and I get some stuff out of storage." Jay's head moved in her peripheral vision. He raised his voice. "I'm thinking that two-seater table and chairs and the small chest of drawers, Henry. You know the ones?"

"Yes, of course." Henry cubed the meat with precision as he spoke. "Alice might like the vanity and bench as well, though perhaps we ought to let her decide before we leave to return the van."

"Wait, wait. You two have already moved me in and fed me. I'm not a stray cat. I'm fine with the furniture I have."

"Jay?" Henry hadn't even looked up.

"A futon, a trunk and a lamp. Unless she's building the rest out of cardboard boxes."

"Unacceptable." Henry stopped working and met her eyes. "Jay and I have furnishings doing nothing but gathering dust in storage. The unfortunate result of merging two households. Please. I would be grateful if you provided a use for them again."

How had he made their generosity to her feel as though it worked the other way around? As though she'd be offending them if she said no?

"I . . . thanks. That would be great."

"Lovely. We'll eat first, if that suits, Alice." Henry filled two trays and draped dishtowels over the top. "The roof deck has both a grill and a breeze to recommend it."

"Fantastic." Jay stood. "The meter on the van's good for another four hours."

One more thing she'd have to owe him.

"And I'm starving."

Alice held in a laugh as Henry gave Jay the once-over. His eyebrows rose, and his nose wrinkled.

"Shower first, Jay, and fresh clothes. With a shirt this time, please. You've inundated us with your scent long enough. Alice will think we're unmannered louts, if she doesn't already."

Jay sighed heavily and feigned a pout as he trudged away. "Shower. Shirt. Anything else?"

"I'm sure you'll manage to think of everything, Jay." Henry winked at Alice. "And you'll be quick about it, or Alice and I will have finished the skewers."

Given the amount of meat he'd piled on the plate, Henry's threat was in vain.

"Yeah, us South Dakota girls can pack away the cow cubes. I might save you a slice of red pepper if you're good."

Henry smiled at her as Jay disappeared around the corner, mumbling about gangs of kitchen bullies with oversensitive noses.

"If I may prevail upon you to carry a tray, we'll adjourn to the roof and start the grill while Jay washes up."

They worked at the grill in comfortable silence, chatting rarely until the door swung open and Jay barreled out, his dark hair wet and dripping on his shirt.

"Did I miss lunch? Is there any left?"

Alice ducked her head to hide her smile. "The most charming eleven-year-old boy I've ever met," she muttered.

Henry let out a soft laugh.

"An excellent description of Jay, to be sure," he murmured. "Though his physique, thankfully, reflects his proper age."

Well, that answered that. Her neighbors were so totally a couple.

Henry raised his voice to a normal volume. "You might have taken the time to dry your hair, Jay. The skewers will be another minute."

"Oh." Jay flopped on a chaise and sighed, an overdramatic gust.

"I'll rest until the food's ready, then. I worked extra-hard moving those boxes. Not that I couldn't handle it. My stamina is massive."

God, if he weren't taken, she'd be all over that, tickling his ribs and straddling his thighs.

Alice flushed the instant she caught Henry watching her.

He tipped his head toward Jay, returned her uncertain smile with a tiny nod, and clapped his hands once.

"Let's get some food on the table, shall we?"

They ate with hands reaching and elbows bumping and Jay stealing pieces from both of their plates. She learned Henry was a well-respected oil painter. Jay owned a messenger service but preferred bike runs to paperwork. She described her work as a mechanical engineer, drafting and design in the office with a team.

Henry, it turned out, was thirty-seven, a little older than she'd thought. Jay was twenty-eight going on twelve, just under eighteen months older than she.

At least Henry didn't mind her ogling his boyfriend over lunch. Unless he was trying to set her up with his roommate. *Which is it, Henry, boyfriend or wingman?*

She drove with an abundance of caution to avoid losing Henry and to control the unfamiliar beast that was Duffy's van. They'd left Jay after lunch with her apartment key, the building's hand truck, and his assurances he'd get the chosen furniture out of storage with no problem.

Well, that and Henry's promise he'd stop for ice cream in Coolidge Corner and bring Jay back "something good."

Fortune smiled on her with a parking space in front of her old building. She fed the meter while Henry slipped into a space down the block. The length in his stride and the breadth of his chest quickened her pulse as he approached.

"This won't take a minute. I just need to run in."

"It's no trouble, Alice. Please, take your time." He scanned the street, no doubt noting the differences she had when she'd hunted for a new apartment.

Goodbye, litter. Goodbye, bars with heavy foot traffic in the middle of the afternoon. Goodbye, flickering neon sex-shop sign.

He turned back to her with a neutral expression. "I'll escort you inside."

She was tempted to ask whether he worried for her safety or his own. She wouldn't blame him for not wanting to stand on this street, but inviting him in made her stomach squirm. His apartment with Jay screamed pristine elegance. Not even a throw pillow out of place. Her old place . . . well.

"Hey, it's your funeral. Just, uh, watch where you step and try not to touch anything. For your own safety." She forced a smile and opened the outer door.

The mailbox vestibule smelled of cat urine. Probably cat urine. Hopefully cat urine.

"You might want to hold your breath, too."

Henry kept his silence as she unlocked the inner door. He held the door for her and followed her down the hall without commenting about the peeling paint or the burned-out bulbs. She almost wished he would, even if his words were scathing.

She unlocked the apartment's three locks and shoved hard with her shoulder. "The door sticks sometimes." Why did she feel she needed to apologize to Henry?

Her foot struck a beer can. She looked toward the sounds of gun-fire. "Hey, Miles."

The man on the couch grunted, staring at the oversize television set. Soldiers in camouflage crouched behind objects on the screen, periodically popping out to fire. "Yeah, hey, Al."

"Winning?"

"Fuck no." His voice raised. "*Some* people can't get their asses in gear and take out that fucking bunker."

He was talking into the headset to his gaming squad. Typical. No point in introducing Henry. "Karen or Duffy around?"

Miles laughed. "You can't hear the moaning? They must be taking a break. No, you fuckwit, I'm not talking to you, I'm talking to the chick in my living room. Yes there is. *Yes*, there is. Fuck you, too. Shoot the damn enemy."

"I'm leaving my apartment keys on the kitchen table, Miles. Don't forget, okay?"

"Sure, Al. Keys on the table."

He'd forget. Karen would see them, at least. But she needed to put the van keys in Duffy's hand, or he'd be fucking pissed and calling her cell at one in the morning when he was half-drunk and couldn't find them.

She looked down the hallway to the bedrooms. The door to the last room, hers and Karen's, was closed. Her new neighbor was doing her a huge favor to be here at all.

He stood unmoving by the door, either disgusted by the apartment or mindful of her warning not to touch anything.

"Sorry. Two minutes, I swear."

She scurried down the hall and banged on the door.

"Duffy! You in there?"

Silence. She leaned closer. No, not silence. The screech of bed-springs. Great. Well, she wasn't waiting all fucking day.

Alice shoved the door half-open.

Duffy knelt behind Karen on the bed, fucking her doggy-style.

Karen dragged her head up from her arms. "What the—"

Alice jangled the keys, attracting their attention like she might wave a chew toy for a dog.

"Yo, Duffy. Keys." She tossed them, underhand, and he swiped them out of the air without missing a beat. Good sense of rhythm. Benefits of fucking a musician? Alice shook her head and smirked. "Van's out front. Meter's good for thirty minutes."

Karen laughed. "More than long enough for studly here."

Duffy leaned down, his chest covering Karen's back. "Just for that, I'll make it *three*."

"Thanks for the loan." Alice stepped back, pulling the door with her. "See ya."

Shit. Henry had stepped farther into the living room, with a per-fect view down the hall. A view that thirty seconds ago had included Karen and Duffy fucking. Way to make a terrible impression on her neighbor.

Fuck if she'd apologize. Sex wasn't anything shameful. She crossed the space between, about to apologize anyway, because her relaxed boundaries didn't mean Henry needed the image of strangers fucking shoved in his head, but he spoke first.

"Ready to make your last exit?"

She scrutinized his face. If her behavior or her ex-roommate's had bothered him, it didn't show. Courteous neutrality. *I'll see your courtesy and raise you a smile, Henry.*

"You bet. Thanks for coming along. Saves me a long subway ride."

Henry snapped his arm out, elbow crooked, and bent toward her. "Shall we, then?"

She stared at him, a single chuckle escaping, and called a goodbye to Miles before wrapping her hand around Henry's arm. "Lead the way, my good man."

Duffy's excited shout followed them out the door. Three minutes. Poor Karen.

Chapter 2

Alice blamed Henry for her uncharacteristic distraction at work all day. If his dinner plans hadn't reminded her of the anniversary, she wouldn't be devoting so much mental space to walking through the last year on memory lane.

She'd been distracted, in those first few weeks, by trying to puzzle out the status of her neighbors' relationship. When she teased Jay about what a cute couple he and Henry made, he hammed it up with boyish charm.

"It's not Henry, Alice, it's me. I make every couple cute." Jay slung his arm around her. "Adorable, right? Wait, where's a mirror?"

When she asked Henry how long he and Jay had been *together*, he was matter of fact.

"Jay moved in nearly three years ago, Alice. He's quite tolerable as a roommate, despite his unseemly boisterousness."

Jay's crab-walking across the roof deck at the time made discerning whether Henry was being dryly sarcastic and twitting him or making a definitive statement about his roommate difficult, if not impossible. A roommate proving something about balancing beer bottles on his abdominal muscles. The precise reason why escaped her, but she wasn't about to ask since the show was free.

She scored a closer look at their apartment when they invited her over for dinner and a movie a few weeks later. Beautiful paintings lined the left side of the hall, including one of a sculpted back she was almost certain was Jay's. The sort to make a girl want to reach out and touch.

Three doors came before the bathroom, the first closed and the second open on a chaotic mess. Jay's bedroom, definitely.

The third matched her impression of Henry's taste. Classy. Den-like. Dark, heavy furniture dominated by an enormous bed. Hello, brandy and cigars. Hello, Henry's deep voice and heavy stare. Hello, fantastic orgasms on high-quality sheets.

Whoa. She stifled a laugh at her outlandish thoughts and hurried into the bathroom before Henry caught her staring into his bedroom.

But after she crawled under the covers on her futon that night, vibrator in hand, it was Henry's bed behind her eyelids when she came.

Fuck. I need to get laid.

The months passed. She finally got laid in December thanks to a bar trivia night out with a couple of coworkers. Not either of the coworkers, God no, but the smart guy at the next table who joined their team. Brandon. Mediocre sex, but human contact won priority over her vibrator, at least for two months. After that, he was more trouble than he was worth. Keeping a lackluster boyfriend through Valentine's Day was begging for problems. She gave him a nice it's-not-you-it's-me blowjob as a going away present. Blowjobs made breakups easier for guys to swallow than speeches did, in her experience.

Seven months of fantasizing hadn't yet answered the question dogging her. Single again, and she didn't know if Henry or Jay would be open to some fun. If they were committed to each other the way they seemed to be, dropping a hint might lose her their friendship, and she didn't make lasting friends easily.

"I want to fuck them." She shoved her covers down with her toes. Post-masturbation sweat, a radiator running hot and a heavy comforter were a little much, even in February. "Either of them. Both of them. Because they are sexy and sweet and not knowing is killing me, and I'm too polite to ask. Because if they haven't flat-out said they're a couple by now, either they aren't or they're in the closet and it's none of my business. Except in my fantasies."

She let loose a frustrated growl. *My maybegayboys don't like to make things easy for a girl.*

When March rolled around, Jay clued her in about Henry's upcoming birthday and invited her over for the occasion.

"You know, wine. Birthday singing. Cake. Store-bought, I'm not making it, so don't worry."

Texts flurried between them as she tried to decide on a gift when gift-buying wasn't in her budget. She settled on a birthday card and a promise in the form of a floor plan sketched on heavy cardstock inside.

Henry looked perplexed but pleased upon opening it. His fingers ran along the edges of the inner card repeatedly as he turned it this way and that.

"This is the layout of the MFA building. You drew it?"

She tried not to let nerves get the better of her. Her offer wasn't a present, exactly, but she didn't know what kind of art supplies he used, he owned everything he needed in the kitchen, and God forbid she try to dress him. He dressed better than she did anyway. And she couldn't afford those things. But her time, well, that she could give him.

"From a reference." She'd studied the Museum of Fine Arts floor plan online. "Jay says you go there a lot."

"I do."

"By yourself."

He'd also said Henry had a membership to get other people in free, too. She'd lived in Boston since starting college, more than eight years now, and hadn't set foot inside.

"Yes."

"But you like to teach, and I've never been."

"Are you offering yourself up as my pupil, Alice?" Henry leaned forward, his elbows resting on the table. "For the entire day?"

"Dangerous, I know, but yes. I think it'll be fun." She shrugged as if his reaction didn't matter. "But if you don't want to—"

"On the contrary, I very much do want to. Shall we say next Saturday?"

She agreed, and Henry opened his present from Jay. A succession of gag gifts, each one worse than the last. A t-shirt with "Munch makes me want to Scream" on the front and an image of the famous painting on the back. Another read "Artists do it with a broad brush and a fine tip." Jay and Alice were breathless with laughter by the time Henry reached the end and thanked Jay for his thoughtfulness in getting him fresh cleanup rags.

The following Saturday, Alice fake-pouted at Henry on their way to the museum.

"You're not wearing one of your gifts. Jay must be so disappointed."

"Alas, they're covered in paint." Henry shook his head in mock sorrow. "A tragic, tragic accident."

"Accident. Uh-huh." She wondered what Jay had actually gotten Henry for his birthday.

They spent all day at the museum. Henry took her arm the moment they stepped inside and held her enraptured for the next six hours. They never made it past the European collection.

Every painting prompted a discussion, and they weren't lectures from expert to novice. He asked detailed questions about her thoughts on composition and color and theme. Invited her to consider the intersection of their worlds, of engineering and artistry.

"Where do you find beauty, Alice?"

"Clean lines. Efficient output." She narrowly missed his shoulder with her chin as she turned. "Not that I'm not enjoying this, because you make it fascinating."

He patted her arm. "Yes, yes. Sops to my ego aside, tell me what beauty is to *you*. My aesthetic is in the form of things. The look, captured in a single moment. But for you?"

"I like it when things fit. Everything has a place, and it contributes to every other piece in the whole. The structure is disciplined and orderly. It has its own . . . music, I guess. Rhythm. And together they all work. And when it's seamless, effortless, when they create or accomplish something together, when everything is in the perfect place, that's beautiful."

"It's important to you they work smoothly together, then. Not merely the facsimile of it, the empty shell." Henry nodded, his voice slightly distant. "Harmonious function. You find beauty in understanding where things belong. How they come together as one. Everything has a place. Hmm. And do you define that place, Alice?"

"At work? Sure, for whatever section of the problem I'm assigned to tackle. I work up my design and bring it to the team. The team leader helps us coordinate a way to bring those designs together. Harmonious function, like you said."

"A hierarchy, then. You define a place for the objects, and your leader defines a place for you."

"I guess so. Isn't that what a boss is supposed to do?"

They'd gone a fair distance from defining beauty. She rolled her shoulders. Where was he going with this?

Henry chuckled. "I'm afraid I wouldn't know. I've never had one."

He guided her out of the gallery. "They'll be closing soon. I hope I haven't kept you too long today. It's early yet, but perhaps you'd care for dinner out?"

A quick bit of mental math. Henry and Jay were the closest things she had to best friends. Splurging on one dinner wouldn't break the bank, so long as they didn't go overboard. It would just set back her budgeting schedule a smidge.

"You bet. Where am I taking you?"

He glanced at her with one eyebrow raised. "My treat, my dear."

"No, this is your birthday present. If we're going to dinner, I'm buying." She was prepared to be stubborn. Recipients didn't pay for their gifts.

"Ah, but this isn't within the scope of your gift to me, Alice. This is the transparent ploy of a man feeling his age, enjoying the attentive company of an attractive younger woman and hoping to extend that time in a public setting to boost his own ego. Please, allow me to take you to dinner."

They stepped out into the cloudy chill of early March. She fumbled to get her mittens on, and Henry tucked the ends of her scarf at her throat. His fingers, encased in dark brown driving gloves, smelled of leather as he raised the scarf over her nose.

She blinked, shivering from his touch rather than the cold, and forced a laugh. "Fine. Your treat. Do people ever tell you you're honest to a fault, Henry?"

"Honesty is important to me, Alice. Lies can be dangerous, painful things, both for those who lie and those to whom they lie."

"Sounds personal."

"Mmm. Too personal for today, perhaps."

Jay's birthday arrived on the horizon in June, though she needed no clue from Henry, since Jay mentioned the fact from mid-May onward. Her office came through with the perfect free gift.

"But my birthday's not for another three weeks." Jay grinned at the cupcake with its lone candle. "Am I getting one of these every day until my birthday?" He jumped out of his seat and hugged her. "Sugar! The perfect gift."

"Sit down and eat your cupcake, you crazy person. That's not your gift, and you're not getting any more unless Henry has plans he hasn't mentioned."

They both looked at Henry, who shook his head with perfect innocence.

"What's my gift, then?" Jay sat back in his chair, blew out the candle and took a bite that encompassed half the cupcake. "I made a wish, so it better come true."

"My company's having an employee field day next Friday. If you wanted to take off—"

"You want me on your team?" Jay preened, puffing out his chest. "It's because I'm such a hot athlete, isn't it."

"Yup," she agreed. "That's it exactly. I thought I'd parade you in front of my coworkers, win some trophies and earn my team's adulation for bringing in a ringer."

"I'm totally there. Sign me up."

She added Jay's name to the list as her "plus one," which for some of her teammates was plus three or four, since families were welcome. They did win some events, though not the piggyback race. Jay allowed a huffing and puffing father with his cheering six-year-old daughter on his back to pass them once Alice whispered in his ear that he was her boss.

A mournful Jay set her back on her feet.

"But now you won't get the prize, Alice. What will you cuddle at night?"

She eyed the oversize stuffed tiger clutched in the child's hands and nearly dragging on the ground. "I don't think that thing would even fit in my bed."

"You need to find a bigger bed, then." Jay tapped his finger on his nose. "I know! I'll make room in mine. Problem solved."

She laughed. Jay's over-the-top flirting was a staple of their friendship. So long as she never told him what they did in bed in her fantasies, it could stay that way.

Besides, his attention span was ridiculously short. He'd find something else to amuse himself in thirty seconds.

"I bet you think a bigger bed is the answer to everything."

"It isn't?" Jay scanned the field. "Wait, I'm wrong. Sometimes a bigger buffet table is the answer."

He grabbed her hand and tugged her along. "C'mon, we need more lunch before volleyball."

When she brought him home, she was certain she knew how a divorced parent felt dropping off her child with the custodial parent. Jay insisted she have a bowl of ice cream with Henry while he reenacted every activity, complete with sound effects and props. She and Henry delivered lavish praise for the accomplishments and the creative theater.

"It was a fantastic birthday gift, Alice." Jay crouched behind her chair and wrapped his arms around her shoulders. "Thanks."

"Hey, you're the one who made it fun. Thanks for hanging out with me."

"I'll have to second Jay's commendation, Alice." Henry's lips twitched. "It's amazing how much one can accomplish when he's out of the house all day."

Alice laughed.

Jay sauntered to his own chair, turned it around and straddled it backward. He crossed his arms atop the back.

"It's okay, Henry. It's probably tough for your old bones to keep up with us young whippersnappers. Did you want us to yell at some kids to get off your lawn?"

Henry smirked. "I'll tell you what I want when you're older. Isn't it past your bedtime, young man? The sun will be setting soon."

They played board games and traded insults for the rest of the night. The hour was late when she went home to her futon, where there was no room for tigers or Jays or Henrys.

A formal invitation appeared on her door two weeks later, requesting her presence for a Fourth of July evening of dinner and fireworks-watching. As if they even had to ask. Had she turned down an invitation yet?

Henry opened the door at her knock, casually dressed, for him, in khakis and a short-sleeved green polo shirt that matched his eyes. She let her gaze roam, flirtatiously, because it was Henry, and he was as safe and harmless as they came.

"Looking sharp. Testing out new date threads?" She circled him as he closed the door.

Exquisite. The slacks hugged him enough to remind her of his masculinity but not enough to feel obscene. The shirt draped just so across the breadth of his shoulders. *Yum.*

Not that his attractiveness surprised her.

No, the only surprising thing was that he'd opened the door himself. Usually that task fell to Jay while Henry cooked.

"Jay on strike tonight? Or busy sampling the food while your back is turned?"

Henry smiled. His gaze skated over her own form, lingering on the scoop neck of her top, presumably because the view wasn't one Jay's lanky body offered. She hid her smirk.

"You're looking lovely this evening as well, Alice. Perhaps you're intending to test your date-appropriate clothing out on me? I deem it a smashing success." He gestured her toward the kitchen. "Although I wouldn't put it past Jay to sample the food behind my back, he is not doing so at the moment. It's rather difficult to do when one is not present."

Jay wasn't here? That couldn't be right. She'd shared meals with just Jay or just Henry before, but never at their apartment and always while they were out doing friend stuff.

"What, you ran out of wine and sent him for a bottle?"

"No, I have a delightful bottle of wine for us right here, a Chablis, to complement the cream sauce for the scallops and linguine."

Henry raised the heat beneath a saucepan simmering on the stove, drained pasta water in the sink and added the noodles to the sauce. He was quick and competent, with elegant motions that always made her wonder if he'd taken dance lessons, though she still hadn't asked.

"There's a bit of the wine in the sauce, actually. If you'll open the refrigerator, you'll find our salads. Would you mind bringing them to the table?"

"As long as you don't tell Jay I'm usurping his role as waiter."

She opened the refrigerator and scooped up two salad plates. No third, not on any shelf. She closed the door, carried the plates to the table and attempted a casual tone. "So where is he tonight, anyway?"

"Help yourself to some cutlery, Alice. You know where everything is."

She carried forks. Napkins. Wine and glasses.

Henry sliced bread fresh from the oven and plated their pasta. He seated her formally, holding her chair for her, and followed up by pouring the wine before seating himself.

They'd both had a few bites, and she'd expressed her appreciation for the rich sauce and the wine's tart citrus before she asked again.

"So Jay's not watching the fireworks with us?"

"I'm beginning to think you're unhappy to be dining with me, Alice."

His smile told her he was joking, though she cringed at her own rudeness.

"No, sorry, not at all. I'm just intensely nosy. When you invited me over for the Fourth, I assumed . . ."

"That Jay and I were joined at the hip?"

Literally. She sipped her wine to stop the laughter bubbling in her gut.

"Something like that, I guess."

"Ah. Well. As it happens, Jay will be taking in the fireworks picnic-style in the park with a young woman he met while kayaking last month. I packed them a superb supper, if I do say so myself."

"He's on a *date*?" Fuck. She hadn't meant to sound quite so disbelieving.

But Jay? On a date? With a woman? Okay, he flirted with every woman he saw, but he was *with* Henry, wasn't he?

"He is, yes. Since early this afternoon in fact, as the wristbands for the best seating go quickly." He continued to eat his pasta and drink his wine as though nothing were amiss.

She wasn't quite so sanguine.

"It doesn't bother you?" Did they have some kind of open relationship?

"Not at all, Alice. Should it? Companionship is a joy wherever one finds it, and long-term friends are surely more significant in one's life than short-term sexual titillations."

"You mean the two of you aren't—"

Their sex life was none of her business, and Henry was shy about that sort of thing anyway. No. Not shy. But something. Private. Maybe he just didn't kiss and tell. A gentleman. A real one.

"It's a poor friend who cannot understand and accept the needs of others." Henry's tone was thoughtful, not chiding, and she relaxed.

She hadn't offended him. He would politely ignore her gaffe.

"Jay is positively in his element when in the company of a beautiful woman."

"He does know how to turn on the charm."

Jay had done it before, with waitresses and instructors and with her, even, but she'd assumed it was a game for him. Damn. Maybe he'd been serious and she'd blown her chance.

The corollary wormed its way into her skull. Tonight's dinner might be a serious effort from Henry. Was she blowing this, too?

She studied him with new eyes, hoping he hadn't noticed the shift in her thoughts. She couldn't help thinking of the last time she'd come with his name on her lips, her vibrator purring between her legs.

He wasn't so obviously sexual as Jay, throwing out innuendo and showing off his body, but his quiet reserve made him all the more tempting. Repressed. Sexy librarian. She ducked her head to hide her smile.

She resolved to pay more attention, to see what kind of signs Henry was giving off, but he was frustratingly himself. He remained polite through dinner, charming, but nothing she could construe as an overture. She sure as hell wasn't about to make a move on him first.

How awkward would that be if he was in a committed relationship with Jay? Even if Jay liked women on the side, that didn't mean Henry did.

They adjourned to the rooftop afterward, where a number of the building's residents had gathered. The sea of buildings stretching northeast grew taller beyond the lightless swath marking the fenway as the marsh wound through the city.

Henry assured her the downtown fireworks would be visible despite the obstructions.

A neighbor was streaming the radio broadcast of the concert from his laptop. They didn't have long to wait before the first burst of red and white streaked across the sky and fell to earth.

Booming pops cascaded. Colors dazzled. Henry's shoulder brushed her back, his fingers grazing her hip.

The contact jolted her, forcing out a gasp.

"Beautiful, wouldn't you say?"

Christ, had his lips touched her ear? Was she reading too much into it? Henry's courtesy surely extended to not disturbing the other watchers. Maybe he'd dislodged a strand of her hair.

She nodded, mute. If he thought her reaction owing to the fireworks rather than his nearness, so much the better.

"Powerful," he murmured. His breath ghosted down the side of her neck.

Please God, don't let him notice the stiffening under her shirt. Next time she'd wear a bra with thicker fabric.

She resisted the urge to push back into his groin and find out if his body's reaction mirrored her own. A forward move with a reserved guy like Henry blared louder warnings than a tornado siren. *Fuck, might as well strip in front of the neighbors and ask if he sees something he likes.*

Neither romantic nothings nor crude suggestions dropped in her ear. No, he talked about seeing fireworks as a child in Maine. The festival in Augusta, where he'd grown up, was a two-week affair leading up to the fireworks, and he'd gone often.

She told him about summers in South Dakota and the fireworks show at Lake Mitchell. How she and her little sister would run around writing their names in the air with sparklers. It wasn't even an option in Boston. The whole state had banned fireworks except in large-scale municipal shows with professionals at the fuses.

The finale crashed across the sky at eleven o'clock. They mingled a few minutes more with the neighbors before he ushered her downstairs with the promise of dessert.

She'd seen the brandy-style glasses of chocolate mousse in the refrigerator earlier. Three of them. Either he thought Jay would join them for dessert, or he'd made him one anyway because Jay loved dessert.

Henry added a dish of fresh local raspberries, and he and Alice shared it between them on the couch. She stayed until well after midnight, enjoying the dessert, the company, and the conversation, expecting Jay to get home any minute.

By one in the morning, it seemed obvious Jay wasn't coming home. And Henry hadn't given her any clear sign of *his* intentions, either. Had this been a date? Or was he lonely because Jay was out with a woman?

When she yawned for the third time in five minutes, Henry's hand came to rest on her shoulder in a light squeeze.

"Go on, Alice, off to bed with you. Your company has been a splendid diversion, but I've ideas swimming in my head for a new project that I believe is about ready to begin."

She smiled at him, untucking her legs and stretching before trying to stand. "Happy painting, Henry."

He returned her smile and stood when she did, a gentleman's gesture. "A properly prepared canvas and a vision of beauty are all I require, my dear."

Chapter 3

"We're on Henry's turf now, Alice. He's the culinary genius. I just do what I'm told."

She stood in Henry and Jay's kitchen enjoying Jay's chatter and Henry's quiet expertise. Henry had heightened his polite reserve for this moving-in anniversary dinner. A chaperone, almost, for a weird date with Jay.

Yeah, keep dreaming, girl.

Despite the backless halter she'd worn, a flowing, flirty, knee-length black dress, this was not a date. Dinner, yes. Date, no. Just her considerate, across-the-hall neighbors inviting her to their apartment for a celebratory meal.

Even if Jay went out with women. Even if maybe Henry had been kind of dating her last month with the dinner and fireworks. This was not a date. Henry was not setting her up with his boyfriend. Probably.

Henry spoke while he worked. "Jay, open the wine, please. It needs a few minutes to breathe."

Jay carried the bottle to the table, raising his eyebrows as he passed her.

"See what I mean?" Jay whispered, but she caught the small twist in Henry's lips.

He stood behind the kitchen island, a commander overseeing the final inspection of his troops, adjusting this dish and that one. He had beautiful hands, long, slender fingers, nimble and strong.

"Woolgathering, Alice?"

She jerked her head up. Henry no longer hid his smile.

"I . . . everything looks fantastic. I can't wait to eat."

"Ah. Of course. Excellent timing, my dear. If you'll allow me to escort you?"

She worked to bring her heart rate down as he approached.

"You've selected a beautiful dress, Alice. Entirely too fine for Jay's benefit, I'm afraid. He's rather immune to fashion." He threaded her hand through his arm and led her to the table. "Myself, on the other hand . . . Mmm. Let's just say I appreciate the thought that went into your choice, hmm?"

Oh God. She'd been way too fucking obvious with the dress and the staring, and he'd tired of her attention whore routine.

"Uh, I, it's not often a girl has the chance to dress up for dinner."

Henry clicked his tongue. "Jay and I have both noticed your interest, Alice. It's nothing of which you need be ashamed. We're flattered."

She waited for his gentle brush-off. God, why couldn't she meet any *available* nice guys? Ones who could dress themselves in the morning and put a meal on the table once in a while? Ones who could hold her attention for more than three dates but wouldn't pressure her for commitment?

"Definitely flattered," Jay chimed in. His gaze raked over her body.

The move might've earned a stranger a drink in the face, but not Jay, her de facto best friend. His look was what she'd wanted when she put the dress on. Even if he was untouchable.

No rule against fantasizing. She'd apologize and promise to rein it in and everything would be fine.

"Manners, Jay." Henry released her arm to pull out her chair. "I won't tolerate such boorish behavior. Alice deserves more dignified attentions."

She studied her sandals against the dining room rug. Dignified, undignified . . . hell, she liked 'em both.

"She wants to play, Henry. You know she does, even if she hasn't said so."

Jay rarely sounded so serious. She opened her mouth to ask about their game when Henry spoke.

"*Enough*, Jay. Sit down and keep your eyes on your plate if you can't be polite."

Jay's eyes, defiant, lusting, caught hers. And then he sat and stared at his plate. What the hell had she walked into tonight?

"Alice. Please accept my apologies for Jay's rather forward behavior." Henry took a softer tone with her than with Jay, gentler, and his hand grazed her bare back. "The young are always in such a rush."

She would've smiled if she weren't so confused by their behavior tonight. Jay might have her birthday beat by eighteen months, but the impatience and immaturity she had shed still clung to him. Henry had a decade on Jay, but age wasn't what set him apart. She imagined him mature and controlled even as a child. Dignified.

Henry tipped his head and captured her gaze. He was taller than she was. Not much. She might match him in heels, not that it mattered, since they weren't dating and never would be. His height hit the sweet spot that made standing beside him exquisite, even if she'd never admit it aloud to the ones she turned down, the ones who weren't the perfect fit.

Henry's fingertips trailed over her spine, and she shivered.

"Except when they're a bit skittish," he murmured. "Is that what you are, Alice? Perhaps you're feeling unsure of your place here?"

She couldn't meet his gaze for long. His eyes invited her to drown in tender concern, implied an intimacy that made her nervous and needy. Jay proved no help, his focus locked to his plate.

"If you don't wish to play, my dear, that's fine. We three may still have a lovely dinner, and your longing looks will be no less welcome for the declined invitation."

Her gaze flicked back to Henry's. She wet her lips. Beneath the nerves welled a thrilling jolt, an anticipatory burst of glee.

"But there could be more if I want it?"

More. Like Jay's fling last month? A one-night affair? With Jay or Henry? *Why not both?*

He smiled, his fingers tracing lines on her back. Pride coursed through her, as though she'd asked an astute question and now basked in the professor's praise.

"Precisely. If you want to play, you must say so explicitly. I value our friendship. I won't have misunderstanding lead to fear or ill will between us."

"And by 'play' you mean . . ."

She couldn't finish the sentence. Was he serious? Were *they*?

Sure, she'd fantasized about her neighbors a hundred times in the last year while her fingers and her vibe gave her the pleasure she craved. Not once had she expected to stand in their dining room with an open invitation to their bed. If that's what this was.

Henry's hand stopped moving on her back. Pursing his lips, he gave an absentminded nod.

"Of course. It's too soon. Forgive me, Alice. I'll have dinner on the table in a moment. Jay, if you'll entertain our guest, *politely,* while I bring out the salad."

She sat, because he turned her with gentle hands and pushed the chair beneath her.

He walked away, around the table, past Jay, and her gaze followed him. Why was he leaving? What had she done? What could she say to bring him back and make him touch her again, make her skin tingle and the fine hairs on the back of her neck stand on end?

"He means we want to fuck you. You don't have to say yes, but I really wish you would."

"*Jay.*" Henry stopped dead, his back stiff, and spoke in a low, clipped tone. "We will discuss this behavior later, you may be assured."

"Wait."

Both men looked at her, Jay eagerly, Henry with suppressed anger.

She fortified herself with a glance at Jay before meeting Henry's eyes. He made the decisions here. She'd figured out that much, at least.

"Is Jay right? Is that what you want?"

Henry closed his eyes and bowed his head. When he faced her again, he'd regained his neutral composure.

"Though crude, Jay is not entirely incorrect. You are quite lovely,

Alice, and I confess, I should like to see that loveliness flushed with pleasure, wanton and needy, and to satisfy those desires for you. But we will *not*—"

He gave Jay a hard look, one that made Alice squirm. The slipperiness against her skin suggested her panties wouldn't last the night.

"We will not force a decision upon you. The choice must be yours. It need not be made tonight."

She pressed her thighs together and bit back a gasp.

"If I wanted to make that decision now, you wouldn't turn me away?"

"If you are capable of articulating what you want, then no, I will not turn you away. Please be certain, however. If this is something you haven't considered before, something perhaps you want someday but not yet, do not feel you need to rush your decision. The offer does not expire at midnight."

"I, I *have* considered it." She'd need to do better than a choppy whisper if she wanted Henry to let her play. She cleared her throat, forced herself to enunciate. "I do want it. Now. Tonight. I want to play, Henry. I want you to make me feel wanton, and I want you to satisfy my needs."

She'd never spoken quite so bluntly to a prospective sex partner. An odd lightness, a liberation, filled her chest.

Henry's face glowed.

Jay nodded enthusiastically in her peripheral vision.

"Very well. In that case, I believe dinner will keep."

She sat taller in her seat as Henry studied her, stretching her spine, wanting even her posture to be perfection in his eyes. She waited in silence.

"Alice. Stand up and step to your right, please."

She did so. Her heart thumped faster. She had next to no idea of what she'd agreed to, but she knew these men. Henry's courtesy, Jay's sweet wit, their thoughtful concern and willingness to help her out whenever she needed.

Henry's eyes, a calm green sea, reassured. She trusted him to keep her safe.

Henry stepped up to the table across from her and held out his arms.

"Give me your hands, please, Alice."

Her palms were sweaty. Henry's were warm and dry. His fingers clasped her own, and he rolled his thumbs across her knuckles in soothing repetitions.

"You'll need a word, Alice. If you wish to stop, at any time, for any reason, simply say your word." He raised his voice, his gaze fixed on her. "Jay, what's your word?"

"Tilt-A-Whirl."

"Thank you, Jay." Henry smiled. "He hates carnivals. Your word, Alice?"

She took a moment to think.

"Pistachio."

"Good. Say it again, please."

"Pistachio," she promptly repeated.

"Delightful." He drew her hands toward him until she lay bent across the table alongside her place setting, hips crowding one edge and fingers curving around the other. "You'll leave these here, Alice."

The rough touch of the tablecloth reached through the fabric of her dress. Anticipation and the friction hardened her nipples. Had she ever been this turned on before a man had even truly touched her? No. No, not unless she was by herself, eyes screwed shut, fantasies playing out behind her lids.

Hands reached for her face, turning her toward the foot of the table where Jay sat. Fingers swept her hair out of her eyes, draping it down her neck to fall to the table.

"Can you see Jay, Alice? He greatly enjoys watching you."

"I see him." God, her throat was dry. She swallowed. "I see him."

Henry's hands left her and he walked around the table, ruffling Jay's hair while Jay leaned into the touch. His hands, too, gripped the table's edge. They didn't move.

Henry passed out of her sight. Behind her, somewhere. Silent. Should she turn and look for him? What was he doing?

Jay watched her with knowing eyes. A little smirk. The barest shake of his head.

No. Best not to look, his eyes said.

She gasped when a hand touched her foot. The left one, first. Her sandals slid off, one at a time. Warm hands curved around the arches of her feet and danced up her calves.

"Better without these, I think." Henry's voice conveyed calm, thoughtful precision as his hands trailed up the outside of her thighs, beneath her dress.

He pulled her underwear down, down, down to the floor and off, raising each foot once more. Black panties. To match the dress. Date panties, silk with brocade embroidery. Soaking wet, now. Had she hoped this would happen? Hell yes.

Palms stroked between her knees.

Henry spoke, deep and commanding. "Spread your legs for me, Alice."

She couldn't disobey. Didn't want to. She wanted his hands to keep moving. She spread her legs.

He inhaled, loud enough for her to imagine his chest filling out, broad and deep. A soft sound of satisfaction followed. His hands lifted her dress with them as they rose over the backs of her thighs. The summer-weight cotton tickled sensitive skin, whispered against her back in a flowing bunch as he draped it above her ass. Her skin was hot, the air cool. The fabric settled. She shivered.

"Beautiful," Henry murmured. "Slick and heavy with need. Such an intoxicating blush. You feel it, don't you, Alice? The blood racing through you? Settling here and throbbing, aching? Waiting?"

"I feel it," she said, and she wasn't ashamed.

Jay smiled, his eyes eager. Pleased. Proud.

"You smell her, don't you, Jay? That thick, sweet musk in the air that slips in through your nostrils and coats your tongue? Makes you hunger for her?" He traced the seam of her lips with a single finger. They parted under his touch, wetness rushing forth as she clenched. "She's so very wet, Jay. Hot and slippery."

A pause. Henry exhaled, his breath cool against her heat. "Are you hard for her, Jay?"

Jay's eyes wouldn't let hers go. His voice was strained. "Yeah. God, yeah."

"Good boy."

Henry never stopped his gentle stroking, back and forth between her lips, a single finger teasing her entrance, running up and over her clitoral hood. If he didn't do something soon, she would die. Literally die, right on their table.

"Take it out, Jay. Stroke yourself for her."

Jay's hands dropped from the table, and her gaze dropped with them.

Her hands flexed. The damn table blocked her view. Was that frustrated growl hers? A hiss and a clink of metal. His belt. The fastener. A rushed whine, the zipper parting. She shuddered. A soft snap of fabric. Underwear. Waistband. *Boxers or briefs, Jay?*

"Tell me, Jay. Tell her."

"Christ. Wet. Leaking like a fucking faucet."

His arm shifted, a hypnotic, rhythmic, up-anddown motion. She wanted to climb in his lap and move like that. Her muscles knotted. Her toes curved into the rug.

"So goddamn hard, just want—"

"*Slowly*, Jay. Nice and slow."

Jay's arm jerked once and then slowed. His mouth hung open a bit as he panted. He seemed fixated on her ass.

She sensed movement behind her, air shifting. Henry's finger went away. She wanted it back, wanted it now. She shivered at the slow release of a zipper, the slight snap of a condom unrolling.

Henry slipped his hands under the curve of her ass, thumbs stroking along her lips, pulling her open for him. He nudged her with his erection, teasing, the tip dipping inside.

"Like Alice, Jay. She's a good girl, isn't she? See how patient she is? Good things come to those who wait."

He pushed, a long, slow thrust, and her legs quaked as he filled her.

Jesus Christ. She trembled right on the fucking edge, and he hadn't even pulled back yet. Was it possible to come from one stroke? God knew none of her former lovers had managed it. For themselves, sure, but for her? Not even close.

She watched Jay, his gaze glued to what she couldn't see, to the place where she and Henry joined.

She whimpered as Henry withdrew, her hips trying to follow, her handhold on the table stopping her.

His hands caressed the outside of her thighs. He didn't move other-wise, and her whole body grew attuned to the motion of his fingers sweeping up and down her legs. The speed matched Jay's as he stroked himself.

The sound in her ears wasn't only Jay's panting now but hers, too. The air in her lungs whooshed out as Henry thrust deep and slow.

Jay moaned, a frustrated deep whine.

She wiggled her feet, raising her heels and lowering them, fuck-ing herself on Henry's unmoving cock and watching Jay's arm slide back and forth. *Oh! That's nice. So nice.*

Jay squeezed his eyes shut. His arm paused. "Fuck. She's . . . that's so . . . *fuck*, I can't. Please?"

A heavy hand settled against Alice's tailbone, right on the top of her ass, and she couldn't lift her hips anymore, couldn't force her feet to raise her up. *No, no, please? Let me.*

But the hand was inflexible.

"Mmm, yes, our girl is quite creative, isn't she? So very lovely. Wet and tight and eager."

Henry greeted her with that same pleasant, composed voice in the hallway. He breathed easy even when the forceful thrusts punctuating his words left her shaking with need.

"You're eager yourself, aren't you, Jay?"

"Eager," he rasped. "Really, really eager."

Henry's steady thrusts built a solid pressure between Alice's legs.

"Stand up, Jay. Show us how eager you are. Alice is quite keen for a look, isn't that right, Alice?"

Nodding vigorously, she fixed her gaze on the table's edge.

"Uh-huh. Keen. Good word. So keen." God, she couldn't stop her-self from babbling.

None of her ex-lovers had stroked off for her. "Fucking is better," they said. "You wouldn't like it," they said. "It's personal," they said. But here was Jay, practically dying to do it while Henry kept her wound up with fullness and friction and anticipation.

"So keen," she gasped.

Henry chuckled.

Jay stood, resting his left hand flat on the table. His right hand gripped his cock at the base, a pale circle against its dark magenta, almost aubergine, flush. Thick and hard, angled up toward his stomach, unmoving above its furred trim. Waiting.

She busied herself staring at his muscled hips and the smooth, slick cock standing between them.

"You've been very patient, Jay, and so polite. Perhaps Alice's example is good for you. Go ahead, my boy. Show her what you'd like to give her. You've wanted to for months, haven't you? Flaunting yourself in front of her, begging her to notice you?"

Henry's hypnotic voice, as steady as his thrusting, prodded Jay to action. His right hand darted forward, smooth skin sliding with him, not quite to the tip and back again.

His twitches and jerks caused a cascading rhythm in her lungs, an answering hitch in her breath. The slight twist his fingers added brought her tongue to her lips. Her thumbs drummed on the table.

Jay's near silence exaggerated the harsh weight of his breaths and the constant enticement of Henry's words. He encouraged. Goaded. Described her in such detail that she shivered and bucked beneath his hands, a willing narcissist soaking in the knowledge that he'd been paying attention long before tonight.

When Jay came, splashing white across the festive orange plate in front of him, a low whine in his throat, she soared with him in spirit if not body.

He slumped in his chair, licking his fingers. His gaze met hers. *Your turn*, he mouthed.

Sweat settled on her back, dryness in her mouth, as if she'd run a marathon while standing still. She flexed against the table, seeking that pressure, the right angle. She'd never been the kind of girl to come from penetration alone, but she'd never had anyone like Henry, either, patient, deliberate, focused.

He moved with confidence, as though she couldn't possibly do anything but what he expected. The finish line loomed close now, so close she'd die from burst lungs if something didn't set her off first.

Specks of light danced around Jay's face. Numbness overtook her fingers. She couldn't be sure she stood on the floor because she couldn't feel her toes, only the shaking in her legs and the tightness stretching like a rubber band to every place in her body, hell, through the pores of her skin, even, and she wanted it to let go.

Henry's pace never changed, but his fingers-yes, God, his fingers, please-please-please—slipped beneath her, feather light, teasing. *Harder, Henry, oh God, I need it, I need it.*

He squeezed, hard, around her clitoris, as if in answer to her silent prayer.

The rubber band snapped. Her legs and hips rocked the table with their vibration, and her body arched, back flexing like a bow.

Her hands, though, never moved from the place Henry had laid them so gently.

His thrusts never became the all-too-familiar desperate, frenzied pounding. The moment when she faked it with moans and shuddering and a voice in her head saying, *Jesus, hurry the fuck up so I can send you home and take care of this myself,* and *Are you so fucking dumb you can't tell the difference? You've never felt a woman coming, have you?*

Henry thrust with wicked slowness when her rubber band fell slack and left her boneless. Eyes half shut. Breathing harsh. Unsure yet if the pressure of his hips against hers alone held her upright.

His shadow fell across her face as he stretched forward, a pause in his steady motion. His lips touched her for the first time, pressed to her spine between her shoulder blades.

"Magnificent."

The praise sent a ripple of pleasure through her, an after-tremble as she caught her breath, before an unhappy thought intruded. Satisfied as she was, she hadn't satisfied him in return.

"But you didn't—"

"No, not yet, my dear." Henry's tolerant tone wrapped a hint of chiding in fond amusement.

She flushed.

"Jay helped me take the edge off before you arrived. It wouldn't do to have disappointed the guest of honor before she'd had her fill."

He emphasized the source of her satisfaction with a gentle thrust, his body still curved over hers.

"My dear Alice, it is not any deficiency of yours. We'll work on these misguided feelings of inadequacy you have, hmm? If you'd care to make this a regular arrangement?"

She smiled at Jay sprawled in his chair and wiggled her hips for the man pressed to her back.

"I'd care, definitely." Hell yeah. A man who cooked and teased and set dinner aside to fuck her senseless? Times two? She'd be an idiot to say no.

As a bonus, Henry and Jay had each other for the crazy declarations of love shit. This was just fucking. Okay, not just, because Henry was the best fuck she'd ever had, but nothing to get emotional about.

She coughed. "I believe I was promised dinner?"

"An excellent suggestion. Time to discuss and process events would be welcome, I think." Henry brushed her back with his lips. "Jay, washcloths, if you would."

Jay stood, lazily, pants open and hanging from his hips. His penis lay against his pubic hair, settling left, the light catching wet streaks as they dried on his skin. He seemed unselfconscious about his nudity. A Jay trait or a male trait in general? They never felt they had any reason to hide themselves. Why should they?

"If my legs'll hold me," he joked. "It was good, Henry. I'm still feeling it." He laughed. "Not as much as Alice is, though. I can almost see her legs vibrating from here. I think she moved the table an inch off-center."

His knowing, intimate tone made her want to hide. A mocking evaluation of her performance wasn't something she'd expected from Jay.

Two rapid thrusts from Henry sent her thoughts skittering away.

"Alice is receiving compensations your behavior does not yet merit this evening, Jay." Henry's voice held an edge. "Perhaps you've forgotten how vulnerable and exposed you felt at your first scene?"

Jay collapsed into a crouch, his eyes level with her own. Deep brown pools of apology studied her face.

She gazed at the tablecloth.

"Damn. I . . . Alice, I talk a lot. I mean, *a lot*. You know that. I wasn't laughing at you or trying to say you've been anything less

She startled a laugh out of Jay.

"Oh, she's good. More than a match for our self-flagellation."

Henry pressed a kiss to her right temple.

"Well said, my dear." He straightened up and stretched out his right arm.

Jay laid the washcloth across his palm.

Even propped on her elbows, she couldn't see far enough over her shoulder to watch Henry then, but she felt his hands. One on himself, his knuckles brushing her swollen lips, probably holding the condom in place, while the other pressed the washcloth against her, encompassing her sex in its warmth. She held back a whine at the loss of fullness and connection as he pulled out.

He cradled her with the washcloth, clearing away the evidence of her enthusiastic response to his touch.

Cherished. The feeling she hadn't been able to name. Something previous partners had never accomplished. She stood still and let him make her fresh and clean and relaxed in their company once more. He seemed to think the responsibility was his. She wasn't sure where the boundaries were yet, but she was beginning to feel them out.

Henry excused himself, walking away with the washcloth in one hand, pants held up with the other.

She stretched her back as she straightened and allowed her dress to fall into place.

Looking at the table, Jay sighed. "I'm gonna need a new plate. This one's got a little something on it."

She chuckled at the understatement. Drying lines and drops of ejaculate had liberally splattered the plate.

"Are you sure you aren't the artist? The plate makes a good canvas for your work."

"Naw, these are just cheap reproductions. I'm like Thomas Kinkade. I could churn out three, maybe four of these a day."

She laughed even before he'd finished speaking.

"If you want real artistry, you'll have to ask Henry. I'm sure he picked brightly colored plates on purpose when he had me set the table."

"He's always thinking ahead, huh?" She turned her gaze to the floor, searching for her underwear. They'd be uncomfortable now, cool and sticky, but she supposed she ought to put them on. Going without wasn't ladylike.

"Always. And you won't find them there, your little black panties. They're in Henry's pocket."

"He took them with him?"

The presumption left her flattered, a bit, that he wanted them. Irritated, a bit, because they were her nicest pair. Nervous, a bit, and aroused, because she was keenly aware of the air moving against her labia every time she shifted her legs.

"He might launder them and give them back to you later. Or he might keep them as a memento or to use in some other game. Who knows?" Jay seemed unconcerned by the prospect. "You can always ask him. No guarantees he'll answer, though."

"Ah, gone three minutes and Jay is giving all of my secrets away, I see."

Henry, like Jay, was now fastened and buttoned away. The formality seemed more appropriate on him, though she flashed on an image of him disheveled and lying beneath her, sweaty and sated, atop green silk sheets that matched his eyes.

"Jay, if you'll replace your plate—unless you prefer the personalized design—I'll put the finishing touches on dinner. It won't take but a moment. And Alice, though you haven't asked, you are, of course, free to do so. If you want your underwear returned for the rest of the evening, however, you'll need to say your word."

Was he serious? Firm gaze, one eyebrow arched. Waiting for her reply. Yes, definitely serious. Did she want to use her word to stop him? Hadn't things stopped already? Or had they started again now? Fuck it. She didn't want to stop.

"It's that important to you?"

"The important question for you, Alice, is which is more important to *you*. How attached are you to the idea of wearing underwear? Is this something you feel you cannot sacrifice? Search yourself for your boundaries. Whatever the answer, you will find no judgment here."

"I've never . . . no one's ever asked me to . . ." She paused, considering, grateful when Henry didn't rush to fill the silence and Jay picked up his plate and moved into the kitchen. *No pressure.*

She meant it sarcastically, but the thought rang true. Henry would accept her choice either way, and maybe he'd rearrange his thoughts about her comfort level, but he wouldn't be angry with her. She shifted her legs and found her answer.

"No. You keep 'em. I'm okay with that, I think." She smiled. "As long as your chairs are okay with that."

Henry winked. "The slipcovers are more than decorative, my dear. They're also washable."

Hell, if things had stopped, they'd started again. She'd be lucky to get through dinner with the renewed tingling in her pussy. Even distracted by a mix of satisfaction and arousal, though, she couldn't fault Henry's hospitality or his cooking.

He served up a tart, crunchy salad with pears and blue cheese and almonds. Not something she'd have taken the time to make herself, but then she didn't always take the time to make breakfast, either, and he'd brought her an apple fritter this morning. She'd never had less than a fantastic meal any time they'd extended the invitation. *Must add sex to the list of things Henry does well. Really well.*

Henry didn't talk about the sex, though. He talked about the meal. Shared amusing details of his trip to the fish market to buy the lobster, cod and clams for the main dish, a colorful seafood paella she'd have considered the highlight of the evening if not for the sex.

She excused herself to use the bathroom while Henry cut the dessert, a decadent strawberry-pineapple cheesecake she couldn't wait to taste. She stared at the soap bubbles on her hands as she washed them.

Henry must've spent the whole day in the kitchen. The dinner was important to him. Because she was? What had he said about Jay having wanted her for months? Or wanting her to see him sexually, at least.

"He didn't pack us a lunch."

She shut off the water, dried her hands and took her time rehanging the towel.

"If it was just about letting Jay play with a girl, Henry could've done his behind-the-scenes thing and I never would've known."

What made the most sense?

She studied herself in the mirror, considering.

"Jay said something to Henry the day we met. Henry knew the neighbor thing would make this more complicated than some Fourth of July fling for Jay. If Henry said no, Jay would accept his decision."

She didn't know what had prompted Henry to allow this tonight if Jay had been asking all year. Or why Henry had fucked her but Jay hadn't. Some kind of control thing?

She tapped the counter, losing herself in the clicking echoes off the tile. "Henry's showing Jay he's still in charge, even if he approves of Jay pursuing meaningless sex with me now?"

No matter what he said, Henry was absolutely in charge. She'd never had such an instantaneous response to a man or behaved so out of control, as if her body wasn't even hers then but his. She'd worked hard to climax with previous partners, when she'd made it happen at all, but with Henry the surrender was effortless.

"Never spent most of a year fantasizing about a guy before, either. Face it, Allie-girl, you did this to yourself. He snaps his fingers, and it's all arousal avalanche."

She shook her head and blew out a breath. Henry, at least, would realize she was having a complete freak-out in their bathroom if she didn't get back soon.

Satisfaction ran deep in her smile as she pushed the fears away and reminded herself of what mattered.

"Henry gave me an amazing orgasm, and Jay thinks about me when he jacks off. Whatever happens, I refuse to lose their friendship over this. The priority is boundaries. Follow their lead."

She returned to her seat, giving Henry a small smile and a nod when his sharp-eyed gaze landed on her, and she dug into the cheesecake with enthusiasm.

Jay confessed he'd hated pineapple as a child.

Alice shared a story about her little sister's failed attempt to make their mom's pineapple upside-down cake.

Henry slyly inquired whether his dessert was more acceptable, and Alice's and Jay's voices tumbled over each other's in their haste to express their delight.

As Jay started clearing plates, Alice half rose to carry her dishes to the kitchen.

"You needn't trouble yourself, Alice. Jay will clear tonight."

"Is handling the dishes, umm." She stopped.

Whatever arrangement Jay and Henry had was *theirs*, wasn't it? Not her business. She was a bit of excitement. Like they were for her, right? Temporary. Friends with occasional benefits.

Jay swooped in and snatched up her plate.

"Is busing tables one of my kinks, you mean? I promise, it's not." He kissed her cheek before sailing off with her dishes.

"It's not a formal part of my contract with Jay, Alice, no. It's more in the nature of a roommate exchange, as Jay's cooking is . . . hmm. 'Inedible' would be the politest term, I believe. Setting the table and clearing is a much safer contribution to mealtimes for him."

"Hey, now, no need to sling personal insults," Jay called from the kitchen. "My dry toast is fantastic. Fan-tas-tic."

Henry smiled at Jay's chatter, but Alice frowned. Henry's statement made no sense, unless she didn't know them as well as she thought.

"You have a contract with Jay? He's paying you?"

Henry's eyes widened. His eyebrows lifted.

"Oh, my dear Alice, no, not at all. I'm afraid I've given you the wrong impression entirely by handling everything backward this evening. Not that that sort of thing isn't done. It is, and the pay for professionals can be quite handsome indeed. But my arrangement with Jay is much less formal and more personal. No, the contract I'm referring to isn't a business contract. It's a statement of intention, a delineation of desires, a promise of fidelity and trust. The contract exists to protect Jay and guide my interpretation of his needs. Something like a prenuptial agreement with an erotic focus."

He paused to sip his wine, still on his first glass. Was sobriety, too, part of his responsibilities to Jay? And to her, tonight at least.

"If you wish to extend this relationship beyond tonight, Alice, you will also need a contract."

"Earlier, you said . . . when I said you were in charge, you said that wasn't quite right. But Jay listens to you. Does what you say. And I listened to you and did what you said."

"Mmm. Yes, you did so quite well, dearest. But what Jay and I do and what the three of us have begun this evening is not about me. I am in the dominant role, directing the action, yes, but the goal is not to fulfill my desires at the expense of yours or Jay's. Rather the opposite, in fact. My primary goal is to ensure that your experience is exciting and memorable, meeting your needs and testing your boundaries without causing physical or emotional harm not expressly requested in your contract.

"In a sense, one might say my role is to serve, though properly the role you and Jay have accepted is termed the submissive one. I take my responsibilities as a dominant quite seriously, Alice, which is why I am ashamed to see I have begun your instruction in such haphazard fashion. You deserve better from me."

"I'm the one who said I was ready. That I wanted to . . . well, okay, I didn't know exactly what you had in mind, but I wanted it. And I knew I trusted you."

"Then I have doubly failed you, Alice. You had already granted me your trust, based upon our friendship, and still I neglected to be certain you understood the game you were stepping into. I am the expert. You are the novice. The responsibility was mine."

"Are you saying that this—" She gestured at Henry, at the table between them, at Jay, standing in the kitchen, watching them talk. "That it can't happen again? Because you feel guilty about how it started?"

Wow, she sounded more angry and panicked than she intended. Just because she wouldn't be fucking them again didn't mean she couldn't keep their friendship. Once was enough, wasn't it? *No. I want that again.*

Henry replied with quiet restraint, his voice as fluid as ever. "I'm saying I've inadvertently abused your trust, Alice. I will atone for that, as I'm able."

He studied her in stillness as she trembled on the edge of certainty that he would send her away, to her empty bed across the hall. Pushing his chair back, he stretched out his hand instead.

"But at the moment, I've compounded the problem by allowing this distance between us. Come here, my dear. Please."

She went without hesitation, surprised by how much her worries eased when he pulled her into his lap, settling her legs sideways across his and wrapping his left arm around her back. His right hand stroked the outside of her left thigh. She shifted into his touch and inhaled sharply as the bare skin of her labia grazed the fabric of his pants. A deliberate roll of her hips rubbed her against him.

He chuckled. "Such initiative. Is that a request for more?"

Was she being greedy? She'd already had a turn, and Henry hadn't even come.

His voice lowered to a whisper. "It's quite all right, Alice. You've done nothing wrong. I'm still learning to read your needs. It's to be expected that I'll question you far more often than I do Jay until I am able to anticipate what you desire most at any given moment."

Oh. Of course. "Is that what the contract will tell you?"

"Precisely. The document provides a starting point for understanding. You've decided, then? You wish to go forward?" His fingers mimicked his words, sliding under her dress, slipping over the top of her thigh until they rested so close to her lips the heat warmed her.

She spread her legs wider, biting her lip at the rush of sensation, the not-quite-scratchy, not-quite-soft fabric and the nudging against her right leg as his cock swelled in his pants beneath her.

"Yes, please."

He brushed her lips with his fingers, parting them easily. She was already wet, already plump and eager for his touch, and he didn't make her wait. He sank a finger into her, and she gasped. He added a second without pausing.

Her hips rocked.

"Jay," Henry's hushed call vibrated past her ear. "At my side, please."

Her eyelids drifted shut.

Henry's palm rubbed over her clit with each thrust of his fingers. His left arm cradling her back, he delved beneath her dress under her arm and cupped her left breast. She hadn't worn a bra, judging a backless halter bra too much trouble, the black dress enough concealment and her breasts not requiring the support. His hand fell on bare skin, thumb tracing her nipple as his fingers held the weight of her breast in a secure grip.

Sighing, she leaned into his chest and pressed her left cheek to his. New warmth settled alongside her legs. She was too comfortable to investigate. No one here but Jay, and he would do . . .

Whatever Henry tells him to.

Alice giggled.

Henry murmured in her left ear, his fingers slow and steady between her legs. "Now that's a happy sound from our sweet girl."

The soft warmth of his lips as he kissed the corner of her jaw made her shiver. He nuzzled her ear. "Jay must be feeling exceptionally contrite for upsetting you, Alice. He's never quite so patient. Shall we give him a chance to redeem himself?"

Henry pulled his head back from hers.

She opened her eyes and followed his gaze, angled to the floor where Jay knelt back on his heels alongside the chair.

He raised his bowed head to meet their inspection, laying his cheek against her left knee and delivering silent pleas with puppy-dog eyes.

"We should," she said.

She wasn't mad at Jay. If he hadn't spoken, she wouldn't have had the courage to tell Henry she wanted this. His teasing had been exuberant, not mocking. She wasn't so thin-skinned. Besides, he was so damn cute down on his knees, all boyish charm and puppy pleading folded into a grown man's body.

She smiled at him. "He wants to be a good boy."

Henry chuckled. His left hand briefly tightened on her left breast.

"You've found favor with the lady, Jay. You mustn't squander the opportunity. Hands and mouth only. Practice, slowly, what you plan to say as you work from the farthest reaches of exile to the sweet depths of forgiveness. You may begin."

Jay lifted her right foot. His fingers stroked and massaged, in lines and circles, in incomprehensible patterns, at times firmly and others gently.

All the while, Henry's fingers provided torment of their own, unmoving inside her except when her body clenched around them.

When he allowed a slow thrust or two as he murmured to Jay, "More of that, yes" or "Our girl prefers a firm hand, Jay."

The slow pace, the restraint they showed, confused and aroused in equal measure. Tortured anticipation kept her nipples hard and breasts aching, satisfaction waiting miles down a twisting road. Her body threatened to wiggle right off Henry's lap. Involuntary shivers coursed through her, as if she teetered on the cusp of sleep and jerked herself awake again and again.

She had to be dripping all over his left leg given the wetness sliding down her thighs. His pants were probably dry-clean only. She didn't care. She wanted to leave a mark on him, on them both, something to prove she wasn't dreaming.

Jay kissed the top of her right foot with light, fluttering kisses. He suckled at her toes, twining his tongue around them and tugging. He bit lightly into the arch of her foot, and Henry urged him to do so harder when her toes curved around Jay's cheek and her thighs tightened and her body trembled with near-orgasmic pleasure.

Her breath came hard.

Henry laid his lips against her neck. A kiss? No, feeling her pulse. An excruciating wait, and bliss denied.

"Go on, Jay. The left, now."

Her left foot received more focused treatment, every brush of finger and tongue a certain, sure movement ratcheting up her desire. When Jay's touch made her gasp or shudder, Henry stepped in with his lips on her neck and his fingers in her pussy to coax a moan from her.

She floated on the edge of intensity, her skin hypersensitive to every stimulation as Henry urged Jay on.

Jay hooked his hands behind her knees and slid her across Henry's lap. Her dress rode up her thighs. Her body reclined against Henry's strong left arm.

The tightness spreading through her seemed endless, a pleasure almost painful in its need. She'd beg without shame if Henry asked her.

Jay mouthed her thighs with lips and teeth and tongue, the barest hint of stubble on his cheeks a teasing scratch. She couldn't shift away, as she had nowhere to go. Jay's hands held her knees open, baring her for his mouth, and Henry's body cradled her.

She throbbed around his fingers, wanting more, but his hand slipped free, fingers sliding away and not returning. She whimpered.

"Don't stop, please. Please, more."

Henry raised his fingers to his lips and pulled them in with his tongue. His eyes briefly closed.

The pleasure at pleasing him rippled through her. A breath alone might have served to send her over. When his hand descended, she couldn't control her panting breaths or the moans trapped in her throat.

He brushed her dress aside, and her hips strained toward the movement of air and fabric. His hand flattened against her stomach, holding her dress up and out of the way. Beyond lay the fullness of her labia, flushed rose red and spread wide, shining with desire between close-cropped curls the deep gold of ripe wheat. And an inch away, the back of Jay's head, a shock of dark hair between pale thighs.

"Beautiful," Henry murmured, and she wondered if her body had become a canvas in his mind. "Will you accept Jay's apology now, Alice? You're ready for it, I think."

Excitement buzzed in her ears and through her brain, and every spark directly connected to such a tiny patch of flesh between her thighs.

"Wha . . . yes, I . . . yes, now, please, I accept, whatever, whatever he, I don't know what he . . ."

"Jay is making his apology, dearest. It's only fitting he make it with his mouth, as his mouth has given the offense. Go on, Jay. You've practiced enough."

Jay licked along her thigh, lapping at the ready lubrication her body provided, until his mouth closed over her clitoris. The suction from his mouth, the first swipe of his tongue, sent her reeling.

Only his hands at her knees and Henry's grip around her back and stomach held her in place. The rest of her soared and tumbled along cloud lightning that never seemed to strike earth. Jay's tongue kept her from coming down, thrust inside her and swept her clean and drew the rush forth again and again.

And all the while, Henry whispered to her with unfamiliar words, his tongue mastering their cadence and rhythm as surely as he did hers. "'Love is a war of lightning, and two bodies ruined by a single sweetness. Kiss by kiss I cover your tiny infinity, your margins, your rivers . . . '"

When she woke, finally, for it seemed a waking to her, a stepping out onto damp blades of grass after a storm has passed and the sun emerged, Alice lay trembling in Henry's lap still, her head tucked beneath his chin. Her gaze fell on Jay's head, resting on her thigh, Henry stroking his hair.

"Beautifully done, my boy. Quite the incentive for Alice to consider another night like this one has been, hmm?"

Henry thought she'd needed more incentive after the commanding way he'd brought her to orgasm? *Well, it's not as if he knows you've never had it this good, Allie-girl.* Maybe he'd wanted Jay to have a chance to show off some skills, too. She sure as hell hadn't minded.

Jay tilted his face up, brown eyes wide. "Alice?"

He couldn't be worried, not after such a stellar performance. She laid her hand on his forehead and brushed his hair back. Sliding her fingers alongside Henry's, she remembered why he'd allowed Jay to play.

"It was the best apology I've ever gotten, Jay. You didn't actually owe me one." She smirked, ignoring the blush heating her face. "And now you've built up a nice bank, so the next two times you think you owe me an apology, you can remember the extra orgasms this time and forget about it."

Jay pushed against her thigh, snuggling closer. He returned her smirk. "Or I could take it as a challenge. Make the next apology an even better one."

Her body shuddered before she could lock it down. Oh hell yes.

Henry rubbed her left arm, shoulder to elbow and back again. "Jay, if you please—"

"Fresh washcloth, I know. I'm on it." Jay kissed the inside of her right thigh, and her left thigh, and her swollen lips before he climbed to his feet. "Be right back."

He wandered down the hall without saying a single thing about fucking her, even though his pants had done nothing to hide his erection when he stood. He hadn't even hinted. Did he think Henry would tell him no? Did he think she would?

She squirmed on Henry's lap, feeling his still-firm erection, too, and tried not to frown. She wanted to ask—Jay hadn't come, and Henry hadn't come—but the etiquette seemed to be not to.

"It's not a requirement, Alice."

"What?" He couldn't possibly know what she was thinking. But Henry gave a quiet chuckle, and she knew he'd read her mind.

"You're staring, Alice. And squirming. Do you think I don't know why?" Henry kissed the top of her head. "You're not responsible for making certain I achieve orgasm. If I choose to do so, I will. As it happens, I enjoy deferring my pleasures on occasion. And Jay was apologizing, my dear. He ought not benefit *too* terribly much from it."

"But . . . I mean . . ." Was anything ruder than bringing up ex-boyfriends during a postcoital moment with a partner? *For God's sake, Alice, have some tact.*

Glancing down the hall at Jay exiting the bathroom, she yelped when her seat stood. Henry lifted her to sit on the edge of the table, her back to Jay. He pushed her knees apart with gentle hands. Knowing eyes met hers.

"Your previous partners have been more focused on their own needs than on yours, haven't they, Alice?"

She nodded, her mouth dry. "It wasn't their fault or anything. I wasn't looking for anything with them, either. It was just sex. I was thinking about what I wanted, and they were thinking about what they wanted. Pretty standard."

His hands tightened on her knees before he pushed up her dress.

"Only sex," he murmured. "And they couldn't even manage that properly."

Henry reached out with his right hand.

She swiveled her head and came face-to-face with Jay, who delivered a fresh washcloth.

He handed off the towel and hopped up beside her, swinging his legs like a kid. The walk to the bathroom and back seemed to have calmed his arousal some.

"Thank you, Jay." Henry cupped her sex with the washcloth. The warmth made her sigh, and Jay's shoulder bumping hers helped her relax.

She leaned back on her hands and let Henry do as he liked. The cleaning was a personal quirk, she supposed. One she wouldn't mind getting used to if it was always preceded by the amount of pleasure she'd gotten tonight. *Settle down. When-if—they want another night, they'll let me know. With that whole . . . contract thing.*

Henry focused between her legs and kept his silence until he laid the washcloth aside and lowered her dress. When he met her gaze and spoke, his voice held a serious note. "It's not uncommon to experience confusion, guilt, or distress after an encounter like the one we shared this evening, Alice. Even for those who have been playing these games for years."

His left hand grasped her waist, fingers stroking her back. "I want you to promise me, now, that if you do begin to have such feelings, you will come to me with them before they become overwhelming."

"Okay, sure, if you want." She was confused *now*, because his description encompassed every sexual encounter. The disappointing one-nighters that left her wondering why she'd bothered to bring them home. The breakups with the ones who'd hung on long enough for a relationship but never fulfilled her.

She sure as hell wouldn't be depressed and shoveling in ice cream after a successful, satisfying sexual encounter with not one but two considerate guys.

Henry frowned. "I don't make this request lightly, Alice, and I want you to treat it seriously as well. You will call me, or you will present yourself at our door, if you find yourself overly emotional this weekend. Is that understood?"

His voice held the hard edge he'd used with Jay earlier, the one that had spurred Jay's instantaneous apology for upsetting her. The forcefulness of Henry's concern for her stirred a startling arousal. He had a way of asking questions and making requests that weren't questions or requests at all, his politeness covering a demand that commanded obedience.

"I promise, Henry. I will."

But when she lay in bed later, alone, wondering whether Henry and Jay were giving each other the orgasms they'd denied themselves in her presence, she didn't reach for her phone. She didn't cross the hall to knock at Henry's door.

She wasn't overly emotional; she was *just right* emotional. It was natural to be unsettled. To question whether they thought of her at all while they tenderly made love or fucked each other hard in their bed. Where they slept. Together. Because they were lovers, and she was . . . *what am I?*

She rolled on her side, wrapping the sheet around her.

"I am one well-fucked woman," she said to the darkness. "I don't need to be anything else to them."

Chapter 4

Alice slept late Saturday.

Her slumber had at first been the dead-to-theworld sleep of the sexually satisfied, a change she appreciated. God, seven months? Brandon shouldn't count anyway, because those two months had fallen short of expectations, which meant way too long, if she had to think to count that high.

She'd woken at a decent hour, well rested and lazy, so she'd let herself drift. And drifting had taken her mind to the night before, to Henry and Jay. Which naturally had taken her fingers to her panties and invited them inside.

The result had satisfied as well as it could when the principal actors were in her head. But she'd fallen asleep again afterward.

She jolted awake to knocking, well into the afternoon.

"Alice?" Henry's voice, coming through the door.

Oh, fuck me sideways.

"I'll wait, if you're presently indisposed, but I would like to see you for a moment."

She tried to scramble out of bed and tangled herself in the sheet, narrowly missing a face-first drop to the hardwood floor. At least the futon was low to the ground.

"Just a minute, Henry." *Yeah, just a minute, Henry, while I pull on pajama pants and wash my hands and pretend I didn't come twice this morning thinking about you fucking me.*

It was more like three minutes after she ran a brush through her hair and splashed water on her face. Taking a deep breath, she opened the door.

"Checking up on me?" She managed a casual smile, or what she thought was one. *I am completely unflustered. See how you don't fluster me, Henry?*

"I am, yes, though I realize you haven't yet given me that right." He frowned. "Nor are you required to do so, of course. But as you showed an interest in pursuing something beyond last night, I've brought you papers I'd like you to peruse."

Papers. "A contract?"

Henry held up a manila envelope. "Precisely that, my dear." He tipped it forward. "If you'd care to have a look?"

"Sure." She took the envelope as if she didn't want to tear it open and start reading. "Did you . . . want to come in and talk about it?" *While I am in pajamas my sister bought me? With little icons of gears and rulers and hard hats all over them? No, really, Henry, please come in.*

He shook his head. "No, thank you, Alice. I won't intrude upon your territory. I would prefer you take the time to look at the contract privately, so you won't feel unduly influenced to accept."

He clasped his hands behind his back. "If, after reading, you find you are no longer interested in furthering this experience, we need not speak of it again. Our interaction will return to the friendship we already enjoy with no questions asked. However, if you find you are interested in moving forward, contact me in whatever way feels most appropriate to you, and we will discuss it further."

"You're awfully formal today." She was aiming for lighthearted, but he tilted his head and studied her until she dropped her gaze to the envelope.

"Does that distress you, Alice?" His voice was soft. Kind. "If you're feeling unbalanced after last night, perhaps—"

"Nope. No. Balance is just fine. Not even walking funny. You're not taking this offer back that easily, mister." Ugh. She'd caught the babbling disease. Time to get her shit together. "So I'll take a look at your proposal—" Fuck, no, that was a terrible word for it. "I mean, the contract, and get back to you."

There. Crisp. Professional. If Henry wanted formal, she'd do formal.

He nodded, slowly. "Of course. Please do take your time, Alice. There's no need to rush things."

"Right. No need to rush. Got it." She smiled at him. No need to rush. Unless she wanted to get in his pants again. And Jay's. Two reasons to rush.

"Very well. I expect you'll contact me if you need anything, including if you simply wish to talk."

"Yup. If I need anything." Which she would do her damnedest not to. She wasn't some clingy basket case or a stalker chick who couldn't separate a night of great sex from a declaration of love.

"Have a pleasant afternoon, then, Alice." Henry stepped back from the door.

"Will do. I've got reading material to keep me busy." She waved the envelope. "Homework assignment."

He chuckled.

"Hopefully not quite so onerous, though you're not far off the mark, my dear." He inclined his head.

She was positive he'd have doffed his cap if he'd been wearing one. He behaved so adorably polite and old-fashioned sometimes. *Sometimes? Try most of the time. Except when he's ordering me to spread my legs so he can fuck me.* She took a deep breath.

"Bye, Henry."

"Alice."

She watched him walk down the hall, closing her door after he'd opened his. Her fingers raced to unfasten the envelope's metal prongs and slide out the contents.

The word "contract" had pushed an image into her brain of comically thick piles of legal paper. Henry had given her four sheets of paper. Four. She skimmed. Two held nothing but questions.

The questions they contained made her flinch. Fuck, had she considered her sexual boundaries relaxed? Henry must think them nonexistent.

Why the fuck did he need to know how often she looked in a mirror or what phobias she might harbor? Or how her parents had disciplined her? Jesus Christ.

At least the sex ones made sense. Her preferred frequency for intercourse. Intrusive, sure, but logical. He'd need to know how often to fuck her, wouldn't he?

The extent of her previous sexual experience. What, he wanted a laundry list of every guy she'd taken to her bed and how they'd screwed her? *To fill in the gaps in my education.* Nervous laughter spilled out.

Masturbation. Telling him how often, fine. But telling him *how* she touched herself? The toys she used? Her thoughts and feelings during the act?

The whole damn thing was horribly invasive, not only sexually but emotionally. Psychologically.

Alice tossed the papers on her kitchen table—*Henry's* table, the sturdy, antique wooden two-seater he'd loaned her—and refused to look at them. She needed food. And a shower. She did not need pieces of paper defining when and how she got laid. She did not need some huge mind-fuck from her neighbors.

She'd go back to finding guys the old-fashioned way, with blind dates set up online, and fuck them whenever she chose to.

Mind churning, she jumped in the shower. Dating was such a chore. Meeting new people. Rejecting the incompatible ones as politely as possible and hoping they weren't the sort of nutjobs who stalked people afterward. Negotiating the tentative back-and-forth of early dates wasn't all that different from a contract, was it?

She already knew Henry and Jay, and she'd sampled the sex. She'd never come so hard or so often. Skip the awkwardness, keep the fantastic fucking.

Her fuzzy outline in the fogged mirror agreed with her.

Henry wouldn't ask such personal questions without a reason.

"He wants me to be satisfied."

Why bother? The guys she'd dated hadn't given a shit.

"It's an ego trip. A power thing." Her reflection nodded. "Right. That's why he's in control, why there's a contract. He gets off on satisfying me because it makes him feel like some huge fucking stud."

Which he is. It was totally fucking hot, and you know it was.

Looking over the contract again wouldn't hurt.

She pulled on comfortable shorts and an old t-shirt, a soft one with a faded logo from too many washings, before she microwaved a frozen meal and sat at the table to read.

Henry would take the primary responsibility for preventing both pregnancy and disease. She'd be welcome to supplement his precautions with hormonal birth control or some other method if she liked, but he'd supply condoms and arrange for regular testing.

She snorted. All well and good, condoms being an absolute must in her book, but she wasn't dropping her birth control, either.

Thinking of him as solely in charge of such things seemed odd. None of her previous lovers had wanted the responsibility. As if they thought she magically wouldn't insist on a condom when they couldn't produce one. She scanned the page. What else would he be in charge of?

He guaranteed her physical safety. What the hell did that mean? Sex complicated enough to require a disclaimer sounded like more than the occasional rug burn or bruised back.

She shuffled to the last two pages, the questions. Nothing but questions.

The first one requested she indicate whether she *had* tried, was *interested* in trying, or *refused* to try—four columns, eight rows, minus one blank spot—thirty-one. Thirty-one different sex acts, some of which she didn't even recognize.

She laughed. Side-achingly hard, folded over in the chair.

She'd been nine. The summer after third grade. She had informed her parents with solemn dignity of her intent to sample every option at the ice-cream parlor. Thirty-one flavors before the end of the summer. Lacking a computer at home, she'd gone to the library to make her chart professional. Grown-up. Used her allowance to buy a pack of star stickers to rate each flavor in her experiment.

A single scoop, every other day, allowing time for her palate to refresh itself, of course. All summer. She'd tried every flavor. Some lasted only four bites, her minimum sample size for an accurate ranking, but she hadn't skipped a single one.

Was she less adventurous at twenty-seven than she'd been at nine?

If things got to be too much, she could stop, right? She flipped back to the first page. Item one. Either party would be permitted to reopen negotiations at any time, for any reason, or end the contract at will. Right. If she didn't like it, she'd say *see ya* and struggle through awkward greetings in the hall and strained friendships like a grown-up. No big deal.

She reread item two. Henry asked for a specific window of time. He agreed her life outside those hours was her own. Although he encouraged her to eat regular meals and get enough sleep, he wouldn't interfere if she didn't. He just reserved the right to judge her health for himself when she arrived and refuse her if he believed her too tired, ill or otherwise unprepared for playtime.

His protectiveness might be frustrating, if he underestimated her capability, but it was for her benefit. If she was honest with him about her physical condition, he wouldn't need to step in for her. Okay. Good. Item two was not a problem, either.

Item three. As Henry's long-term partner, Jay would participate in their activities and be allowed sexual access to her during their time together, at Henry's discretion. A fancy way of saying she had no say in how she was fucked or even in who was doing the fucking. The contract was careful to note that this courtesy—

She snickered. Courtesy? Henry made sex sound like helping her with her coat.

This courtesy would only be extended to Jay and not to any other potential sexual partners. Was Henry expecting to have other partners?

Well, why not? Jay did sometimes. He'd probably had sex with that woman on the Fourth of July.

She'd stuck to monogamous relationships before, but an open one wasn't an automatic deal breaker. Did she need exclusivity if this was no more than an excuse to get laid regularly and try out some kinks?

Food for thought while she skipped to the questions. If she decided not to go through with this, Henry would never see her answers anyway. If she did, he'd have incredibly intimate knowledge of her, and she'd know nothing she didn't already. Where was *his* questionnaire?

"Right. Like he's just gonna hand over information."

The contract allowed him to hide behind the dominant label while she exposed herself. Divulged everything. She wouldn't learn the reasons for his actions unless he chose to tell her. The inherent unfairness of the inequality itched at her.

"That's why he called it a submissive role. I have to trust he'll act in my best interests."

Alice tipped her head back and stared at the ceiling. White. Smooth. Not like the popcorn ceiling in her childhood home. The more accurate data she gave Henry, the better understanding he'd have of her best interests.

She started on the questions. Answers went on a separate notepad, as the pages themselves didn't leave enough room. The first answer had an embarrassingly small number of *have tried,* but the small number of *won't try* made her proud. Most things fell under *willing to try,* especially since she was confident she could stop things at any time.

The second question was a big one. Previous lovers. He didn't care about their names. Just how many she'd had, how long the relationships had lasted, why they'd ended and whether she'd been in love with them. What a preposterous question. Of course she hadn't been in love with them. Love didn't exist, not like that.

She gave them numbers and wrote out complete answers. If Henry wanted thorough, he'd get *thorough*. Assuming she showed him the answers at all.

More than eight years of sexual activity since she'd given it up as a college freshman. Two relationships longer than six months. A handful of flings. Two one-night stands. Not a single sexually satisfying one in the bunch.

She'd kicked them all to the curb. Politely, for the most part. It was just sex, and lousy sex at that. What was the point of the sweating and heaving if she got nothing in exchange? Her own fingers and her vibrator knew her a hell of a lot better than those men had. Even Adam, and they'd been together two years before she broke it off for good. He'd been convenient. For a while.

Sexual compatibility had always seemed out of reach. Until Henry had sized her up for ten seconds last night and fucked her brains out. He was *good*. If he taught her how to make satisfaction happen with any partner, the experience would be a valuable one.

Worth handing over all of this information? Worth handing over control?

She tapped the pen against her notepad.

"Yes."

Her hand was cramped and frozen in position by the time her answers satisfied her. Henry wouldn't have a single reason to reject her, even if she brought nothing to this arrangement beyond inexperience and enthusiasm. Maybe he'd let her put a chart on his fridge. *Note to self: Buy some star stickers. A lot of star stickers. Buy stock in a sticker company.*

"Because I am going to fucking ace this."

She waited until Sunday morning to call Henry's cell.

He picked up on the second ring. "Hello, Alice. It's lovely to hear from you."

"Hi, Henry. I'm—I finished. I'm ready to talk about the contract. If you are."

"Certainly, my dear. Bring it over and we'll chat now. I'll leave the door unlocked for you."

He hung up before she could respond.

Now. Now? She'd thought this afternoon. Or tomorrow. Tomorrow was good.

The pages she'd filled with her writing lay loose on the table. She rushed to tidy them, to create a neat stack and slide them into the envelope he'd used.

She tapped the envelope like a telegraph operator. Was it too businesslike? Maybe she should be more casual.

Out came the pages.

"Relax." Her voice sounded loud to her ears. "It's a chat with Henry. We've had dozens of chats."

Oh yeah? Before or after he'd fucked her senseless?

"Right. Right. This'll be a little different. I'm prepared for that."

Sure. Because a woman freaking out over an envelope screamed Boy Scout levels of preparation. She blamed Henry. If his interview process was anything like his application form for sexual partner-hood, it'd be more intensive than a Secret Service background check and astronaut training put together.

Sure you wanna go through with this?

She stared down at the pages and blew out a breath.

"Henry and Jay are good guys, and this is temporary. An experimental phase. I never did the whole girl thing at college. Maybe sex under contract with two guys is my kissed-a-girl moment. I'll either like it or I won't. No harm, no foul, right?"

She scooped up the pages, left the envelope, and marched down the hall. She rapped twice before pushing the door open. "Henry?"

"Here, Alice. Come in, please."

His voice had come from the kitchen. A deliberate move on his part? Passing the dining room table aroused vivid memories, the thrill of being splayed across it Friday night. His slight smile had to mean he was thinking of it too. Or at least he was amused to have made her think of it.

Aside from the small sounds as Henry poured juice and set plates on the breakfast bar, the apartment was quiet. Two plates.

"Isn't Jay here?"

"Not for this, my dear. You might desire privacy in this discussion. But if you wish for Jay to be here, it's an easy matter to fix."

"No, it's just it affects him, too, right?" His boisterousness might've made her less nervous. A welcome distraction.

Henry nodded and gestured her toward a seat. "It does, that's true, but I have his consent to make determinations about what will be best for him in these matters."

Oh. Right. She was about to hand over that same consent. Was she crazy?

She slid into the seat, awareness of his scrutiny running like a current under her skin.

"The things you choose to consent to may be entirely different from Jay's, Alice. Though you are younger, you're also more settled in your skin than he was at your age. The two of you may need different things from me. I will work to provide them to you accordingly."

How was he the one in charge if he catered to their whims? Better to ask while she had the chance. So she did.

68 · M.Q. Barber

The question hung unanswered.

Henry set a slice of coffee cake on her plate. The scent of warm apples and cinnamon rose between them.

Streusel covered the braided top, and juice from the apples flowed through open slits in the dough. Her mind flashed on Jay's tongue sliding along the lips of her sex, lapping at her flowing center. She shifted in her seat.

She needed to stop thinking about sex while looking at food. This would be a serious discussion. *Yeah, a serious discussion about sex.*

He served himself as well before claiming the seat to her left.

"Alice, dominance takes many forms. Not all require that the dominant partner make the submissive one lick his shoes or receive a spanking. I have no need to humiliate you." He gestured to the papers she'd laid on the counter. "Unless it's something you have indicated you desire."

"It's not," she answered, quick as a cat. "I want to know what makes you tick, I guess. It can't all be black leather and snapping whips, but when you say 'dominant,' that's the picture that comes to mind."

"I'm not surprised, my dear. It's rather the iconic image in mainstream consciousness. But there are as many variations on play as there are dominants to direct and desire them. What Jay and I share is a relaxed, personal relationship. We do not give our games as much formality as you would find were you to visit local clubs catering to those in the scene."

He stopped to eat a piece of coffee cake, and she copied his movements. She'd forgotten about brunch altogether until his fork had approached his mouth.

He sipped his juice.

She sipped hers.

"You would have a great deal more freedom in a relationship with us than you would in formal training as a submissive. And although you have some submissive tendencies . . ." He smiled, a small, private smile he did not explain. "I don't believe you truly desire to be commanded by another's will at all times, in all aspects of your life."

She shook her head. "No, that's not me at all. I don't need some-one telling me what to do all of the time." Just some of the time.

"Mmm. No. Just some of the time, yes?"

She laughed. "Stop being psychic."

"Am I? Good. You ought not wish for me to stop that, Alice. It's precisely what our contract will demand of me. To anticipate your needs, your desires, your limits. To judge when you have had enough and when you hunger for more." His sensual cadence reeled her in. "To read your body, your intonations and inflections and minuscule movements, and to understand and interpret the information prop-erly."

"You'll be . . . watching me." She held back a shiver and toyed with her fork, rolling it over the remains of her coffee cake.

"Intently, my dear. Intimately. I will make a veritable study of you, a philosophical dissertation." He leaned toward her and lowered his voice. "The thought excites you. I know it does."

He returned to eating his brunch as she pressed her thighs to-gether and stared, unseeing, at her plate. He wasn't wrong. The thought of him paying such close attention to her was a heady one.

They finished their meal in silence. She carried her plate, fork and glass to the small dishwasher and loaded them in, and did the same for his while he wrapped up the remaining cake.

Picking up her papers, he smiled and gestured her into the living room.

"What?"

"Pardon?"

"The smile. For what?" She sat on the couch, turning her body sideways.

"A simple answer for a simple question, my dear. You display comfort and familiarity in my home, behaving as a close friend rather than as a guest waiting to be served. It pleases me."

He'd chosen to sit at the far end of the couch. Laying one arm along the back, he tapped the pages in his lap with the other hand.

"Have you questions or concerns to raise about the contract be-fore we go any further, Alice? Any generalized confusion or anxiety you wish to express?"

"It's not exclusive." That sure as hell confused her. The contract didn't require monogamy or celibacy or whatever the hell you called it when you had two sexual partners and handed over control of your sex life to one of them. "We can all see other people? I mean, *see* see."

"You mean fuck."

The word from his lips shocked and aroused. She wanted to hear it in another context, in the quiet growl he'd used Friday when he'd told her to spread her legs. His eyes told her he knew exactly what she was thinking as she shifted in her seat and refused to look away.

"Yeah. I mean fuck."

He smiled. "You're a young woman, Alice. You may meet someone you wish to date. I would not interfere in the natural progression of events should that be the case. Either of us may end this contract at any time. Your consent would only belong to me on the days and times we outline here. You would be required to keep me informed, of course, and to take steps for health and safety, but you would be free to pursue other relationships, so long as you did not engage another dominant for play."

Good. She wasn't tied down to this thing with Henry and Jay. Her dating life remained her own. This was just sex. Fucking. Less complicated, and more complicated. So what if he didn't want to be exclusive. She didn't either, did she?

No. No, this was better. He wasn't trying to control her.

"Right. Okay. That's good." Not that she'd need another partner. If she signed this contract, if Henry signed, she'd be guaranteed sex on a regular basis until they broke things off. And it wasn't likely to get dull, either, if he'd done even half the things mentioned in those four pages. "So, that list you gave me, you've done everything on it?"

"No, not at all, my dear. Some I've tried briefly. Others I have not endeavored to attempt at all. But if you wish to do so, when you are ready, I will make arrangements for another dominant to step in."

"You'd give me away?" Her horror sounded in her voice. "Let someone else . . ."

"No." Henry's reply came swift and vehement, a low utterance as though he cursed the idea. "You would have to choose to break our contract for that to happen, dearest. Should you find you wish to try something beyond my skills, however, the responsibility to make certain you do so safely would be mine. That would necessitate engaging an expert to teach me to find your limits in such games. The contact needn't be sexual, Alice. Professional courtesies are not always, and rules would be strictly set. No one would touch you unless you first gave me your consent for them to do so."

She digested the idea in silence.

"We'd talk about it first, though, right?"

Henry released a soft chuckle. "You'll find much of what we do will involve talking. Before, during, and after." He resettled himself against the cushions. "Do you have other questions before we discuss details?"

"Would I have to call you master?"

A slow blink. "Do you want to?"

"I will if I have to." She didn't want to end this before it started. Not for something so trivial.

"That's not what I asked."

She studied him. Formal, but relaxed, too. Henryish. She tested the word in her mouth. "Master."

He didn't even twitch.

She frowned.

"Master." Her nose wrinkled.

"Try my name." A quiet command.

She closed her eyes. Took a breath. "Henry."

Damn if she didn't deliver his name in the low, warm tone she used in her head on those nights when the thought of him and the touch of her fingers brought her to climax. She opened her eyes, heat flooding her face.

A smile crossed his, there and then gone.

"You'll use my name, Alice. I expect that will suffice for respect." He tilted his head. "Any other questions?

"Just one." The one she almost feared to ask. "We're . . . we'd still be friends, wouldn't we? I mean, for the hours outside the contract, we could still . . ." She had no idea where her mouth was going. "Um . . . do . . . stuff? Without it being weird?"

Henry did not break into laughter at her pitiful attempt at a coherent question, a muddle of nerves she was glad Jay wasn't present to hear. No, Henry nodded, thoughtful, his gaze intent on her.

"It's an important question to ask, and I'm pleased that you are comfortable enough in our friendship to ask it now. The answer . . ." He pursed his lips and exhaled through his nose, a puffing sigh. "I believe so, yes, but it may require the occasional mental adjustment, particularly as this will be a new experience for you. Unless there's a much larger surprise awaiting me in your pages than I expect."

His fingers tapped the papers lying in his lap, and he flashed her a wicked grin.

She shivered.

"But I will not treat you as a sexual object should we choose to go to dinner or visit a museum or do any number of other activities we have previously enjoyed. Nor will Jay. We will continue to treat you as the friend you are. Sexual advances will be limited to the contract conditions. Excepting Jay's flirting, of course. It's impossible to stop his mouth from running away with him."

She laughed, because he was right, and wondered if he'd said it to break the tension. But the lightness faded.

He dove into her answers, confirming she still agreed with what she'd written and probing for additional information. More than four hours passed before they reached the end, and not once did he express surprise, concern or disappointment about anything she'd said.

His methodical, scientific approach reassured her. *He knew I'd appreciate that.* He'd been right, too, to keep this discussion between the two of them.

Jay's unabashed enthusiasm, though relaxing at first, would've grown difficult to manage as Henry's questions went on and on into the afternoon. Jay wouldn't have been able to control his emotional responses, and she might've modified her replies in turn, and Henry wouldn't have gotten the honesty from her he wanted. She had no idea yet what he thought of her replies, but she hadn't censored herself.

By the end, she sat utterly exhausted. Emotionally and mentally wrung out like a dishcloth at a twenty-four-hour diner. But appraisal gleamed in Henry's eyes, so she forced her back to straighten and her eyes to open wide.

He stroked her nose from bridge to tip and tapped once before pulling back. "Perhaps you'd care to nap here? Stretch out on the couch and stay for dinner?"

"I probably shouldn't. I don't want to be a bother." Besides, if Jay came home now, his attitude would overwhelm her. She wasn't up to it, not while waiting for Henry's decision.

"You are not a bother, my dear. You are a friend. And right now, you are exhausted." He paused, smiled gently. "Much as you will be after our evenings together. You'll require time to recover your equilibrium before you depart."

"I will?" She leaned toward him. "You're saying 'yes'?"

"I'm saying yes," he confirmed. "I believe this arrangement will work out well for all of us."

He scrawled his signature on the last page, and she followed suit. Elation coursed through her.

"How do you know?"

"You didn't balk at any of my questions, Alice. Either you're exceptionally open and forthright about your sexuality with everyone you meet, in which case you're likely to be compatible with any number of partners who could introduce you to this lifestyle, or you're exceptionally open and forthright with *me* because of our existing friendship and your trust in me. In which case, we shall do quite well together. Your candor is merely one sign of the sincerity of your interest in pursuing this arrangement."

He stood. "I won't force you to stay. The choice is yours. But I intend to put on some Mozart and prepare dinner. I would very much enjoy being able to look across the room and find you sleeping comfortably on the couch."

He wanted to watch her sleep? She stifled a yawn, considering. Nothing urgent to do today. And she *was* tired. Henry was looking out for her best interests, as a friend. Wasn't that what she'd been so worried about losing?

She nodded. "I'll stay, then."

He nodded in return, raising a single eyebrow. "You do realize, of course, that were now a contract-specified time, I could demand you do exactly that, and you would be obliged to do so unless you chose to use your safeword."

As he walked away, she slid down until she lay curled on her side. He could order her to sleep. To do anything, truthfully, sexual or non-sexual, for the five hours between seven and midnight every other Friday night, unless the contract explicitly forbade it.

The thought distressed her less than she'd feared it might. An oddly soothing thought, in fact. Within minutes, classical music and the clink of cutlery and dishes merged into a lullaby that sent her drifting toward sleep.

Chapter 5

Friday dragged with all the speed of water rolling uphill. Work on the new project hadn't ramped up yet, which left her sitting at her desk studying vague design notes and thinking of nothing so much as seven PM. She had no idea of what to expect. None.

Was she an idiot for agreeing to this? Christ, she'd handed over so much intimate information that Henry now knew her better than any of her previous lovers. Better than she did, maybe.

Yeah, and he made it good before he had any of that information. Oh God. She'd die tonight. He'd kill her with great sex.

When five o'clock arrived, she sped from her office to the T stop. Craned her neck and stared down the track, willing the rattling old train to hurry. Skipped a seat in favor of standing, rocking in the rush hour crush, all to save those few precious seconds and be the first out the door at her stop. She ran the four blocks home like she'd left the iron on. The stairs slowed her steps but not her anticipation.

An envelope graced the center of her door. A dot of cream atop dark-stained oak.

She forced herself to walk. If she ran, Henry and Jay might take note of her thudding footsteps.

She'd found Henry's favored communication style quaint at first. Why leave her handwritten notes when he could text her like Jay did?

But the charm couldn't be denied. She'd long since admitted to herself she enjoyed his thoughtfulness. The pile of notes taking up space in the vanity he'd loaned her proved it.

Henry's flowing script formed her first name across the front of the envelope. Was he canceling? Utter panic.

She snatched the envelope free, wrestled with her key in the lock and managed to get inside. Whereupon she dropped her bag and herself to the floor.

The letter contained no greeting, no salutation. The first line was merely this:

> *Breathe, Alice.*
>
> *My intent is to alleviate your concerns, not to alarm you. I would like you relaxed—though not too relaxed, hmm?—when you present yourself this evening.*
>
> *Eat lightly, if at all. Bathe or shower, as you prefer. Whatever emotions you feel, allow yourself to feel them fully. When you come to me, you will not hide.*
>
> *Do not engage in any sexual stimulation, Alice. Those actions properly belong to me tonight.*
>
> *Wear a sundress. The white with the red hibiscus blossoms you wore in May when we attended the concert in the park, please. Leave your hair down.*
>
> *We'll see you promptly at 7, my dear.*
>
> *H.*

Her first thought was to thank God he wasn't canceling. Her second was that it was nearly six, and she had exactly seventy-three minutes to get ready.

Relaxed, right. If she even managed it, a huge fucking "if," she'd get excited all over again the instant he opened the door.

Shaving her legs in the shower, she nicked herself as his instruction registered. He remembered the specific dress she'd worn on a friendly night out three months ago?

The invitation hadn't been romantic. Henry hadn't wanted to go alone, and Jay had never enjoyed sitting still for two hours. A free classical concert, with amateur community musicians, in the park less than six blocks from their building. She'd kept the note. He'd mentioned how much fun they'd had at the museum for his birthday and what a lovely student she made and did she want to expand her art education to music as well? Nothing sexual about it.

Except now he wanted her to wear that dress. For a sex thing. A sex thing in which he was, for all intents and purposes, her instructor. What had he said the other night, after . . . *after he bent me over the table and fucked me?* Right, after that. Something about Jay being interested in her from day one.

Had Henry been evaluating her this whole time to see if she'd make a suitable playmate for his lover? And now he'd train her to be one? Expand her education.

She took her time drying off, leaving her hair loose, and dug through her underwear drawers for a matching set. The black ones had been her best, but Henry still had the bottoms. They wouldn't have worked under the white dress anyway. Somewhere in the drawer had to be—ah-ha. White satin demicup and matching panties with lace trim. If he took those, too, he'd better start replacing them, or she'd show up in cotton three-packs from a discount store.

Calm descended as she dressed. He'd asked for this outfit, and whatever his reasons, the request comforted her. She couldn't go wrong by following his instructions. She wouldn't spend the night wondering if her clothing flattered her, if she'd reel in her date, because this wasn't a date and the sex was guaranteed.

The mirror was kind as she did her last look. The white linen dress was heavy enough to hide the outline of her underthings, but still flowing. The red sandals matched the blossoms scattered across the dress, and so did the touch of lipstick she'd put on. Her hair grazed her shoulders, hanging straight and flat, as he'd asked.

She was ready.

Butterflies chewed at her stomach. She was so not ready for this. *But I want to be.*

Seven o'clock. She counted the eight steps to their door, raised her hand and rapped twice.

The door opened, and Henry stood before her with a welcoming smile broad enough to show his teeth.

"Alice. It's lovely to see you, my dear. I'm delighted you could make it this evening." He stretched out his hands.

She took them automatically, allowing him to pull her inside.

He set her purse beside the men's keys and phone chargers on the side table and closed the door. His left hand stayed fused to her right.

"I've saved a place just this way." He led her into the living room, his feet bare beneath white linen trousers and a soothing blue shirt, untucked, the color of a dusky sky fading into night.

She followed, keenly aware of the clasp of his hand.

Her eyes widened. The living room furniture had been pushed aside to create an open expanse of floor. At the center lay a checkered blanket with pillows, a picnic basket, and Henry's sandals lying near the edge.

"Sit, Alice, please." He lowered her to the blanket.

She tucked her legs beside herself, her back ruler-straight, and willed herself to relax as he settled next to her.

He flipped open the picnic basket and withdrew a cut flower. A fresh hibiscus blossom. Red. On a comb.

"It matches my dress," she blurted. *Way to state the obvious.*

He smiled and tucked the comb over her right ear, pulling some of her hair back to hold it in place. "So it does, my dear. I must let the other concertgoers know you're my girl, mustn't I? It's traditional."

When he drew his hand back, his knuckles skated across her cheek. The anxiety in her ebbed, a new, more pleasant tension flowing in to replace it.

He was treating this like a date. A concert in the park with Henry. Familiar and unfamiliar, because now his attention was more than friendly, raising an awareness in her skin that these touches meant something. The arousal they woke wasn't accidental or unwanted. He intended to cause such a reaction in her.

"Now, the musicians"—he tapped one finger against the stereo remote lying beside the picnic basket, and she smiled—"aren't quite ready to begin, which gives us a few moments to take care of important matters, Alice."

She nodded despite her uncertainty over what those matters

would be. He couldn't have more questions, not after his exhaustive interrogation last week. Maybe he'd tell her where Jay was.

"You recall your safeword from the other night?"

"Yes, of course."

"Tell it to me now, please, Alice."

"Pistachio." Silly. As if Henry would become some abusive monster she needed to stop.

He studied her for a long moment. "Something's on your mind, some question, perhaps. Tell me."

"I just . . . don't see why it's necessary."

"The safeword?"

"Yeah. I mean, I trust you. I don't think you want to hurt me or anything. And why does it have to be a special word? Why can't we use 'no' or 'stop'?"

His calm nod made it seem he'd expected her questions.

"Because eventually you may wish to play games in which you are free to say 'no' or 'stop' all you like and have me continue despite your pleas. When you feel safe enough to allow *me* to determine your limits. At that point, should a difficulty arise, you will need to have trained your subconscious mind to recognize your safeword and deliver it in an instant. So I will ask you each time we play, Alice. Now, tell me your safeword."

"Pistachio."

"Good girl. And when will you use it?"

She paused to consider her answer as he watched her.

"Whenever I feel like things need to stop."

"Good. And will you be afraid to use it?"

"No." That was an easy answer. She'd never be afraid of Henry. "Because you want me to feel safe, and you won't be angry with me if I need to stop."

"Wonderful. I think we're ready to play now, hmm?"

He made an adjustment on the remote, and music played. Light and flowing.

Violins, she thought, though she didn't recognize the piece. She turned to ask, but he'd anticipated her.

"Dvorak," he murmured. "*Serenade for Strings*, my dear."

He leaned in and placed his lips against hers. A soft kiss. Undemanding. Gone too soon.

He removed items from the picnic basket and poured white wine, handing her a glass, half-full.

She sipped. A light flavor, like melon for breakfast.

Henry held a cracker to her lips, and she ate. Herbs and creamy cheese, with a hint of sharpness at the end.

A small white cube next. Sweet. Juicy. Buttery. A pear.

Another kiss, this time with his tongue swiping across her lips. He pulled away as soon as she parted them.

"Nothing to fear, is there, Alice? Some cause for eagerness, hmm?"

She smiled, meeting his eyes with her own. He'd relaxed her effortlessly. "Yes, Henry."

"Lovely." He reached into the picnic basket. "Then let's heighten the experience, shall we?"

His hand emerged with something thin and black, which he brushed across her arm. Soft fabric. Padded. He held it up.

"A blindfold?" None of her previous lovers had been creative enough to try one, but she'd closed her eyes during sex before. How different could it be?

"You'll find it easier to enjoy the concert if you aren't distracted, my dear."

Oh. Right. He was building this date fantasy for her, maybe because he thought she'd be uncomfortable otherwise. She nodded, slipping a teasing note into her voice when she replied. "We wouldn't want me distracted."

"Mmm. No. We want you very focused. In all of the right places." Henry adjusted the strap around the flower with care as he settled the blindfold over her eyes.

Fabric rustled, soft beneath the strings playing through the stereo, and shifting air raised the delicate hairs on her arms. Henry had moved, but where? She opened her eyes. Her lashes brushed padded darkness. The blindfold closed off all light.

The scent of melon grew stronger. She startled back from a brush against her mouth.

Henry coaxed her with a hushed hum, and the touch came again. The wine glass, its rim smooth, tipped as she opened her mouth.

The cool rush of wine covered her tongue with a hint of honeyed sweetness and a finishing spike of citrus. Delicious, but she had no control. None at all. She wasn't trying to shut out stimuli in a vain attempt to reach orgasm with a clumsy partner now, and she couldn't choose to see him. Couldn't open her eyes for a moment of reassurance. Her right hand rose on instinct, aiming for her face, for the padded darkness.

Henry's hand encircled her wrist, squeezing once before his thumb stroked her pulse point.

"That's no longer your decision to make, Alice." His voice, soft but stern, chided her. "You recall you have a word to use if the experience is too overwhelming?"

She flushed. For a moment, she hadn't remembered at all. His reminder calmed her, and her response was subdued. "Yes, Henry."

"Good girl." His mouth closed over her fingertips, one by one, in quick, sucking kisses while he held her wrist immobile. "Did you wish to use your word now, Alice?"

A vigorous shake of her head. Hell no.

"Good. I haven't nearly finished enjoying you yet."

His voice did things to her. Wriggly, giddy, shivery things. She couldn't get enough of the low tone, or the confidence, or the promise of satisfaction.

He caressed her right ankle, and she fought not to startle at his touch. He shushed her, a whispering hum, as one hand curved around her calf before sliding back down.

"Your legs are lovely, Alice. Sleek and strong." Her right shoe glided away, followed by the left. "There, that's better, isn't it? Shall we relax and listen to the music? Yes?"

She didn't jump when his hand moved to the outside of her right arm. Nor when his fingers traced paths of their own design from the strap of her sleeveless sundress to her elbow and back again. It seemed natural that he should touch her thus. When his other hand lay against her spine, that, too, seemed natural and right, a press of heat below her shoulder blades.

The hand on her arm drifted into new territory. Fingers teased her collarbone until his hand lay flat below her neck, above the swell of her breasts, only his thumb in motion.

At his steady push, she leaned against the hand on her spine.

"I have you, Alice," he murmured, not far from her right ear. "Lie back and listen, my dear."

He guided her to the blanket, until she lay on her back, her head on a pillow, her legs curled to her left. His hands moved away.

A frisson of vulnerable awareness coursed through her. About to ask where he'd gone, she sensed him leaning close to her ear.

"Are you cold, my dear? I thought I saw you shiver. The night air is a bit chilly, hmm? Shall I warm you? No one is looking in our direction. They've eyes only for the stage and its musicians. Perhaps you'd be more comfortable in my arms."

Rubbing soft circles on her right shoulder with the back of his hand, he trailed the touch downward to brush the outer curve of her breast.

She breathed deeply as her body shivered again.

"Yes, you're much too cold, my dear. But we'll fix that." His tone, a mixture of teasing and solicitous, told her he knew quite well what he was doing to her. Temperature had nothing to do with it.

But his insistence conspired with the music and the blindfold to paint a picture on the padded blackness. One in which she lay in the park, surrounded by the hushed whispers of other attendees as the orchestra played and the air cooled with approaching night.

His left arm slipped beneath her, and his chest braced her back with warmth. His legs nestled in behind her own. The music concluded as his right hand grazed her hip.

"Mendelssohn next." His mouth hovered at her ear, his every breath a vibration. "The Violin Concerto. A quick opening, stimulating, plaintive, passionate."

The music began. His fingers danced along her side, and his lips fell upon her neck below her ear, moving in a slow counterpoint to the speed of the violin. His thorough, unhurried appreciation claimed her full attention.

But the press of his fingers against her inner thigh forced a sound from her mouth, a mixture of pleasure and alarm. The hem of her dress had risen without her notice. The tightening in her body illuminated exactly how arousing she found his voice and his touch.

He paused in his worship of her neckline.

"You'll need to be much quieter than that, dearest, unless you wish an audience. I confess . . ." His fingers teased higher with tiny circles. "I myself find nothing troubling in the thought. Your beauty in ecstasy may rival the concert itself. Certainly a show worth witnessing."

He stroked over her panties, his fingers outlining her lips.

Her mind chased the taunting familiarity of his touch as he varied the speed.

The violin. His fingers matched its rhythm. She wished she knew the piece, which stroke would come next. Her hips rocked steadily, a metronome for his variation.

His fingers slipped under the edge of her panties. She freed her sighing moan, the relief as he pushed into her with no resistance. Pushed until his palm lay flat against her sex, his fingers moving within her, his thumb circling her clitoris.

"Please," she gasped. "Please, Henry."

His thumb pressed.

Her hips jerked.

"You want to come here, Alice? In the middle of the park, with people all around us? With my hand between your legs? Is that what you want?" His voice, warm and knowing, told her she did.

"Yes, yes, please."

He obliged her. His mouth returned to her neck, her throat, her collarbone, tasting and teasing. His fingers slicked over her clitoris, dancing in and out.

The blackness in her vision grew bright as tension squeezed her eyes shut, made her body rigid with need. When she came for him, her climax unraveled long and shuddering, her panting breaths becoming soft cries on every exhale. She shook as the music drifted into silence.

A new piece began. Henry rolled them and sat up. His hands took hold of her panties.

She lifted her hips to help, pulling in her legs as he directed until he'd slipped her underwear over her feet and off. She imagined him stuffing them in his pocket, though she couldn't tell from his movements.

He settled her in his lap, draping her legs atop his own and encouraging her to relax and lay her head against his neck.

"You've drawn another gentleman's attention with your enthusiasm, Alice."

Surprise and panic jolted her forward, but his hand on her chest pressed her back.

"Shhh. I warned you what would happen if you couldn't keep quiet, my dear. Shall we show him how wet and ready you are?"

He raised his knees, allowing her legs to fall on the outside of his own, and spread them. Her dress rode up her thighs. Her body lay back, cradled between his chest and his thighs, his erection firm and pressing against her ass through their clothes.

Her heart thumped as a rabbit's must when danger is near. She was open, exposed, and blind. The music dulled her ability to hear much beyond her own breathing and his. She'd become utterly dependent on Henry. Her safety rested in his hands.

His left hand rubbed her chest, a soothing motion. His right made itself known between her legs, fingers spreading her lips open.

She sensed movement in front of her, and instinct urged her to close her legs, but his knees never wavered. Something stroked between her lips. Not fingers. Henry's hadn't moved, and hers worried at the blanket. She whimpered.

"You have a safeword, Alice," Henry whispered in her ear. "If you cannot trust me, it's time to stop."

She took a deep breath through her nose, reaching for calm, and the woodsy scent of bodywash flooded her senses. Jay. Kneeling in front of her, in front of Henry, waiting for her decision.

"No. I trust you." Her hips flexed forward, a slight motion hampered by Henry's legs holding her back. "Don't stop."

She was filled, then, her first experience of Jay's cock as he steadily pushed into her. Different from Henry, not as thick but equally welcome.

"Christ, that's beautiful."

Jay's voice, a harsh rasp, and she wondered if he was watching himself slide in and out, his thrusts starting slowly but gaining speed.

Henry startled her, moving his fingers to massage her while Jay fucked her, putting direct pressure above her clit.

Jay's rhythm wasn't as attuned to her body, wasn't guiding her along with it, but the disconnect didn't matter. Henry's fingers met her needs before she knew she had them, and his voice coaxed her higher.

"That's it, Alice, my brave girl, trusting and giving, let go a little more for me, hmm? You'll fall from a glorious height, and I'll be right here to catch you."

Her fingers clutched at the blanket beneath them.

Henry nuzzled her face. "Let go, Alice. There's nothing you need to control here. I feel the struggle, the tension aching in you, the trembling need in your thighs. Show me what you're holding back."

Jay's rhythm stuttered. He would come soon, she thought, before her mind stopped functioning altogether as Henry's fingers found the perfect pressure. Her body attempted to surge away from his, held tightly in place and shaking uncontrollably as Jay groaned and thrust forward, pinning her body between theirs.

Exhausted satisfaction left her limp against Henry's chest. She turned her face into his neck and nuzzled his skin. She couldn't define his scent the way she could Jay's, but it soothed her, the mix of dark leather and light citrus and everything else that said *Henry* to her nose.

Her hips shifted as Jay left her, and though she felt empty at the loss of him, Henry's body against her back was a comfort. He didn't seem inclined to move despite the erection prodding at her. He hadn't come. He hadn't come the other night, either. He claimed she bore no responsibility for his satisfaction, and maybe she didn't, but leaving him unfulfilled still felt wrong.

He gave her pleasure, and she gave him nothing in return. Trust. Control. Was that all he wanted from her? Maybe putting on a show for Jay, knowing his lover was watching him with her, and seeing the same in return, aroused Henry more than her body did. Maybe that was why he wasn't fucking her now, despite his erection, and why he wouldn't come with her. She might be just a friend to him. A friend and now something of a student.

She sensed Jay moving closer.

His mouth touched hers in a brief kiss. "Thank you, Alice."

His hair brushed her cheek, followed by the sound of another kiss near her ear but not against her skin. He was kissing Henry, and she was missing it.

Her fingers twitched, but she resisted the urge to reach for the blindfold. Henry had already warned her once.

She counted the seconds, listening to the soft sounds as they kissed.

Jay spoke. "Thank you, Henry."

"You're welcome, my boy. Now, if you would be so kind—"

"Washcloth, I know. Gotta look out for Alice's comfort."

Another kiss, this one to her cheek. The blanket rustled. Her sense of Jay disappeared altogether.

Henry lowered his legs, allowing hers to relax, though she couldn't close them. He curved his arms around her, one at her hips and the other under her breasts, a tight clasp she welcomed as she giggled.

Henry rubbed his cheek against hers. "Share what's brought your sweet laughter, my dear, and I'll be certain to repeat the cause so I might enjoy the effect." A small thrust of his hips reminded her she rested fully in his lap. Her movements undoubtedly teased him, even if it wasn't her he wanted to fuck.

"It's just, probably the two best nights of sex in my life, and . . ." She laughed again, not ashamed to admit it. He knew from his questionnaire how lackluster her previous sex partners had been. "It's just I still haven't even taken my dress off."

He chuckled beside her ear, the sound deep and rich, and his arms squeezed her. The fabric slipped against her skin again, the oddity that had amused her.

"Aside from the lack of clothing removal, did you enjoy our game tonight?"

She nodded. The blindfold scratched against something. Henry's cheek or hair, she assumed. "It felt . . . real."

"How so, sweet girl?" His fingers strayed to her side, gliding up and down over her ribcage, and the movement of his arm shifted her breasts with it.

"The blindfold. I didn't know it would be so intense. So different from just closing my eyes." She shivered, though not from a chill. "And your voice. It was . . . it was everything."

"Everything, Alice?"

She shivered again, because his voice was low and teasing and right there beside her ear, his lips brushing her skin. "You're doing that on purpose."

"I am, yes. Do you want to ask me to stop?"

Maybe it was the privacy of the blindfold, or the surreal nature of the whole night, or the safe feeling she had in his arms. Whatever the reason, she didn't stop to think.

"I don't think so," she murmured. "I can't imagine ever asking you to stop." She flushed and tried to backtrack. "I mean—"

"I think you've already said what you mean, Alice, and that's as it should be. You needn't censor your initial reactions, and you needn't be embarrassed by them, either. If all goes well, you'll end each of our nights together with that feeling, which will leave me well satisfied as your dominant."

She smiled. "You love it when a plan comes together?"

A short, sharp laugh from Henry. "More than you know, my dear. I'm rather fond of the moments when my submissives come together as well."

She giggled, and he unwrapped his right arm from around her hips.

"Thank you, Jay." Henry raised his knees, spreading her legs once more.

The warmth of the washcloth between her thighs drew a quiet moan from her throat.

"It seems you've been keeping secrets, Alice."

She sifted through her brain, trying to determine what he meant. "Not that I know of, Henry."

A kiss on her cheek. A steady hand stroking between her legs, patient and thorough. "I would've thought you too young to have watched *The A-Team*."

She laughed.

Henry raised the blindfold in time for her to see a naked Jay kneel beside them. Lowering his legs, Henry allowed hers to slide closed.

"Syndication." She couldn't count the number of times she'd spouted the line along with the actor. It was on the tip of her tongue to blame her dad, the fan, but right now? In the middle—okay, the end—of a sex thing? No matter how relaxed Henry was about the whole dominant thing, she doubted he wanted her bringing up her father on his time. That was one for the friend zone, and this was sex time.

While she watched, Henry bathed Jay as he'd done for her. He laid the washcloth aside on the picnic blanket. "Up you go, my dear. Jay, if you'll offer a hand, please?"

Jay bounced to his feet and grasped her hands, pulling her to her feet.

She flicked her gaze over the blanket.

Jay snickered. "Told you so."

"Again?"

Henry rose to stand in front of her, his hands settling on her waist. "And now the two of you are speaking a secret language, I see."

"You know, Henry . . ."

"Yes, my dear?"

"My underwear drawer doesn't have deep pockets." She smirked at him. "If you're keeping my panties every night I'm here, you'll have to start replacing them, too. Unless you want to see white cotton from now on."

"Or perhaps you'll show up with none at all, sweet girl." He kissed her while she was still digesting *that* idea. "Is there anything you wish to discuss before I release you for the night?"

She shook her head. "It was wonderful. Thank you, Henry." A new thought struck her. "Can I . . . can I kiss Jay good night, too?"

Henry smiled, a wider grin than usual. "What a lovely suggestion. You may, Alice."

She found Jay leaning toward her. "I guess you're okay with that idea, too," she teased. She didn't leave him time to answer, kissing him with firm lips and a hint of tongue.

She slipped her sandals on.

Henry walked her to the door, giving her a final kiss and handing over her purse. "Thank you for your trust and attention this evening." He stroked her back. "If you encounter any difficulties processing events as you reflect further on the experience, bring them to me and we will discuss them together. Am I understood?"

"I understand, Henry."

"Good girl. Then you are released from our game, Alice." He stepped back, allowing her to pass him.

A few strides found her at her own door, opening the lock and stepping inside. She closed the door on Henry's gaze and tossed her things aside. Stripped to her skin and lay on her futon.

Henry and Jay had done all the work. She'd hardly moved. Yet she thought she might sleep for a week.

"Signing that contract might be the best decision you've ever made, Allie-girl."

Henry hewed rather close to the scenario he'd given her with the concert during their next three nights together. The evening always started with role-play, something almost romantic, and led to her, blindfolded, having energetic sex with Jay while Henry directed them and made certain she enjoyed herself.

But he didn't fuck her. Didn't use his mouth on her. He left those things to Jay.

So even though she grew intimate with the clasp of his body and the scent of his skin and—God yes—the sound of his voice, and even though he'd told her to come to him if she needed him, she avoided asking about his distance. Just because Henry treated her as a lover as part of their arrangement didn't mean that's what she was to him.

As long as she kept the distinction firm in her head, she'd be fine. What did she need beyond the exciting-but-safe sex? Nothing, that was what. She had no need to go running to Henry about her confusion. He was available if she had a real problem. Crying to him about every stray thought that passed through her head would abuse his generosity, his willingness to split his attention between his real lover and her.

Besides, Jay seemed to be making some extra effort to maintain their friendship, and he provided comical entertainment at its finest. Every week, not just every other week, his delivery route brought him out near her office complex. Somehow, he always had time to stop for lunch, texting to say he'd be down the street in five and did she want to join him?

So every Tuesday for six weeks, she'd eaten lunch with Jay. During which he talked about anything and everything except the fact that he was fucking her on alternate Fridays. He flirted, though. At least until he'd get a half-panicked look on his face and change the subject.

Maybe Henry had given him a list of acceptable topics.

Henry himself hadn't approached her outside of their contract nights. But twice now he'd left her gifts with the notes he placed on her door before their nights together. The first, a small metal sculpture of a hibiscus in bloom, graced her desk at work. The second? A box of replacements. Bra and panty sets in six shades.

She wore them when she went to him now.

He did eventually remove all of her clothes. He tormented her with a vibrator while Jay gripped her wrists. He always stopped before she came. That, she only ever did with his fingers inside her, or with Jay's fingers, or tongue, or cock.

Overall, the arrangement wasn't so different from her past experiences. Except for the blindfold. The excitement. The satisfaction. The two guys.

Right. Except for all of that. But otherwise? Completely the same.

No whips or chains or that Japanese rope thing that seemed all the rage on the sex blogs she'd studied while reading the contract terms. From her unscientific study, he was pretty lenient for a dominant and taking excellent care of her needs. She considered asking him about the vibe, though, because it felt fantastic. Maybe she'd replace her current favorite.

On the other hand, Henry wielding it made for a fabulous benefits package. He always made sure she was satisfied before he let Jay fuck her. And even then, he stepped in with his voice frequently, with his hands when necessary, to make sure Jay pleased her, too.

He acted almost as if testing her responses. Putting her on a long line and watching her gait. She'd spent plenty of summers on her aunt and uncle's ranch watching them train up the horses for sale. Henry was taking her measure, seeing if she'd fight the bit, tossing a blanket across her back until she was ready for the saddle—and the rider.

Teaching Jay, too, maybe. Every night they met, Jay grew more attuned to her. Needed less help from Henry to find her rhythms. Maybe Henry meant to pair them. Carriage horses. A matched set.

She laughed at the thought, but it was true, wasn't it? Henry was the driver, and they were his team. Someday, he'd be holding the whip.

Anticipation made her clench with a whisper of fear and an avalanche of arousal.

Chapter 6

Jay opened the door at her knock, held it wide enough for her to step past him and closed it behind her. He didn't touch her, and though she smiled at him, he didn't greet her. Was he already playing?

In the living room, Henry stood and approached her, gesturing for her to remain still. "Alice. Punctual as always. How lovely."

He didn't make small talk. His time started now, and on these nights, she was not Alice the neighbor and friend who might need to talk about her day. Such things belonged outside the door.

Anything that demanded responsibility or concern was Henry's to handle. She needed only to listen and obey. Outside this carefully controlled place, she still squirmed at the thought on occasion. But here, he'd instructed her to accept herself and her desires without shame.

"Are you ready to play, Alice?"

"Yes, Henry."

"Go to the bedroom. Remove your clothes, all of them. Leave them on the chair. Lie on your back in the center of the bed and wait for me."

She acknowledged him with a sharp nod and turned down the hall, away from them both. The eager anticipation she'd leashed all day broke free and danced in her muscles. It was permitted here. She was done hiding for the day.

She placed her clothes on the chair and climbed onto the bed. No top sheets, no comforter, no pillows. Just the fitted sheet and a vast expanse she alone couldn't fill. She lay back and waited, her pulse picking up speed.

Henry almost always made her wait. It made the reward sweeter, he said, and she agreed. Waiting was hard, but it felt very, very good.

A footstep. Her breath caught.

Sweeping into the bedroom, Henry radiated confidence and calm beneath his oh-so-proper attire. The collar flaps on his dress shirt, a purple so deep it flirted with black, stood crisp and buttoned. The shining clasp of his belt taunted her fingers. Dared her to open his pants and see what he refused to give her.

Jay, following, was as naked as she, and half-hard already.

"Stand at the foot of the bed, please, Jay. I'll call for you when you're needed."

As Jay obeyed, Henry strode closer, near the head of the bed to her left. "Tell me your word, Alice."

"Pistachio."

"Good. And when will you use your word?"

"Anytime I want things to stop, for any reason."

"Will I be angry with you if you use your word?"

"No. You'll be proud of me for recognizing my limits and being honest with you."

"Correct. Very good, Alice."

The ritual played out nearly word for word every time. Henry's way of reassuring her, she supposed. As a tactic, it was effective. She never doubted her ability to stop things. He prompted her himself sometimes, reminded her to use her word if their games skirted the edges of her boundaries. Thus far, she hadn't needed to.

"We're playing a new game tonight, Alice." Bending over, Henry retrieved something from under the mattress. "Extend your left arm toward me, please."

She did, without hesitation, though he held some kind of strap. Black, with a metal ring at the end and a shorter strap hooked on it with a metal clasp. At the opposite end of the short strap was a wider piece of black fabric, perpendicular to the rest.

He folded the soft, padded fabric up and around her wrist, and she shivered as Velcro closed. A handcuff. Something designed to keep her in place. They hadn't experimented with bondage, at least not aside from the weight of hands and hips.

"Tug for me, please, Alice."

The strap gave a bit, but the cuff remained strong around her wrist.

"All right?"

She nodded, a shaky jerk, as her excitement gained a new, nervous edge. She was breathing through her mouth now. When had she parted her lips?

Henry guided her fingers to a small loop. "Pull sharply."

She yanked. The Velcro peeled back to free her hand. No matter what happened, she wasn't trapped here.

He refastened the cuff. "Are you confident of your safety, Alice? Do you wish to continue?"

"Yes, please."

Her breath calmed as Henry kissed her open palm. He secured her ankles and right wrist, until she lay naked and spread, arms straight out from her sides, feet pointing at the far corners of the bed.

He stepped back, studying her in silence.

Jay, too, stood still and silent, his erection firm and bobbing against his stomach.

Henry began to walk, pacing around the bed, and her eyes followed his movement.

"Tell me, Alice, when did you first experience intercourse?"

He knew the answer, of course. He'd asked the question as they'd created the outlines of her contract with him. Of what she wanted and why, of what she'd tried before and liked or disliked.

"College. Freshman year. It was finals week, before Christmas break."

"Did you know the boy well?"

"We'd been dating for a couple of months."

"Were you in love?"

"No." The idea had seemed ridiculous at the time. In some ways, it still did. Love was chemistry, all pheromones and neurotransmitters, sexual attraction calling itself by a romantic name. Chemistry and stupidity and people fooling themselves. "I just wanted to know what everybody else knew. To figure out how everything worked. I was tired of theory and guesswork. I wanted a practical."

"And where did you plan this tryst? Or did it simply . . . fall into your lap?"

The men wore identical smirks.

She wasn't embarrassed. Not of this.

"No, I planned it. My dorm room. My roommate had a bio lab final. I knew she'd be there for the whole three hours."

"You wanted to be able to take your time."

"Yes."

"Did he? This boy of yours?"

"He tried. We made out for a while. Clothes got tossed. Condom went on. After that, it was about three minutes." He'd been sweet, if not satisfying. She didn't regret the experience, though if she'd known then what she knew now, she might've chosen a partner with more care. Someone older. More knowledgeable. More Henry.

"Did he rectify the situation?"

"He apologized. We cuddled and fooled around some more, until he was ready to go again." At that age, recovery hadn't taken long, though he'd claimed to find it distracting that she wanted to watch, to catalog every twitch as he stiffened. In the end, he'd plastered his mouth to hers and ground himself against her stomach. Forgot the condom in his rush to get inside her again. Thank God she'd been levelheaded enough to remember.

"He came twice in those three hours?"

"Yes."

"And how many times did you reach orgasm?"

"I didn't." That had been disappointing, sure. But even now—well, up until this thing, whatever it was, with Henry and Jay—she counted on two hands the number of times she'd come with a partner. In the nearly nine years since that Thursday afternoon on a crowded single bed, it hadn't been for lack of trying.

"You had been able to do so previously on your own?"

"Yes."

"The intercourse wasn't stimulating enough?"

"No." It was never stimulating enough. *Had* never been stimulating enough, she corrected. Now she expected more. If . . . when . . . Henry and Jay tired of her and these Friday nights came to an end, her next partner would have to work damn hard to meet the new standard.

"And this boy, did he put his mouth and fingers to work to please you?"

"No." Awkward groping, yes. Oral sex hadn't been on the menu.

"So in those three hours, you received some insufficient foreplay, some apologetic cuddling, and some small bit of pain?"

She smiled. She'd complained, later, of the same disappointments, though in more colorful terms. "Yes."

"Ah. You deserve better than that, my dear. Much better."

Henry stopped his pacing and stood behind Jay, almost invisible. His mouth hovered at Jay's ear, though his eyes watched her.

"No toys, Jay. You may use your body to stimulate Alice however you like, within the restrictions already agreed upon. You may come twice. Your goal, however, is to please Alice. Make her come, Jay. Make her come as many times as her body can manage. I want our girl thoroughly satisfied and entirely exhausted, is that understood?"

"Yes, Henry." Jay wet his lips.

"Good. You have three hours. Begin."

Henry stepped back, and she mentally nicknamed him the professor in this scenario. Would he grade Jay's performance? Oh shit. Maybe this was Jay's final exam. *Henry ought to wear one of those jackets with the patched elbows.*

Her thought stuttered as Jay dropped beside her in full exuberant-puppy mode, kissing her cheek. Nuzzling her face. Wiggling his groin against her left hip.

"You know it's not just the sex, right?" His voice was earnest and loud and punctuated by kisses to her neck and bites to her earlobe.

What is he . . .

"I mean, I really like you, and it's so fucking hot that you want me to be your first."

Ohhh. The scenario wasn't merely a setup for him. He was going with it, role-playing it to the hilt. Recreating the anxious excitement, the unknowing of that first time.

"God, Alice, sometimes I see you across the room, and it's just . . ."

He stopped to suckle at her neck. His left hand stroked her belly. Up and down her side. A squeeze at her hip. A circling at her breast.

"I practically come in my pants I'm so hard. But I'm gonna make it good for you, I promise. You know that, right?"

"I know." She tried to think herself back to that girl, imagining Jay as an upperclassman. A frat boy. She smirked. "It's why I picked you. I like the way you look at me. And your reputation gets around."

"I'm just a hard cock to you?" His voice was a teasing pout. He thrust his hips, and her clit throbbed in echoing reply. "What have you heard?"

His hand stroked lower, teasing the crease of her thigh, dangerously close to—for tonight, anyway—virgin territory.

"That you take your time. And that you have a lot more to offer than just a hard cock."

He chuckled against her throat. "I've got two hands and a mouth, sweetheart, and I'm gonna use them all on you. How long did you say your roommate was gonna be out?"

Jay rose over her, weight balanced on one arm while the other lay across her abdomen and curved upward so his hand cupped her right breast. He planted sucking kisses along her collarbone.

"Three hours." She gasped at the firm tug of his mouth, wondered if he might be inclined to repeat it on her breasts or between her legs. If there was a God, he would. "She's at a lab final."

"What if her professor's sick? Or the fire alarm gets pulled?" The hand at her breast pulled away, her nipple taut between thumb and forefinger as he plucked at her. "Then she'd be back early. With a key to get in. And she'd be watching you, all naked and flushed and beautiful, panting and trembling and needy."

He lifted his head from her chest and stared down into her face.

"You'd like that, wouldn't you, Alice? You like being watched."

God, Jay sounded almost like Henry then, confident and in control, and she wondered how well he'd learned his lessons.

He swept his tongue into her mouth when she opened it to speak. Her body rolled, undulating to the same rhythm. One of his legs pinned her left hip to the mattress. The straps tugged against her wrists and ankles when she arched up to meet him.

It hadn't happened that way. Her roommate hadn't come back until well after Alice's first lover had left. But the possibility alone fed her arousal. A need grew in her to know if Henry was hard, watching them from a dark corner.

She twisted and came up short. The cuffs rasped against the sheets. She shuddered. No control. No fulfilling her own needs. She tugged again and gloried in the drag of the cuffs.

Jay's mouth left hers. He rolled off and settled beside her, his breath fast. Too close, maybe? He'd pulled his hips back, and his erection no longer pressed against her flesh. His left hand hovered above her stomach.

"It's okay if you're nervous, Alice. We don't have to rush, right? If you wanna stop, you can tell me."

Damn, he's adorable.

"No, I wanna do this." She didn't have to pretend to be in earnest. That part came easily. Pretending to have a virgin's nerves came harder. She softened her voice. "I just wanted to touch you. Silly, right? 'Cause *you* were already touching *me*. Only now you're not."

Jay breathed out. Resting his face on her shoulder, he lowered his left hand and rubbed her stomach in a slow circle. "I am now. Is that better?"

"Yeah. Yeah, I like it when you touch me." She took a deep breath, and his head shifted. He'd be watching her breasts, of course. He never seemed to get enough of them. *So adorable.* "It makes me want more."

He slid closer, his lower body touching hers again, left leg covering hers, cock brushing her hip. "More like this?"

"Mm-hmm." She buried her face in his hair. "Maybe even more than that. I get all wet sometimes, thinking about . . . more."

"You can tell me about it if you want." Jay rolled on top of her, straddling her left leg, and stared into her eyes. "Just 'cause you can't touch me doesn't mean you can't guide me. I'm here for your pleasure. Whatever you want."

She smiled and let herself go with the role-playing. Tried to look suitably starry-eyed. "I've never done this before. I don't know what I want. But you do. You know how to make me feel good."

He did. He'd paid attention on all of their Fridays. She knew he had, because he was putting that knowledge to use now. He might love her breasts, but he didn't limit himself to touching them and nothing else. And he might want to bury his cock in her, but he didn't immediately reach for a condom, either.

He ran his palms over her arms, one at a time, from her wrists all the way to her shoulders, and followed the same path with his mouth. He spent time appreciating her neck. Her jaw. Her ears. He stroked her sides and kissed her ribs, his hair tickling her breasts. By the time he turned his attention to her breasts, her nipples stood hard and waiting.

"You're so beautiful," he murmured.

"Not too small?" She wasn't normally self-conscious about her breasts, but it was nice to be appreciated sometimes.

"Christ, no. Just right." Jay cupped her right breast. His mouth descended on her left.

She moaned as his fingers massaged her and his mouth sucked at her.

Desire wound its way down her stomach and pulsed between her legs. She couldn't close them, couldn't bring her thighs together to find relief, and Jay's weight rested at her left side rather than over her. He'd curled one leg around her, a pleasant weight on her thigh, but she needed more now. Her hips squirmed. Her hands clenched and released.

The edge of panic, desperation, heightened the sensation when Jay's teeth grazed her left nipple. Orgasm hovered just out of reach. She couldn't get the pressure she needed by herself, not with her hands and feet bound. During her real first time, she hadn't tried. Nerves, or the naive belief that orgasms should magically happen without help. But since then, if she was anywhere near close, she gave herself a hand. Until Henry and Jay.

A whimper escaped her throat, a tiny plea, and Jay stopped massaging her breast. He lifted his head.

"More?"

She almost complimented him on his uncertain expression. As if he couldn't tell.

"More," she agreed. "Definitely more."

He gave her a boyish little smile and lowered his head to her breasts. His mouth switched sides to take the place of his hand on her right, his body leaning across her, putting more weight on her. He tugged at her right nipple with his teeth.

Oh God fuck yes.

His fingers brushed over her clit, back and forth, slow at first, and his mouth sucked at her breast, and she couldn't stop thinking. Not just that Jay had read her need and moved his fingers to help her. Not just that the cuffs added excitement. No. It was the knowledge that she was going to climax, and Jay was going to make it happen without her help, and Henry was watching her. Listening to her. Silently willing her to come, maybe.

Her brain buzzed. *He wants to see it. They both do.*

She moaned, low and needy, when Jay's firm touch sped up and her hips bucked under him. The harder he sucked at her breasts, the deeper the throb between her legs. Her eyelids dropped shut. Her back arched.

For a split second, she imagined he held her open for Henry. Henry, who hadn't fucked her since that first night. Henry, who'd almost made her come with a single thrust.

The fingers on her clit squeezed, the way Henry had that night, and she gasped as she came, her toes curling, hips shaking, arms pulling at the restraints.

Jay's fingers stopped moving. His hand curved protectively over her sex, a warm and gentle touch. He kissed her breasts, the right and then the left, and wriggled until his face lay alongside hers.

She didn't wait. Unable to wrap her arms around him or slide her fingers through his hair, she stretched to reach his mouth and kiss him appreciatively. He surrendered, letting her control the kiss, though the hand between her legs cupped her more tightly, covering her while the last shudders spiraled through her.

Sweet. The sort of thing she imagined Henry would do. Give her a safe space to feel vulnerable. Wasn't that what he'd already done here, in his home? She gentled the kiss and let Jay go, but he stayed close, his mouth brushing her cheek when he spoke.

"Did you like that?"

"It was amazing." Virgin thoughts. Role-play. Her brain bouncing in orgasm-land didn't signal the end of the game. "Your fingers felt so good on me. I love the way you touch me."

Jay's voice dropped to a conspiratorial whisper, but his smirk made it clear he was keeping it loud enough for Henry to hear. "I learned that move from a friend."

She giggled. "Your friend had a hand in teaching you?"

"More than a hand," Jay whispered, and she moaned.

Oh God that's hot.

"Do you . . . still want more than a hand tonight? It's okay if you don't, sweetheart. We'll go at your pace."

No horny college guy was that considerate. No, not true. Henry had coached Jay for this role. And Henry might've been exactly that sort of considerate guy.

Jay pulled back to look at her. The hand on her sex drifted to her right hip and rolled in a slow circle. Waiting all night for her answer wouldn't faze him.

"I want to try more," she whispered, trying to strike a balance between shy virgin and eager coed. "I want you to make me feel that way again. Is that okay? Do you want to touch me?"

She expected a joke. Giving Jay a straight line was dangerous.

"I always want to touch you." The utter seriousness in his voice floored her. He kissed her mouth, a chaste touch. "And I'm all yours right now, Alice. Whatever you want, remember? It's your special night."

His words were true outside tonight's role-playing game, too. Every other Friday was her special night. Although she never asked for things she wanted. Henry just knew. He decided the flow of the evening, and she submitted to it. This, tonight, was different.

She and Jay lacked the smooth, even flow of Henry's direction. She kept expecting his voice but heard only the rustle of the sheets and restraints and the throaty murmurs of her pleasure and Jay's.

Unlike Henry, Jay seemed to want her to request things. Well. She knew one way he'd have no trouble getting her off again, though previous partners had never offered and rejection marred her lone request. The uncomfortable look and halfhearted "I could try if you gotta have it, but, I mean, I'd rather not" had been such a turnoff she'd never bothered asking again.

She didn't want some guy she couldn't trust sticking his head between her legs. Or to make oral some obligatory chore he thought he had to do before he could fuck her.

But if she'd learned one thing from her nights with them so far, it was that Jay had a fantastic tongue. What would encourage him to use it? She needed to think like a virgin. A nervous, not-too-experienced virgin.

"Would you . . ." She couldn't force a blush, but she lowered her eyelids. "If I wanted . . ."

Jay's hips gave a little thrust. Involuntary, probably, like the tiny moan he breathed in her ear. His cock pressed hard against her side.

Bingo. I'll take "Shy Virgin Requests" for $500, Alex.

"Anything you want, sweetheart."

"Maybe you could use your mouth to touch me? I heard it can hurt the first time if I'm not ready."

Jay beamed as if she'd voiced the best idea he'd ever heard. Like he wanted to patent it. Here was the confident-swagger Jay she'd expected. She'd been wrong to imagine him as a frat boy in this scenario. She should've known that if Henry was grading this performance, Jay would channel the sensitive artist, not the preening jock.

He scrambled to his knees and moved back on the bed, navigating between her spread legs with care.

"I don't want this to hurt, Alice, so let's get you nice and relaxed for my cock." Jay dipped his head between her thighs. His tongue probed along her lips, easing them open. He flicked his tongue against her clit, just once, and she jerked toward him. "Has anyone touched you like this before?"

"No." She shook her head. "You're the first."

That was even true. She giggled.

"Mmm." He licked her, a slow glide, his tongue flat. "I'm glad I can be the first to taste you."

"You already are," she murmured, lost in the memory. "I was pretty fucking happy about it, too."

He paused, and she shivered with the remembered sensation. The way Henry had held her open while Jay made her come again and again with his skilled tongue. Before the contract, before the questions, before Henry had known what he offered with Jay's mouth.

"You mean . . . the first time we . . . that was . . ."

She must've broken his brain. Not that it was hard to do with Jay. But he wouldn't have broken character otherwise. Her fault. She'd started it.

"Mm-hmm. It was one hell of an apology." She damn well wouldn't forget it, being cradled in Henry's arms while Jay teased his way up her legs and tasted her. She'd trusted Henry, trusted them both, enough to let it happen. Her first time on the receiving end.

Jay's low, drawn-out "*fuck*" pushed his breath over her clit, but it was Henry's unseen reaction that made her shiver. An indrawn hiss followed by a rumbling growl that woke a sleeping corner of her mind. A possessive, fierce sound as if he wanted to taste her immediately. Or turn the clock back ten weeks and taste her first. Alpha male. Ego thing. His dominant growl made her walls clench. Made her body demand to be under his, *now*, filled and sheltered and shuddering toward ecstasy.

She squirmed, restless, her hips rocking.

Jay didn't hesitate to take advantage of the jump in her arousal. He thrust two fingers into her without preamble. He latched onto her clit and sucked hard, teeth grazing her, and she bucked beneath him. The straps pulled taut against her wrists and ankles and gave her hips little space to maneuver.

She wanted to touch him, to encourage him with her hands in his hair and her legs around his back, but lacked the option. Unless she rotated her wrist and yanked the panic loop brushing the back of her hand. Ended the game. No fucking way.

When she forgot and tried to reach for him, every attempt reminded her of her own vulnerability. Which heightened her fear, which heightened her arousal and sent two thoughts pounding through her brain. Jay would never hurt her, and Henry had guaranteed her safety. They'd proved their trustworthiness on every night she'd spent here and in the year of friendship beforehand.

Tied down, she was perfectly free. Allowed to express herself in ways she usually didn't. If she couldn't make her appreciation felt, she could at least make it heard.

So when Jay's fingers thrust, she babbled her pleasure and urged him to move faster. She moaned as his mouth tugged the top of her sex inside and his tongue rubbed her clit. She sighed in the aftermath of orgasm when he showed the good sense to stop stimulating her clit and instead lapped at her pussy.

He raised his head, his mouth wet with her and his hair falling across his forehead.

"Alice, I was, umm, thinking we should make extra sure you're relaxed enough. To be sure you want this." His face beamed with hope, and she ached to offer proper encouragement. "So maybe I could . . . again?"

"I like *again*," she murmured. "Your mouth is even better than just your fingers. If I'd have known sex could feel this good, I'd have done it ages ago."

The moment his hopefulness turned to determination played out on his face, in his lowered brows and pursed lips. He had this roleplaying thing nailed. Better than her, certainly. A scenario he played out for Henry often? With every new partner?

Jay flashed a smile. "I'm glad you waited to try this. It's . . . really important to start with a good teacher."

He ducked his head between her legs and started slow, kissing her thighs, using his hands to stroke her hips and waist and belly.

She let her thoughts slip away. Did it matter what he'd done with other girls? What Henry might have done? The two of them were hers for now, and the sex was fantastic.

Jay's tongue and fingers made finding the edge of orgasm again easy. The cuffs tugging at her and the memory of Henry's gentle touch as he tied her down made it even easier to tumble over. Her landing would always be a soft one in this bed, she thought. She rested on a high plateau, basking in arousal and sensitized to Jay's gentle kisses as he worked his way up her body.

He'd taken Henry's directive to make her climax to heart, but she wanted his cock. Wanted to share that moment when her body tightened and her movements surpassed conscious control. She wasn't going to take no for an answer.

If this was supposed to be her virgin night and he'd been ordered to do whatever she wanted, then by God he'd fuck her now. *Try to be a little more virginal and lot less demanding when you tell him, Allie-girl.*

He settled against her side, his erection an obvious need pressed to her hip, but he seemed content kissing her neck and shoulders. She rolled her face left and nudged his head.

"You have protection, right? I mean, of course you do, because you want us both to be safe."

"I do, yeah." Jay raised his head. "I want us both to be safe."

"I think it's time to put it on." She pushed her hips sideways, adding pressure against his cock. "So I can feel what I've been waiting for."

Jay kissed her cheek before he rolled away.

Twisting her head far left brought the edge of the nightstand into view. The condoms lay on top. The packet ripping open seemed loud in the silence.

He put it on with his back to her. His muscles moved in a lovely play of shadow and light, a sight Henry must appreciate daily, but she would've preferred a front-row seat when Jay held his cock in his hand.

He turned to her, and this time he didn't stop at her side. Centering his weight over her, he aligned their hips. He stared into her eyes, and she produced a soft, trusting smile. He wet his lips.

"You're sure you want to give me this? You can still say 'no' if you want. Don't be afraid to tell me, okay? You don't have to worry. There's no shame in stopping if you're not ready."

Oh God, he was sweet. And that made it so much better. Making sure she was ready for him. Letting her know, again and again, he'd stop if she said the word. As if she were a nervous virgin in truth, and this their first union, and Jay the considerate, compassionate lover going slowly for her.

She hadn't played the shy virgin before. Her first time had been methodical and decisive, at her instigation, and her partner surprised but enthusiastic, if ultimately incompetent. But Jay's performance went beyond competence. Maybe he heard Henry's guidance in his head. Like Henry shared the bed with them, even in his absence.

Was it wrong that the idea made her hips buck? Jay seemed to like it, though he probably thought her just answering his question. He held his cock in a firm grip and rubbed the head between her lips without entering.

She rolled her hips to encourage him.

"I feel like I want it." She couldn't pretend shyness anymore. "You make me feel wonderful, Jay. I want to feel all of it. I'm not afraid."

He nudged, and they both gasped.

She fought not to giggle. He'd sunk farther than he meant to. All the role-playing in the world couldn't change the fact that she wasn't a nervous, dry virgin suffering from inadequate foreplay. She was an aroused woman eager to welcome her partner. *Go with it. Don't make him feel like he did something wrong.*

"Yeah, like that, I want to feel you. It's better than I imagined." That sounded virginal, didn't it? As if they hadn't had sex two weeks ago or two weeks before that or . . .

He bracketed her body with his arms. Lifted his hips. Pulled almost out before pushing in deeper.

She tried to raise her legs, but the soft cuffs held her back. She'd have to go at his pace. A tremor rolled through her, and she moaned.

"You thought about it?" Jay kissed her cheek. "You like it nice and deep? Like that, Alice?"

"Just like that. I think about it a lot. When I'm by myself. Touching."

"About me?" He thrust again, still slow and deep. In deference to her pretend-virgin status, maybe, or a result of focusing on their conversation. Or he feared he'd come too soon if he rushed the pace.

She nodded, but some wicked impulse wouldn't let her leave it there. "About you, yeah. You and your friend. The one who had more than a hand in teaching you."

Jay's slow withdrawal became a quick thrust, hard and rocking her hips as he ground against her. He panted across her cheek.

"Jesus." He gulped in a breath. "Fuck, you gotta stop telling me things like that, Alice. I don't . . . I don't wanna hurt you or leave you unsatisfied."

She nuzzled his ear, a gentle apology. "Jay, sweetheart, I can't help it. I want you to know how excited I am. How much I want this. Just because it's something new doesn't mean I'm afraid of it."

A pleased hum—not Jay's—rolled from the darkness.

A secret thrill shot through her. "You're not hurting me. I'm not unsatisfied. Even if I didn't come again tonight, I'd still be satisfied. It's my best first time ever."

Jay groaned, turned his head, and kissed her. Not a peck this time. A hard, thorough, Henry-like kiss. His hand snaked between their bodies and rubbed her clit. His hips thrust.

"But *I'd* be unsatisfied if I couldn't make you feel good again. And my friend would be unsatisfied." His fingers circled. He settled more heavily on her with only one arm to hold him up, and she welcomed his weight. "I bet he'd love to be watching you right now."

"I'd like that," she confessed.

Jay kissed her again, like a reward. His fingers gained pressure and speed. His hips, too, moved faster, and she felt the vibration of the moan emerging from his throat before she heard it. Jay was close.

She could be, with a little thought. She didn't want Jay to fail his final exam.

Maybe Henry would give a textbook demonstration afterward. Leave her tied down and open to him. Walk Jay through every section of the exam and show how he might've done things differently. Henry would talk all the way through. He'd use his voice to question her, to tell her of his arousal and her own. Heighten the intensity until she thought she'd die.

Her orgasm hit as Jay thrust again, and she gripped his cock over and over. The only part of him she could reach. Her legs, held fast at the ankles, couldn't rise no matter how hard she pulled, and her arms strained uselessly against the cuffs while she shook.

The helplessness beat at her mind, a panic that made Jay's finishing thrusts and his hard kisses at her throat more intense, more pleasurable. Henry must've known that, he must've known when he'd set up their game tonight. She lay safe in his bed, with him watching to see how much she enjoyed this.

She tipped her head back and shrieked, a drawn-out *yes*, her body stiffening under Jay's as a second orgasm followed hard on the heels of the first.

He groaned and held her tight, done but not leaving her. He clung to her while she trembled, and he kissed her cheeks and the corners of her mouth when she panted for air. He rested his elbows on the mattress, his fingers smoothing her hair from her face.

When she could breathe, she lifted her head to rub her cheek against his, nudging him into a kiss. Slow. Gentle. He looked awestruck. Like he needed this more than she did. Maybe his first time had been a wash, too. She'd ask him if she got the chance. But not now, with his tongue sliding along hers and his thumbs gliding across her cheeks.

She let her head fall back to the mattress, and he followed her down. This was already miles better than her real first time. Jay was much cuddlier. He didn't roll over and flop on his back without touching her like her first sexual partner had. Of course, Jay didn't have anything to apologize for, either. She grinned. *Thank the nice boy, Allie-girl.*

She whispered into his ear as he nuzzled her neck. "Does it always feel this good?"

He sucked in a breath. His body trembled once, and he pressed his face hard against her neck. "It will for you, Alice. Every time."

Wow. Talk about a serious answer. If she were a virgin and he her first, she'd be melting. Hell, she practically was anyway.

A soft sound she couldn't place had an immediate effect on Jay, his head popping up like a dog hearing its master's call. Ah. Henry clearing his throat.

Jay seemed to flip through something in his head before his eyes widened.

"Are you comfortable, Alice? Do you need a break? A snack? Or the bathroom?" His hand fumbled between them as he pulled out.

"Nope." She shook her head. "I'm good. Feeling spectacular." She smiled to shore up his nerves. *First time directing things, Jay?*

She couldn't imagine him directing things with Henry. Even tonight, Henry hadn't abandoned him. He'd just retreated to the shadows. If the lights hadn't been angled toward the bed, she might've been able to find him.

Jay sat up. "Okay. Can you ... umm ..." He took a breath. "Wiggle your right hand for me?"

She did.

"And the left?" Again, his head turning. "Feet, too, please?"

Repeating the safety check Henry had gone through, but with less confidence. *Adorable.*

Did Jay behave this way in bed with all the women he'd dated with Henry's blessing? He might falter without Henry to coach him, unless he received instructions beforehand. Homework assignments.

She pushed the stray thoughts aside as Jay stripped off the condom and disposed of it before he curled up with her.

He lay on his side, his body perpendicular to hers, legs tucked alongside her outstretched left arm. His head rested on her chest, facing her. His left arm curved over her and wrapped under her back. He stroked her skin with his right hand, fingers tracing her collarbone out to her left shoulder and back to her throat, outlining every dip and curve.

"You're sure you're okay, Alice?"

She tipped her chin down to look at him. Warm brown eyes met hers, a vivid reminder of the first day they'd met, of the way Jay had continually sought Henry's approval and praise. Henry was quiet tonight. A background player in this game. If Jay needed praise and reassurance, it would have to come from her.

"Kiss me?"

He leaned forward to fulfill her request in an instant, as if he'd been waiting for her to ask. She took control, keeping the kiss soft and soothing, a series of nibbles and tugs and light touches ending with a firm press of closed lips.

"I'm better than okay, Jay, all because of you." She ached to touch him, to wrap her arms around him and roll him underneath her. To protect him. Flexing her hands, she flirted with temptation. But pulling the release loops would be cheating. Jay would feel like a failure, and Henry would worry she'd been injured in some way.

She rubbed Jay's legs with her left arm, a small motion, but the best one she could manage. "Because you took your time and made me feel special. Because you're sweet, and funny . . ." She smirked at him and lowered her tone. "And really, really fun in bed."

He kissed her face, a dozen happy pecks, in full exuberant-puppy-Jay mode. At least he wasn't licking her. Although she wouldn't mind if he wanted to hump her leg.

She eyed Jay's cock, lying soft against his left thigh. Henry had given Jay permission to come twice. And she wasn't exhausted yet.

She nudged his face and kissed him again, deeper, moaning when his right hand wandered across her breasts. She encouraged him to keep going with a steady stream of soft noises, and Jay didn't disappoint.

He massaged her neck and breasts with hand and mouth together. His left hand, beneath her, flattened against her back and pressed upward, holding her tight. Arousing, but . . .

He said whatever I wanted.

"Jay? Would you—"

"Anything you want. Do you want me to stop?" He pulled back from her breasts. "We don't have to do anything else if you don't want to."

"What if I do want to?" She arched her back to push her breasts toward his hand. *Gently, Alliegirl. Think virginal. Twenty minutes post-deflowering virginal.*

A glance left made her lick her lips. Jay's cock wasn't anywhere near hard yet—she didn't expect it to be—but there was movement there, the potential for more with encouragement. "I heard . . . sometimes . . . a guy can go more than once in one night. If he wanted."

Jay's chest filled out. His fingers trailed over her breasts. "Oh, I *want*, Alice. You don't ever need to feel unwanted, okay?"

She nodded. Unlike her former partners, he wouldn't turn her down. Hell, he'd done it for her before, at Henry's command. She took a breath. "Show me? How you touch yourself? Before we . . ."

"You want to watch me?" Jay's hand dropped to his cock, loosely cupping his balls and stroking upward. She followed his movement. "You . . . anything . . . and you want me to touch myself for you." He sighed and swiftly kissed her cheek.

"Perfect," he murmured.

Laying his head on her breasts, he shifted his right leg back. "Good?"

"*Very* good." She had just enough of his weight on her to feel connected to him. Had the protective embrace of his left arm. Had a fantastic view of every twitch of his cock, every stroke of his fingers. Her happy sigh echoed Jay's.

He started slow. Teasing himself with a flat hand. Only his palm slid over soft flesh. Then fingers, lightly, one at first, running up the underside and around the head. One finger became two. One direction became two as well, his fingers running back and forth in a steady stroke as his cock darkened and swelled.

Her breathing deepened along with his. He was doing this for her.

Enjoying it, absolutely, but he was doing it to please her, and his efforts had a definite effect. Growing wetness between her lips. A pulsing rhythm in her clit.

Jay changed his grip to a circle of finger and thumb. Tiny, fast motions, back and forth. He whimpered, and her hips surged in response.

"Jay, you are so fucking beautiful."

"You like it that much?" He sounded curious, a tad disbelieving, maybe, but sweetly hopeful.

"I could watch you do this for hours." Fascination shackled her attention to the tip of his cock and its growing bead of pre-come. His motions differed from hers, but the desire was the same. The need for friction and sensation and speed.

She wondered if Henry would ever show her . . . no, if they would both, together, side by side . . . and let her watch. See how their strokes differed, or if Jay would follow Henry's lead even in something so personal and intimate.

Jay snorted. "I could manage maybe twenty minutes. And then I wouldn't have anything left for you."

He had plenty for her now, though. He squeezed his cock hard at the base, and her thighs clenched.

"You could wrap it up and give it to me now," she suggested, a hint of teasing in her tone.

He pressed a quick kiss beneath her chin, sat up and reached for the nightstand. Turning toward her, he knelt with cock in one hand and condom in the other.

"I thought you might like to watch." He gave her his little boy smile before it morphed into the Jay-smirk she'd gotten to know well. "Since it's your first time and all. And my cock is mesmerizing."

"Damn right it is," she answered, her gaze glued to his groin.

He unrolled the condom with a slow flourish and finished up with a teasing waggle that made her giggle.

"For me? A gift? How thoughtful. Do you deliver, too?"

He dove on top of her, planting his hands alongside her breasts and grinding their hips together.

She moaned and tipped her pelvis up until his cock settled between her lips.

"Express delivery," he quipped. "Should I leave it at the door, or would you like it inside?"

"Oh, inside, definitely." She raised her head but couldn't quite reach him. He immediately dropped his head closer, and she kissed him, hard and brief. "I need to make sure everything functions as described. The in-store demonstration was seriously impressive. Satisfying."

He smiled against her cheek and shifted his weight to one arm while the other reached for his cock. His fingers bumped her clitoris. Accidental at first, maybe, as he lined up his cock, but repeating with more purpose when she gasped and rolled her hips. The head of his cock nudged inside, but he didn't thrust. His fingers kept working at her as he traced the line of her jaw with gentle kisses.

"All the way in, Jay," she murmured. Her mind flashed on Henry, on that first night. "One thrust. For me."

He obeyed in an instant, sinking deep and rocking her hips, his groan trapped against the curve of her jaw. They moved together, slow and easy.

Jay ducked his head to reach her breasts, teasing her nipples with his tongue. Sucking at them in an alternating rhythm, he carried her higher with his enthusiasm. The friction and warmth and his obvious desire to please her made for welcome additions to her arousal.

But somewhere between the nips at her collarbone and the deep, searching kisses, she hit a wall. Her arousal mimicked a living thing, thick and needy and wanting, but desire didn't coil in her belly like a spring or press at her with urgency. It was . . . everywhere. Mellow.

Dammit. She closed her eyes and tried to focus, but the spark wasn't happening. This would be embarrassing. And Jay . . . *fuck*. He'd blame himself if she didn't come.

He'd done everything right. His deep, steady thrusts rocked her hips against the mattress, and his fingers worked in ceaseless motion over her clit. Having him inside her felt good. But the more she chased the elusive orgasm, the faster it slipped away.

Her hands clenched into fists. She turned her face right, her breathing harsh against her shoulder. She didn't want to look at Jay, to see questions or accusations or confusion in his eyes when she didn't come for him after she'd all but promised she would. Her foot kicked in frustration, and even the tug of the cuff holding her down wasn't enough to bring back the sweet spiraling need.

A soft touch. The stroke of a finger on the top of her right foot. Another. Quick. Fleeting. Intriguing. Her attention sharpened.

Yes, fingers, and now a hand, squeezing her foot, massaging the sole, fingers gripping deep. A second hand slid up the back of her right leg, stroking her calf.

Henry. Her breath caught. Her back arched, legs extending, pushing into the pressure of those hands. She blindly sought Jay's mouth, landing kisses on his jaw, his chin, his cheek before he fused his lips to hers. She let frustration slip away and just let it happen. Let Henry—

Like magic, as her body relaxed, Henry's fingers stroked and Jay's cock thrust forward and rocked her clit against his pubic bone. Orgasm. Bliss. Not as powerful as earlier, not with her body so drained, but her peak sent her straining against the straps holding her down, forcing her body up against Jay's.

She moaned with contentment and he answered with a deep, satisfied groan. Hard, rapid thrusts. A final push, holding her tight as she shuddered and he tensed before their bodies fell slack together.

She blinked, hard, and bit her lip. *Thank you, Henry.* Did Jay realize how close Henry was now? Had he been that close the whole time? Within arm's reach?

The hand squeezed her right foot a final time before disappearing. She stretched her leg, but it didn't return.

Jay sighed against her throat, his nose rubbing her skin in a slow half circle. They were both done for the night. Exhausted. Jay's full weight rested on her now.

She'd found the contact uncomfortable with previous partners. Lying sweaty and unsatisfied and waiting for them to get the fuck off her. But not with Jay. Her body hummed, and his touch soothed rather than annoyed. His scent relaxed her. The only thing missing was Henry.

She kissed Jay's cheek, and he turned to touch her lips with his.

"I had fun, Alice." He sounded almost surprised.

She couldn't help but laugh. "I thought it was pretty wonderful myself."

The bed shifted, sinking near her right foot, and Jay put his left hand on his cock to hold the condom in place while he pulled out. She missed the heat of him and the pressure, the fullness, in an instant.

He settled against her left side, the way he had all night—obvious now. He'd been giving Henry a better view. Not blocking her body with his own. Able to meet Henry's eyes if he wanted reassurance or direction.

Henry sat on the edge of the bed, his body facing away but his torso turned to see them both, his weight resting on his left hand behind him. He squeezed her foot and smiled when she wiggled her toes.

"Quite wonderful," Henry agreed. "Both of you performed beautifully tonight."

"Did we earn an 'A'? Because I think Jay deserves an 'A' for his work."

Henry pinched the skin on the top of her foot. "Eager for a grade, are we, Alice?"

She stretched her legs and pointed her toes. "Just eager to make sure he gets proper credit for his work. It was an exhaustive exam."

Jay buried his face in her neck, and Henry chuckled. "You have no idea, sweet girl. I suspect he's as ready for a cuddle and a nap as you are. Isn't that so, my boy?"

Jay nodded, his voice muffled against her skin. "Yes, Henry. It was . . . a big responsibility."

She pressed her cheek against Jay's head. "But you did a fantastic job reassuring the nervous virgin," she joked.

Jay laughed and slipped his left arm around her waist in a hug. "Yeah. *I'm* the one who played my role perfectly, with the reassurance and the confidence and the sexy talk." He laughed again and shook his head. "You were amazing, Alice. And you didn't even—"

"—need to worry about being graded," Henry finished. "But since you've both done so well, I think we'll hand out an 'E' to both of you. For effort and excellence and extra credit, as you ran three minutes over your allotted time."

Three minutes? Henry's hand on her calf. A signal that time was up. But he'd given her the focus she needed. If he'd stopped things, she'd have missed out. A bonus orgasm. She ought to thank him for that.

"Thank you, Henry."

Wait. That wasn't just her voice. She tipped her head, and Jay lifted his. They traded stares and burst out laughing.

With a quiet hum, Henry opened the cuff on her right ankle. The Velcro crackled as it unwrapped. He examined her ankle with strength and care in every touch. Flexed her foot and pressed a kiss to her skin.

Jay sat up at her side, stripped the condom and disposed of it. "Henry?"

He paused in his study of her foot. "Yes, my boy?"

"Can I help?"

"Certainly you may. That's a lovely thought. I'm sure Alice appreciates your attentiveness to her welfare."

Jay looked down, and she nodded to confirm Henry's words.

"Take her left foot out, please, Jay."

She couldn't stop the giggle.

Henry tapped the bottom of her right foot. "Have I discovered a ticklish spot you neglected to mention in your initial questionnaire responses, my dear?"

She shook her head.

"No? But you won't divulge the source of your amusement?" Henry stroked lighter, and she curled her toes to resist the ticklish sensation. His voice teased. "Careful now, Alice. There's danger afoot."

She shook her head harder, eyes squeezing shut as she mentally groaned at the pun. Henry seemed happy. As playful now as Jay, but in his typically sly way. Still, she wasn't about to tell him she had the hokey pokey playing in her head. *You put your left foot in, you take your left foot out . . .*

Velcro crackled again, and hands cradled her left foot.

"Look for any discoloration, Jay, and rotate and flex the foot to be certain full movement is comfortable for our girl. It's our responsibility now to make certain Alice hasn't injured herself without noticing. She's given us quite a bit of trust this evening. And when we treat our partners with the proper care, that trust is likely to be extended again, hmm?"

Silence fell, but her foot didn't move. She opened her eyes.

Henry had cupped Jay's cheek in his hand. His voice quieted. "I'm very proud of you, my boy. You've treated Alice with every ounce of the care you both deserve."

Henry moved to unfasten her right wrist. His gaze strayed to Jay often, checking his progress on her left foot, which Jay inspected with adorable thoroughness. How the hell did they keep their hands off each other outside the apartment? And why? She'd seen only the most casual of touches between them in the entire first year she'd known them. Yet Henry had touched Jay's face with unmistakable tenderness.

Henry's natural reserve around outsiders might keep them apart. He didn't seem the type to care about projecting a masculine dominant front, but maybe Jay did, if he felt ashamed of being a submissive guy in front of other guys. Maybe the hands-off masculine front was his. She'd never had a front-row seat for relationship dynamics before. Other than her own, of course, and it was impossible to be objective about such things.

She lay tranquil and content while they unbound her hands, wiggling her fingers on command and sighing at the slow, sweet kiss Henry placed against the underside of her right wrist and Jay copied on the left. The sense of liberation in her unbinding carried an upsetting note. As if she'd lost something and she wanted it back.

Jay half rose from the bed. "Should I fetch the washcloth?"

Henry waved him back down, getting up himself and walking around the bed. He pressed a kiss to Jay's forehead and smoothed his hair. "Not tonight, my boy. Cuddle with Alice for a bit, please. She'll want to touch you now. Isn't that so, Alice?"

She nodded. With her hands back under her own control, she wanted to feel skin beneath them. Connection.

"Good girl. Just cuddling, please. No roughhousing, and no sexual teasing. I'll return shortly."

Jay lay down on his side. She rolled onto hers, pressing her hands to his chest and resting her head on his arm. His ribs expanded under her hands when he breathed. She moved her right hand atop the thump of his heartbeat.

Jay pushed aside her hair with his face. No, not pushed aside, exactly. Burrowed. He breathed deep. "You smell good."

"I smell like sex." She rubbed her face against his chest and inhaled. "And so do you."

"You smell like *you*," he insisted. "And sex. It's a great combination."

No teasing, she reminded herself. No grinding her hips against Jay's, even if she didn't let the playfulness go anywhere. She sighed instead, a sound of satisfaction and satiation, and scratched his chest with her fingernails.

"You like it, don't you, Alice?" The unsure question of a little boy.

She wormed her arms around him and hugged him tight.

"I *do* like it," she confirmed.

Even if Henry wasn't going to fuck her again and she couldn't figure out why, she still liked playing with Jay. He was sweet, and fun, and he always tried so hard to please her. Like he didn't know how to do anything half-assed. He threw himself into their games wholeheartedly every time. The no-holds-barred approach had to have gotten him hurt a time or two. Maybe some bitch had broken his heart.

She hugged him tighter. "It's the most fun I've had in bed."

He relaxed into her embrace, arms rubbing against her back.

"It'll get even better," he whispered. "Just wait'll Henry gets you in bed."

Wait'll Henry . . . holy shit. What did Jay know that she didn't? Or was he just talking from personal experience? "Did he—"

"Both behaving, I see."

She almost panicked and pulled away, as if she'd been caught in bed with a married man. Henry might be fine with sharing his lover with her, but only when and how he allowed. She doubted the sharing included his plans for future nights.

But Jay's body hadn't tightened at all, and he hadn't tried to escape her arms. He lay utterly relaxed and snuggly, as if sex and secrets were the last thing on his mind despite their conversation and their position.

Take two orgasms and call me in the morning?

"Are you having a nice cuddle, my dears?"

"Yes, Henry," Jay answered, and she echoed him.

"Lovely. If you'll indulge me a moment, we'll have more time for cuddling afterward."

Alice and Jay unwound their arms and rolled onto their backs. She bit her tongue to stop her mouth from dropping open.

Henry had stripped to his boxers. Not naked, true, but he displayed more skin than she'd seen from him yet. And he wasn't hard when he settled on the bed. The boxers wouldn't have been able to hide that from her.

He hadn't been gone long enough to take care of things himself, but she hadn't heard him while she and Jay were playing. Surely he hadn't spent three hours watching them and not touching himself. That was insane. Torture.

Maybe he got pre-playtime action from Jay every night they were together. Like he'd said the first night, when he took her over the table. Asking a man how many blowjobs he'd gotten from his lover today seemed a sure way to get kicked out of his bed early.

She stared at Henry's chest, unashamedly opening her legs for him when he asked, enjoying the warmth and care with which he applied the washcloth. Henry had more hair and less defined musculature than Jay, but his chest wasn't wooly and his stomach wasn't flabby. He was just . . . male. Wide shoulders. A smattering of brown hair trailing down. Narrow waist. A criminally satisfying cock hidden under those boxers.

She didn't bother to shift her body or close her legs once Henry finished bathing her to his satisfaction. He patted her gently, kissed her knee and moved to attend to Jay.

Jay stretched like a sleepy puppy while Henry gave him the same careful treatment.

Henry patted Jay's hip when he'd finished.

"Under the covers, both of you, and we'll cuddle a while longer tonight." Henry left the room with the washcloth in hand.

Jay scrambled for the sheets, dragging them up and over their bodies, leaving the bondage straps dangling against the side of the bed. Did they stay on the bed all the time? Would Henry tuck them under the mattress in the morning? Not that she'd be there to find out. Once Henry had dissected her experience of the night, he'd thank her for spending the evening with them, and kiss her, and send her home. He'd done it every time so far, getting her home at midnight as the contract promised.

She shifted on her side as Jay snuggled up to her. Curving his body around her back, he dropped his left arm across her waist. His hand stroked her stomach, and his breath warmed the back of her neck. Falling asleep like this would be so easy.

All she needed was Henry's neck to cradle her face. His scent in her nose. His chest against hers, bare skin to bare skin. She blinked as the bed dipped and he was there in front of her, settling on his side, mere inches away. She nearly missed his question, caught up in tracing the exact slope of his collarbone with her eyes.

"Restraint is a pleasurable experience for you, isn't it, Alice?"

He'd pinned her hands or her legs in assorted ways on previous nights. His grip had felt more intimate than the cuffs tonight, but . . . not being able to touch Jay. Having to trust he'd get the job done. And the pull of the cuffs against her skin every time she forgot. Yeah, restraint was pretty fucking pleasurable. Hell, even the way their bodies boxed her between them now was a comfort.

"It makes me nervous at first. But it feels . . . better . . . during."

"Merely nervous, Alice?" Henry's right hand settled on her hip, alongside Jay's arm, his thumb moving in slow strokes that treated them both as one.

She'd known the joy of heart-stopping panic tonight, of panic heightening her senses and connecting her to Jay. No, nervous didn't cover it.

"Frightened," she clarified. "When I forgot. But in a good way. Like a roller coaster."

"A roller coaster?" His voice coaxed her, his smile a silent prod to make her speak the words. To make them real.

"Excited. Knowing something's coming and I can't stop it, but it'll be a rush and it won't hurt. The safety features will protect me.

Only I'm not thinking about them when the car's zipping down the hills and banking around the curves."

"You enjoy that feeling, don't you, Alice? That forgetting?"

"Yes." She wasn't going to be embarrassed about that. Not with Jay nestled behind her and Henry looking into her eyes with understanding. "I was pulling against the cuffs, but sometimes I forgot I could open them myself. And that was more exciting than when I remembered I could stop things."

Henry squeezed her hip. His lips grazed her cheek before he leaned back to study her face. "Lovely. You felt safe allowing yourself to forget?"

She nodded, frowning. She didn't think of herself as *that* girl. She was the responsible one, the designated baby sitter in the group when she'd gone out with her girlfriends in college. "It felt . . . liberating?" Could that even be right?

Jay nodded and wiggled in agreement at her back. "It does for me, when Henry's in charge."

Because you're like a puppy, you ridiculously adorable man. She didn't say it, though. The way he wore his vulnerability so openly in private was one of her favorite things about Jay. She refused to dampen his enthusiasm. Liberation in surrender was just more difficult for her to accept than it was for him, she supposed.

"From the moment you signed our contract, Alice, the ultimate responsibility for your safety during our time together lay with me. It's appropriate for you to feel a sense of freedom in that." Henry kissed her, slow and gentle, and did the same to Jay. He studied them both afterward as she stifled a yawn. Exhaustion had crept up on her. "Perhaps a lighter topic is in order now, hmm?"

Jay's words came in a rush beside her ear. "Did you mean it, Alice? Was I the first tongue between your legs? Not just for tonight?"

She laughed. "You've been waiting to ask that this whole time, haven't you?"

"Not the whole time."

"You were, yeah." Her smile at Henry was a touch sly. "It let me check off an extra line on my contract questions the next day."

Henry shook his head. "I admit, my dear, that was not a revelation I expected this evening. You surprised me." Shaking his head again, he returned her smile. "Delightful."

He caressed her side, his hand following her arm down to her waist, dropping to her hip and thigh. "As Jay chose the first topic, perhaps you'd care to choose a second?"

"First times. How you lost your virginity. You both got to hear mine." Not that she'd feel slighted if they didn't share. She just wanted to know. Had their first times been with men or women? Had they been older or younger than she was her first time? Had theirs been calculated decisions like hers?

"I was sixteen," Jay blurted. "She was a college friend of my sister's."

She raised an eyebrow. This had better not be some setup for a letters to *Penthouse* joke. "Was it good?"

Jay snorted. "I thought it was fantastic. She might not have thought so, since I came after all of four thrusts. But that didn't stop her from coming to visit my sister Nat pretty much every week that summer. She always managed to get there when Nat was out, and we'd walk down by the creek to where the grass made a soft bed. I did eventually satisfy her, too, but the first time? Hell no. She got herself off with her fingers after I was done." His voice dropped to a whisper. "That was pretty hot, too."

She waited for Henry's answer.

Jay leaned in.

"Wait, you don't know, either?"

Jay shook his head against hers. "Not even a hint."

Four years together, and Henry had never told the story? It was either extremely good or excruciatingly bad.

Henry gave an elegant shrug. "A class trip to Paris, my dears. With a classmate, on the balcony of my hotel room. As I recall, she was quite impressed with the view, the flowers, the room service dinner, and the outcome." His lips quirked. "Though my wallet was rather poorer for the experience. I had to pay my roommate to stay out of the room all night and hold his tongue lest the chaperones investigate."

They drifted from topic to topic, the choice rotating among the three of them. At some point, she'd missed half of Jay's story about smashing a kayak and somehow escaping with minor injuries. If Henry had answered the question about getting drunk for the first time, she'd missed that, too. Her eyes wouldn't stay open. But that was okay.

She was still Henry's responsibility. She could nap. He'd wake her and get her home safe when it was time.

Chapter 7

Alice woke to the murmur of low voices and the patter of rain on the windows. No shifting mattress, no other bodies in the bed, but still-warm sheets. Henry's bed. They'd let her stay?

That was a first. If she counted the night Henry had taken her so decisively across the dining room table, last night had been their sixth Friday together. Either Henry had exercised his contract option to extend her playtime into Saturday, or she'd fallen asleep and been too difficult to wake. Not worth the trouble, maybe, and Henry and Jay indifferent to her presence? Shit, that would be embarrassing. A walk of shame.

She cracked open an eyelid.

Henry stood by the window, naked, looking out through the glass. He spoke in a hushed tone, the sort he might expect wouldn't disturb a sleeping partner. Was she obligated to tell him she was awake?

"Not today. The rain would be a bit of a bother, my boy. Though it's a fine idea."

Speaking to Jay, though she couldn't see him from where she lay. Henry would notice her wakefulness eventually. Until then, she wasn't about to move for the world. Not when she had such a beautiful and rare view. Henry watched her all the time in their games, but she'd never had such an opportunity to study him.

Most often he used his voice rather than his body to excite her. He wielded it with precision, blindfolding her or staying behind her. Painting with words in her ears that lit up the pleasure centers in her brain with anticipation.

Her one complaint, one confusion, about the past two and a half months was that Henry hadn't fucked her. Not since that first night.

He often brought her to orgasm with his hands, and God, that was wonderful. His beautifully long fingers stroked and teased and drew out her pleasure until she begged. But he tasted her only by licking his fingers clean or demanding a kiss from Jay after he'd gone down on her. He didn't fuck her, not even when she squirmed against his erection and wished she dared ask for it.

He'd made it clear his orgasms weren't her concern. Maybe that first night had been a test and she'd failed. Maybe his interest in her was limited to providing a regular female sex partner for Jay, to keep him from straying. Jay had fucked her on almost every one of their Fridays, following whatever instructions Henry had given him for the night.

She never went home unsatisfied, but she feared she'd never feel Henry's cock again. The memory of that first thrust, his thick girth and slow, steady, deliberate pace, was enough to make her wet no matter where she was or what she was supposed to be concentrating on.

Like it was doing now, she admitted, as her eyes drank in the planes of Henry's back and her mind begged him to turn and face her. She refused to squirm, though her clit thumped out a demanding rhythm. If Henry knew she was awake, he probably wouldn't allow her to watch him like this.

But Jay had that right. He moved into view, partially hiding Henry's body from her when he laid a hand between the older man's shoulder blades. For one terrible moment, she blazed with jealousy before reason returned.

Henry and Jay had a relationship. A lengthy one. Years of being together, even if they didn't make it obvious in public, and even if they dated other people. The day might come for her, too, when she could approach a nude Henry and touch him without seeking permission. But she didn't want those complications. Did she?

"You're woolgathering, Henry." Jay pressed closer, his body indistinguishable from Henry's, the two of them one outline in the gray light slipping in through the window.

Jay boasted an extra inch of height but with a leaner build, his shoulders and hips narrower than Henry's. Boyish. Coltish. A three-year-old eager to run but not ready to challenge the herd stallion.

She stifled a laugh, certain now wasn't the time to tell them she'd been comparing them to her aunt and uncle's quarter horses.

"I'd be a fool to do so today, my boy. Wool smells awful in the rain."

"You could always come back to bed." Jay nuzzled Henry's neck, and her jealousy ceded space to eagerness. Jay's hand slid down Henry's hip before moving where she couldn't see, though she guessed where it was headed.

She pressed her thighs together and bit her tongue against the rush of pleasure. *Yes. Great idea. Come back to bed.*

Jay poured on the charm, the smooth wheedling tone he used to fluster countless servers and clerks.

"Alice is still sleeping. We could wake her up."

Oh God, yes. Thank you, Jay. You're a genius. No one in the history of the world has had a better idea.

"You know that's where you belong, Henry."

"Mmm. And you belong on your knees with my cock in your mouth." Henry's command voice.

Jesus. Was it wrong to be so aroused when it wasn't even directed at her?

"But only one of those things will be happening now. Would you care to guess which one?"

"The one I like best?" Jay dropped to his knees without waiting for a command and began biting Henry's flanks. "You gonna turn around?"

Please, please, please be yes.

And Henry did, as though he read her mind. Through her half-lowered eyelids, his cock appeared tall and thick, a darker outline standing against his stomach. The clouds outside and the darkness inside conspired to hide the details in shadow, but the fuzziness and her own sleep-fogged brain made it all the more beautiful and surreal to watch Jay's tongue and lips move over Henry's flesh.

She could give in to jealousy, or she could enjoy the gift of watching them together when they believed themselves unobserved. If she let jealousy rule her, this arrangement would never work. She'd have to give them up. No way in hell. She gave jealousy a firm push and slammed the door in its face.

It wasn't like she didn't have options.

Lying partly on her right side, mostly sprawled on her stomach, she shifted her right hand, hidden by the sheet, beneath her. She didn't even have underwear to push out of the way. Her fingers slid down, tips tingling at the fuzzy-scratchy brush of her hair before rubbing across her clitoris. She internalized the instinctive shudder of pleasure.

If she called attention to herself, they might stop. She didn't want that, not when Jay curved his hands around Henry's ass, gripped him, and bobbed his head in a hypnotic rhythm. She'd given plenty of blowjobs, but watching was a first.

Jay started out playful. Not unexpected from such a consummate joker. He pulled back until his lips slipped off. Swiping his tongue across the tip, he leaned back and looked up at Henry. A pause, one, two, three seconds before his lips curled around Henry's cock and sank down once more.

Her idle fingering grew more urgent.

Henry's calm facade showed cracks as Jay worked at him. Every split made her want to match it, as though she were connected to what they shared. Henry's breaths came harshly. He moaned once, a low bass, and she pressed a finger inside herself to feel the echoing vibration as her body responded.

When Henry's hand dropped to Jay's head, dark hair standing up between his fingers as they clenched and released, her own fingers developed a more purposeful motion. Frenzied sweeps, thrusting inside and sliding back up to rub her clitoris as she grew desperate for a release she could almost reach. Jay wasn't protesting the grip, something she'd have batted a lover's hands away for and possibly even stopped for.

Jay moved faster, a happy moaning hum emerging from his lips. What would it feel like? To have Henry's hands in her hair like that, to be allowed to worship him in this way?

Her gaze drifted to Henry's face, to his half-closed eyes and the fierce intensity in his jawline. He was close, and tense with it. She followed that tension along his neck and across his shoulder. Down his arm to where his hand gripped Jay's hair.

Henry's hand clenched and held, and his hips thrust twice, sharply. He growled his pleasure while Jay's throat worked to swallow, and she came too, fingers pressed to her clit and teeth biting her lip. She struggled to keep her body's quivering release beneath the covers from drawing attention.

Her eyes closed and her breath emerged in short puffs she couldn't prevent. When she looked again, Henry was smoothing down Jay's hair.

Jay rested his head against Henry's hip.

Henry's erection held firm despite his release, hardly softening at all yet. He coaxed Jay to his feet, Jay's cock hard and weeping with it.

Henry's hand circled the base of Jay's cock. Would he return the favor? Stroke Jay to his own orgasm? It wouldn't take much, not from the way Jay gasped when Henry squeezed.

"Go on and give this to Alice, my boy. She's started without you."

They turned their heads, Jay in sharp surprise, but Henry . . . he'd known all along. Might have known from the first moment she'd woken up.

Embarrassed panic rushed through her, a hint of shame and fear she might be punished for touching herself without his permission. But he could have stopped her at any time. He hadn't. Maybe because he'd wanted to see what she would do or how she'd react. Had she passed the test?

"On your stomach, Alice." Henry's voice, low and controlling, stirred flutters of anticipation in her. "Hands alongside your head."

She moved into the proper position and waited, face turned toward Henry, eyes watching him as best they could over her left arm. She loved the waiting, the not knowing what would happen next. Her excitement held an extra edge of anxiety, because she didn't yet know whether she'd displeased him.

His voice gave nothing away. The same one he always used with her on her nights. And now mornings, too. Because it was morning. And she was still here. In his bed.

Oh God. She needed to stop thinking these thoughts before she worked herself into some kind of mental orgasm.

"Jay, the sheets. Strip them to the floor, please. I want to see Alice's lovely charms. After all, she's been enjoying ours. You were enjoying the show, weren't you, Alice?"

The sheets slid over her skin. Cooler air caressed her shoulders, her back, the dip in her spine, the curve of her ass. She shivered.

"I liked it. It was beautiful."

Henry had been walking toward the bed with measured steps, but he paused at her answer. The sheets continued their slide down her legs.

"Tell me what was beautiful."

The sheet traveled the last few inches across her bare feet. She whimpered, squirming against the mattress. Naked and exposed to their eyes. She struggled to bring her scattered thoughts together and answer Henry's demand.

"The way he's so eager to touch you . . . his tongue and his mouth and his hands sliding on your skin . . . all that motion focused so tightly, and the window behind you . . ." She was almost breathless, the words tumbling out, truthful and eager to please him. Her pussy throbbed, its renewed slickness rolling down her lips and across her clit. "With the clouds making the light all dim and, and, and flickering. His head moving like a shadow and your hand stroking his hair and the way your knuckles tighten when you come."

The way it's so tender and caring and how it's so obvious in his worship and the look on your face that you think you're in love with each other, she thought but didn't say. It would smack too much of jealousy. Of a place she didn't occupy here, private intimacies that did not belong to her.

Hands, Jay's hands, obvious by the more calloused feel of them, grasped her ankles and pushed them apart.

"Very good, Alice." Henry's praise warmed her. "Quite specific. You were watching closely, hmm? And that's what prompted you to touch yourself?"

"Yes."

The hands moved up her calves. She grew desperate for more, to feel Jay's weight and heat and give him the release Henry had not.

"Even though you're not to do so without my permission?"

God, she wished she could read Henry's tone better.

Jay's hands slipped away. Something rustled behind her. Getting a condom, maybe?

"Yes, Henry."

"Did you believe our time together was over and you were free to do as you pleased?"

An out. To take it, she'd have to lie. Even if she hadn't known he'd chosen to extend their time together, she'd hoped so when she woke and discovered herself still here with them.

"No," she whispered. "I thought I was still yours."

"You are," he confirmed. "Even when you're a disobedient girl. But you're an honest one, Alice, and that pleases me. Just as your intense arousal pleases me. You couldn't stop yourself, hmm?"

She'd pleased him. Even her disobedience pleased him, when it originated in her overwhelming need for him.

"No. I couldn't . . . I *needed*."

"Yes. And you still have that need, don't you? Your fingers alone aren't nearly enough to satisfy it." Henry knelt by the side of the bed, his face inches above her own. He stroked her cheek. "You need something more."

She held her breath, waiting, not daring to ask.

Henry's face turned for a moment. He nodded, and the bed dipped with Jay's weight, his body sliding along hers, up and over until he covered her better than any blanket.

"Jay is going to fuck you now, Alice," Henry murmured. "You're not to come unless I give you permission. Can you do that for me, my dear?"

Her body trembled in reaction, the suggestion itself, that she belonged so utterly to him, enough to bring her closer.

"I . . . I don't know. I don't know." The barest whimper.

"Try, dearest. You'll try for me, hmm?"

Oh God yes. She'd try anything for him.

"Yes, Henry."

"Good girl." He nodded.

Jay sent his right hand diving between their legs, gripping himself and rubbing the head of his cock along her sex. A brush of his knuckles, his wrist sliding along her thigh, and he pressed forward, deeper, burying himself in her with a single stroke. He groaned, his open mouth against the side of her head above her ear.

"Fuck, Henry, she's so wet and open, Jesus, I'm not—"

"Do *not* come, Jay. I'll be forced to punish you if you do, and poor Alice will be disappointed."

The threat of punishment seemed dire enough to stave off Jay's imminent orgasm. He lay motionless and panting above her as she resisted the urge to squeeze. He gained a modicum of more control, and his hands slid along her arms until he covered her there, too. He pressed his fingers between her own.

As if he'd been waiting for Jay's motion, Henry spoke. "You can learn to control this, Alice. To make it stop, and start, when you will it. At the sound of a voice. At the touch of a hand, perhaps."

Henry stared into her eyes, and understanding bloomed. He recognized the trouble she'd had last night. He understood her desperation, her need to try to force herself into orgasm to please her partner. He'd offered his hands to help her focus then. What would he offer now?

"You're designed for this, sweet girl. Engineered to feel this pleasure, hmm? And it's easy when you're by yourself, isn't it? Your fingers know your body intimately. That's how you were able to bring yourself to orgasm with such speed and silence this morning in my bed, isn't it?"

She panted, mouth dry, tongue struggling to find the moisture to speak. Jay's steady thrusts didn't help. "Yes, Henry."

"I want you to imagine your fingers there now, Alice."

Her wrists twitched under Jay's hands, fingers stretching out.

"Don't move them, my dear. Your hands are pinned, and they'll stay that way. Your body is caught under Jay's. Held safe. But when his thrusts drive you down, forward, and the friction moves over you, the slide of the sheets against your lips, the faintest graze across your clitoris, your nerves blazing, I want you to feel your fingers there."

Henry's eyes encouraged her. His words painted a picture. Jay's welcome weight against her back protected her, shielded her from the world. No one could see her touching herself. No one else would see phantom hands. Only she would feel the way they skimmed down her breasts and belly and between her legs to where slick need waited for her expert touch. Recalling the feel of her fingers was simple. Familiar. Yes, she could do that for Henry.

"Can you feel it, Alice? The stroke of a finger? Two? The slow circles when you want to feel lazy and relaxed. The pressure, the rapid side-to-side rush when your need is greater, when your clitoris rocks between and jumps against your fingers."

Staring into Henry's eyes and listening to his voice, was it any wonder her focus strayed? The fingers she imagined between her legs became his. Her body thrust hard against Jay's in response, driving him deeper and drawing a moan from him that vibrated in her left ear.

"That's it. You feel it now. Those fingers moving so expertly over your flesh. Knowing the precise pressure. The exact angle."

And she did. She did. But the fingers weren't hers. They were his, and they were going to make her come.

"Tell me what you're feeling, Alice."

"Building. It's building. I want . . . I want . . ." She breathed hard, and Jay matched her. Awareness narrowed to the slide of Jay's cock, the rumble of Henry's voice, and the phantom touch of fingers on her clit.

"I know, sweet girl. Hold on to the feeling. Keep it on a short leash. You're teasing yourself, fingers bringing you close and backing down, bringing you close and backing down, over and over. Can you feel it?"

Her head slid in a nod under Jay's. She knew that feeling, when she wanted it to last. To hold off her orgasm until it was strong and focused and ready to end with her legs shaking against the sheets or sending bathwater sloshing on the floor. It wasn't unusual to have Henry or Jay in mind when she did. But this, having Jay in her body and Henry in her mind . . . *Jesus, Henry, please. Please please please.*

A whimper stuck in her throat, emerging as a thin whine. Her eyes closed. She struggled not to give in to the feeling, though she'd clamped down so tightly around Jay she thought he wouldn't be able to thrust at all if she weren't so wet, soaking her thighs and the bed beneath.

"Alice."

Her eyes snapped open. Henry had tipped his face sideways, aligned with hers and Jay's.

"You want to come now, don't you, my dear?"

Her garbled moan seemed a suitable substitute for the string of affirmative responses the question deserved. Henry's left hand hovered above hers and Jay's where they lay entwined on the bed, a point of focus between Henry's face and her own.

"Almost there," Henry murmured. His hand lowered, slow and steady. A fraction of an inch above Jay's now.

She stared at Henry's hand and felt the echo of it on her sex, hovering, an instant away from perfect pressure.

Henry growled, a low rumble. His hand pressed hard on theirs, and the intensity of the contact overwhelmed her. "*Now*, Alice. You'll come for me now, dearest. You both will."

She let go with a cry of relief as the phantom hands, Henry's hands, gave her the push she needed. The violence of release drove her into the mattress. Her hips thrust against the sheets, rapid and uncontrolled. Jay stayed with her, stayed deep, less thrusting than rocking without pulling out at all, as quick to come as she was at Henry's low command.

When their rough breathing softened and the rocking of their bodies stilled, the only motion in the room belonged to Henry. He moved his left hand over theirs, his palm rubbing their fingers. He traced shapes on the back of Jay's hand and wrist and dipped his fingers down the side of Jay's wrist to touch hers, trapped beneath it.

His right hand floated toward them in the top edge of her vision. From Jay's quiet hum, she expected Henry had touched his face. Pushed Jay's hair back from his forehead.

Henry leaned forward and pressed his lips to Jay's skin.

She inhaled deeply. None of them had showered since yesterday, before their games had begun, and her nose grazed Henry's throat. Her tongue touched her lips.

"Go and fetch a washcloth, please, my boy."

Jay nodded, his head sliding against hers, before he turned and kissed her cheek. "G'morning, Alice."

She was giggling when he pulled out and left the bed. He'd fucked

her silly this morning without saying a word to her. Now he ad-
dressed her for the first time with a cheerful greeting as if he'd just
woken up. Backward. They were doing everything backward. And
God help her if she didn't like it.

Henry pushed her hair off her face.

"No need to ask if you're enjoying yourself, I suppose. Certainly
we're at least managing to keep you amused, hmm?" He kissed her
forehead at her left temple, whispering in her ear. "Your laughter pleases
me, sweet girl."

His right hand swept down her bare back and squeezed her ass.
"Roll over for me, Alice. We'll have a bit of cleanup before breakfast
today."

She was staying for breakfast? She rolled over in time to catch Jay
strolling naked across the room.

He handed Henry a washcloth.

"Thank you, my boy. Lie down and wait a moment, please."

Jay fell back at her side, making the bed bounce, and thrust his
hands under his head with his elbows out. He rolled his head in her
direction, watching alongside her as Henry gently spread her legs and
raised her knees. The warmth of the washcloth and his light touch
was soothing on her thighs and sex. She sighed, and Jay nudged her
shoulder with his elbow.

"This is the life, right? Just lie back and follow Henry's direc-
tions, and everything else is taken care of."

Henry gave a single quiet laugh. He kissed her upraised left knee
before shifting to give Jay the same treatment. "You ought to be
thinking about what you'd like for breakfast."

"Waffles!" Jay waggled his eyebrows. "You want waffles, too,
right, Alice?"

"You'll let Alice make up her own mind about what she wants,
my boy."

Jay yelped, his body jumping, and she tilted her head to look down
the bed.

Henry had a firm grip on Jay's balls, she thought, though it was
hard to tell with the washcloth in the way. She bit her lip to avoid giggling, imagining Henry leading Jay around with a leash attached to
his cock.

"Sure," she managed. "I don't have anything against waffles. They're good when you want something special. Rare. Not for everyday breakfasts."

"No, not every day," Henry echoed. "Jay, return the washcloth, please, and then go dress. It seems today will be a waffle day."

Jay snatched up the washcloth and headed for the bathroom, flashing a thumbs-up at Alice before he darted out the door.

She started to slide off the bed, but Henry's hands stopped her. "Allow me, Alice."

He retrieved her clothes and dressed her, his hands light and quick, his attention thoughtful and focused. He dressed himself afterward. Casual, for him. Slacks and an untucked button-down shirt, his feet bare. He reached for her hand. "Come along, and we'll start on the waffles. Two for you?"

She slipped her fingers into Henry's and followed him to the kitchen. "Two for me, two for you, six for Jay . . ."

"Only six for me?"

Jay had thrown on a t-shirt and loose gym shorts. Typical Saturday morning attire, she expected.

"But I burned a lot of calories trying not to come before you. It's a tough job, especially when you're all soft and wet and moaning. I'll definitely need a dozen waffles."

"Your waffle craving is my fault now?" She hip-checked Jay at the breakfast bar. It was fun spending the night. Teasing Jay. Watching Henry's hands, whether they were curled in Jay's hair or stroking her swollen sex or washing up at the sink in preparation for making breakfast.

She sat at the breakfast bar while Jay fetched, carried and served her orange juice at Henry's direction. Henry hadn't asked for her help, and Jay seemed at ease in his role as chef's assistant. She was extraneous. Unnecessary. Had the chairs gotten harder? Finding a comfortable position proved impossible.

"Alice, my girl, come and take the first plate, please." Henry beckoned her to the waffle iron, and she held the plate while he peeled the golden circle away from the metal. "Sit at the table. Jay and I will catch up with you soon enough."

She took her plate and glass to the table, to the place where she always sat when she dined with them. The place she'd been sitting ten weeks ago when Henry had ordered her to stand. Her fingers rubbed the edge of the table.

"You're not having toppings?" Jay settled in the seat to her right at the foot of the table, his plate clattering against the wood.

She snatched her fingers back and picked up her fork. "What? No. I mean, yes. Of course I am."

"Uh-huh." He eyed her plate with its bare waffle before he scooped peaches onto his own and topped them with maple syrup and whipped cream. "Have some fruit. Henry will tell you it's good for you."

She gave Jay a wry smile and loaded her waffle with cinnamon apples. Henry always seemed to know what was good for her. "Satisfied?"

"Mmmph." Jay swallowed. "It's been a good morning. And a good night, too."

Alice blushed and avoided his eyes, watching Henry's back as he poured the last of the waffle batter into the iron. "You're just happy you passed your exam with flying colors."

Jay nodded in her peripheral vision. "And this morning's pop quiz. I'm crushing this class."

She was still laughing when Henry arrived at the table bearing a plate of extra waffles. She waited until he sat and fixed his waffle before eating her own.

Breakfast was lazy and relaxed with Henry leading the conversation. He kept the topics light, and Jay remained his charming, playful self. But the meal ended all too soon. She'd cleared her plate. Couldn't hold another bite. She fidgeted with her fork until Henry called her name.

"Come here, sweet girl." He pushed his chair back and settled her in his lap. "Are there any issues you need to discuss with me? Concerns or questions you have?"

Did she? Nothing that warranted Henry's intervention. Typical relationship uncertainties, minimized by the terms of their contract and magnified by the fact that she'd never been the third wheel in a relationship before. It was an adjustment. He'd told her it would be. Of course, he hadn't told her he wasn't planning on fucking her.

But she could hardly say that. As if sex with Jay wasn't fantastic? As if she weren't pleased with the time and attention Henry did give her? As if the lover he'd chosen for himself wasn't good enough for her, too?

She looked at Jay, working his way through a third waffle, and shook her head. "No, Henry. I enjoy our time together. It's nothing I can't handle."

Henry turned her face toward his. Studying her in silence, he leaned in, brushed his nose against hers and kissed her slowly. He tucked her hair behind her ear when he pulled back. "All right. If you're certain. Thank you for sharing yourself with us this morning, my dear. I won't keep you from the rest of your day."

She slid off his lap as he stood. He led her by the hand to the door and kissed her cheek. "If you happen to think of anything you wish to discuss with me, please know you are always welcome."

"I know, Henry." She took her keys and phone from the hall table and kissed his cheek in return. "Thank you."

He held the door, watching until she reached her own apartment, and she gave him a small wave before she shut the door behind her.

She flopped back onto her futon.

"Did I think this would be a walk of shame? Fuck that." She rolled on her side, smiling. "I might not be fucking Henry, but I'm not ashamed of a damn thing."

Chapter 8

Son of a fucking bitch.

She'd known all day. The fatigue, the generalized ache, the uncomfortable tightness at her waistline. A visit to the restroom confirmed it.

Three hours before her scheduled Friday night fun, and she'd have to cancel. Her hand hesitated over her cellphone. Texting Henry was the coward's way out, but she couldn't make herself call.

Need to cancel tonight. Really sorry.

She tried to work, turning back to the breakdown on the Davis project. But concentration eluded her when the analgesics hadn't kicked in yet and she was pissed about having to cancel and nervous about Henry's reaction.

Her phone vibrated. Henry. Of course. Shit.

She'd feel like the worst sort of friend if she let his call go to voicemail.

"Hi, Henry."

"Hello, Alice. You've had an emergency come up?"

"No emergency." Hell if she'd lie, not to him. "I'm fine. I just can't play tonight."

That was safe enough. Any nosy coworkers would think she played on a rec league sports team or had some other nonsalacious, pedestrian pastime.

"You've made other plans?" He sounded no more curious than a coffee-shop barista taking her order.

"No, of course not." She lowered her voice. "I wouldn't do that."

Not on a contract night. She valued their arrangement too much for that. It wasn't like she wanted to miss tonight.

"No, I didn't expect you would." His tone seemed mild yet. "Must I drag the truth from you, Alice?"

She lowered her voice even further. Working in a profession surrounded by men had its downsides. She wasn't embarrassed about being a woman, but she didn't want to advertise her cycle at work.

"Nothing a hot bath, some painkillers and a few days won't cure."

"Is that your usual ritual when you're menstruating?"

Jesus. He hadn't even paused. His unapologetic interest shouldn't have surprised her. The contract questions had included intrusive inquiries about her cycle and the severity of her cramps, if she had them, and whether she'd engaged in intercourse while menstruating. That answer was no, and it was going to stay no.

Her two long-term relationships had been with guys who cared nothing about what was between her legs except whether it was open for business. She hadn't lived with them, so avoiding the subject had been easy.

"I'm at work. I can't talk about this here."

"Do you trust me?"

"You know I do."

"Then arrive at your usual time and leave everything in my hands."

She knocked on Henry's door promptly at seven, her mind a jumble of nervous thoughts layered atop the throbbing bonfire of pain centered below her waist and between her hips. The stress of not knowing what he had planned and never having been in this position with a bedmate weighed on her. Tension gave her a sharp backache, a line of fire to complement the blazing knot twisting up her womb. *Hi, Henry, I'm on fire for you tonight. Please tell me you have a big enough hose to put it out.*

She stifled a laugh. He did. He just hadn't wanted her since that first night.

The door started to open, and she pasted a smile on her face for Jay. No reason to take her crazy, neurotic, bitchy, pain-filled mood out on him. She discovered confident green eyes filled with compassion instead of the dark pools of eagerness she expected.

"Come in, Alice, please." Henry gestured her inside.

She set her purse on the side table and slipped off her shoes while he closed the door. Henry at the door? Where was Jay? She'd gotten accustomed to Jay opening the door after the last four times. To having Jay fuck her. He had it practically perfected. But she couldn't deny that on the nights between their encounters, the long two weeks alone, it was Henry's name she called most often in her head. The memory of his voice and his cock brought her to climax. Subtle glances revealed no clues.

"Jay won't be joining us this evening. Your current circumstances deserve some exclusive attention, hmm? Particularly as it's not an experience you've shared before."

Before. As in, before tonight. So she would be getting . . . well, no, maybe not. Maybe she'd just be getting pampered. Or his fingers. Or toys. *Christ, Henry, why won't you fuck me again?*

Was there something wrong with her? Was he reconsidering the arrangement? It wasn't as if he needed a reason to do so. The option was right there in item one. At will. Any time.

Her body throbbed, and she grit her teeth. She could say her safeword and go home to her standard routine of heat and pressure and exercise and painkillers and chocolate. Or she could stay here and trust him.

Henry touched her face, turning it toward him. She had no doubt he felt the tension in her.

"Pain or nerves, my dear?"

"A bit of both." She wouldn't lie to him. She might leave, but she wouldn't lie.

"Hmm. We'll have to see what we can do about both, then." He curved his hand and slid his knuckles across her cheek. "You're warm. But you'd like to be warmer, wouldn't you?"

He was taking her temperature? He laid his other hand over the ball of heat below her navel and pressed. She swayed into his touch. He wasn't wrong. The best way to fight this fire was with a hotter one. But how had he known to do that? It wasn't as if he went through this with Jay every month.

"Tell me what makes you most nervous about tonight, Alice."

Most nervous. Well, that was a loaded question.

He stepped up behind her as she considered her answer. Trapped her between his body against her back and his left hand on her stomach, palm firm and steady, thumb rubbing across her navel. He laid his head against hers.

"You . . . I mean . . . I know you have a wider range of sexual experiences to draw upon than I do. So it's natural, I guess, to let you lead there. But being a woman is . . . you're not . . ." She shrugged. She couldn't articulate what she wanted to say. It felt rude. "I don't know. It's weird."

"You feel this is your area of expertise." His intimate tone caressed her ear. "That, as a man, particularly one with a longtime male companion, I might be ill-equipped to care for your needs."

Unruffled. She'd called his skills into question, challenged his leadership, and he took it in stride. Maybe he'd bow to her knowledge here. She'd dealt with this every month for fifteen years, and he'd been with Jay practically since she'd graduated from college.

"I . . . yes. I'm sorry, Henry, but I haven't been with anyone who was even remotely interested before, aside from knowing which week I'd be hanging a do-not-disturb sign on my vagina." Crude, but true.

"By your choice or theirs?"

"What?"

"Is your distaste for intimacy at this time a function of your own discomfort with the idea or something imposed upon you by your former partners?"

Of course the idea was hers. It was disgusting and gross and . . . was it? Or had the guys she'd dated just told her it was? Henry was the only one to have asked the question. She squirmed, and he slid his right hand down her right arm. Soothing. Calming.

"I don't know," she admitted.

"All right, Alice. We've established you perhaps aren't the expert you believe yourself to be, hmm?" His voice remained soft and coaxing. "Which makes you uncertain of your own mind but does little to increase your confidence in mine, isn't that so?"

She nodded, reluctantly. She didn't want to alienate him, to give him another reason to end their arrangement, one beyond whatever made him uninterested in fucking her.

"Do you recall our contract talk, dearest?"

Her heart hammered. Was he going to reopen negotiations now? She nodded again, even more slowly, her hair sliding against his.

"I told you it was my responsibility to help you through new experiences, didn't I? And that I would, if necessary, enlist the assistance of an expert in matters beyond my knowledge?"

She went rigid in his grasp. He'd said Jay wouldn't be here tonight, but that didn't mean someone *else*—

"Alice, Alice, relax your muscles, dearest. You're causing yourself more pain. I *spoke* to a colleague of sorts this evening. An expert."

"A woman, you mean." Okay, that was a twinge of jealousy. But he'd consulted with the colleague for her benefit. One chat didn't mean he wanted to fuck that woman any more than he wanted to fuck Alice herself.

"Yes." He nuzzled his cheek against her hair. "Will you trust that I have some knowledge and experience outside your awareness? That I will be as prepared and mindful in my care of you tonight as I am on any other night we spend together?"

She leaned her weight into him, and he supported her easily. Submission meant trusting him to be in control, but giving up control in this was difficult. Sharing something she'd never even spoken with a man about. But Henry wasn't like any man she'd met before, was he? So maybe this, too, would be different, and that was okay. She squeezed her eyes shut.

"Yes, Henry."

"Good girl," he murmured. "Thank you for trusting me, dearest. There are two things I want you to do for me tonight. The first is to obey me, and the second is to enjoy yourself. Those are your only responsibilities. Can you accept them?"

His hand moved in firm circles on her lower abdomen. He still supported her weight. In the darkness behind her eyelids, relaxation grew.

"Yes, Henry." Words tasted lazy and thick.

"My sweet girl." He pressed a kiss to her right temple, and she sighed happily. "Let's get you comfortable before your bathwater cools."

She sank into the water and closed her eyes. He'd led her through their safeword ritual as he undressed her with neither haste nor overt sexuality but a kind of dedicated focus. Given her privacy while he stepped out with her clothes.

The air, heavy and wet, coated her throat as she inhaled. It carried the scent of roses. Her foot brushed something cloth-like on the bottom of the bathtub when she stretched. She opened her eyes to look, leaned forward and lifted the beribboned sachet to her nose. A soft knock came at the door.

"I'm decent," she called. She sniffed the sachet. Strong. Fragrant.

"What a shame. I'd hoped to find you quite *in*decent, my dear."

Her glance stopped at Henry's groin. He'd undressed as well.

"Brother Cadfael," he said.

"Huh?" She tore her attention from his hardening cock as he sat on the edge of the tub. He folded a towel and held it against the tile.

"Lie back, Alice." He adjusted the towel behind her head and plucked the sachet from her hands. "The rose petals. Brother Cadfael. The warmth of the water enhances the scent."

Lowering the bag to the water, he let it sink.

His fingers trailed through the water, skimming the top, coming to rest against her upraised right knee. He stroked her calf with firm, certain pressure.

Why had she thought a bath by herself would be better than this? He sat mostly facing her, and her eyes drifted back to his groin. His cock had grown taller, easily visible over his thigh. Was he going to use it tonight or just tease her with it?

She couldn't ask. He satisfied her at his discretion, not hers. Her job was to obey, not to question. If she didn't like it, she knew where the door was.

But she did like it. He'd never sent her home unsatisfied. His lack of interest in penetration was just confusing.

"You're tensing again." He squeezed her knee. "Close your eyes, dearest. Stop worrying about what will or won't happen and simply allow yourself to enjoy this moment, relaxing in the bath."

She closed her eyes. How did he always know?

"That's better."

A rustle from the shower curtain. Henry's hand left her knee. Water sloshed near her feet, sending gentle waves to lap at her nipples. A quiet crinkling. Paper? Ribbon, maybe? A second slosh between her feet, there and then gone. Water drops falling to the surface. A tickle of scent. Vanilla? Wet shirring. The vanilla scent grew heavier, a heady mix with the rose-scented water.

Her shoulders dropped as she exhaled, muscles loosening. Yeah, relaxing wouldn't be a problem, though falling asleep might be.

"There's an intimacy to bathing, Alice." Henry's voice bounced quietly off the tile, a low and deep rumble. The knots in her abdomen unraveled, leaving behind a growing calm and the faint stirring of desire. An ache, but a welcome one.

Her right hand was lifted, her arm hanging in the air, and she twitched at a light touch. The touch grew firmer, heavier. Moved in small circles on her forearm. Henry's fingertips, encased in the soft, wet warmth of a washcloth. She filled her lungs with vanilla when she inhaled and hummed as she exhaled. Henry had thick, gentle washcloths, not at all like the thin and worn-out pair she'd had for years.

"It's an activity we're accustomed to in early childhood, subconsciously entrusting our bodies to the ones who love us. The ones who care for our needs. But it's a delight we rarely indulge in as adults."

He lowered her right arm and raised her left, soaping and rinsing her skin with gentle, thorough attention.

"Bathing is an opportunity to raise one's awareness of one's partner. It need not be expressly sexual." He lowered her left arm.

The washcloth trailed across the top of her breasts, and she breathed deeply, intensifying the contact.

"But the potential for arousal is implicit."

His attentions turned to her legs, the cloth starting at her left foot and winding up the leg until it ended at her sex. He massaged her through the cotton, a brief tease before he repeated the process on the right. But this time his hand stayed between her thighs. The wet cloth molded to her sex, tugging at her lips, and his strong fingers parted them as he stroked her.

She let her legs drop open, knees falling against the sides of the bathtub. Her mouth, too, fell open, her nose unable to meet her body's increased demand for oxygen. Her exhalations became soft sighs.

Fingers circled her clitoris through wet cloth. Her hips rocked, and the bathwater moved over her body in tiny waves. Pain no longer figured in her thoughts. Now she measured only the pleasure from Henry's expert fingers . . . *so good.*

"You feel that arousal expanding, don't you, Alice? Pushing outward, racing along your every nerve, eager to converge on a single point." His fingers pinched, rolling her clitoris between them. The washcloth drifted away, and she gasped at the brush of his skin on hers. "Your body is a wonder, dearest. There's nothing shameful or wrong in sharing it with me."

His fingers slipped inside. He thrust slow and shallow. She tilted her hips to deepen the contact, moaning as the heel of his hand pressed hard against her clit.

"My beautiful, responsive girl. You'll come for me, won't you, Alice?" His fingers pumped faster, the curve of his hand bumping against her with each stroke. "So sweetly flushed with heat and desire."

His mouth covered hers, swallowing her moans. He moved to her neck, biting and sucking as the pleasure spiraled up and reached a tipping point.

Her moan became a strangled whimper. Her back arched, sending her breasts into the cooler air above the heat of the water. With no room to move, her legs flexed hard against the sides of the tub as her hips shook and his fingers thrust deep and stayed.

His kisses turned softer, gentler, and his voice murmured to her in between. "That's it . . . sweet Alice . . . your body offers its own solutions for pain, hmm?"

Warm and safe and buzzing with the rush, she nodded and

hummed her agreement. Not that she couldn't have done it herself. But that he was willing. That he *wanted* to.

"Thank you, Henry," she mumbled.

He kissed her mouth and forehead. "You are always welcome, my dear girl."

His fingers left her, and she bit down on an unhappy sigh. A metallic *thunk* made her flinch. The water level dropped.

"Open your eyes, Alice."

She blinked at the sudden brightness and allowed him to help her to her feet. Draping a towel around her shoulders, he began drying her with a second. She let her chin drop to her chest. He made no attempt to do anything about the erection he sported as he dried her from head to toe with tender swipes of the towel.

If he wasn't interested in intercourse, maybe he'd allow her to taste him instead. She'd seen him ask it of Jay. Would he grant her that, at least? In three months, it was the only time she'd seen him orgasm.

He hung the towels over the shower rod and stroked her cheek. "Is your pain gone for now?"

"Yes, Henry." The physical pain, anyway.

"I'm pleased."

Maybe his responsibility had ended for the night. Maybe he'd fetch her clothes and send her home so Jay could come back and Henry could get laid. Because the transparent truth was that he only wanted to have sex with Jay.

Even his erection might have nothing to do with her. He might be thinking about Jay right now. A hard cock was a physiological response to stimuli. Meaningless, especially if he didn't want her to do anything about it. He'd tell her if he did. She was bound to obey him. He could ask-demand—anything of her, and he hadn't so much as asked for a handjob.

He scooped her up in his arms, bridal-style, and she squealed in surprise. Such a Jay move from Henry was unprecedented. He carried her sideways through the door and across to his bedroom, where the covers had been pulled back, and laid her on the bed.

She wanted to scramble to her feet, to eliminate any chance of bleeding onto his wonderfully soft, undoubtedly expensive bedding. "But, your sheets—"

"Are neither your concern nor your responsibility, Alice," he chided. "You have two responsibilities tonight. Name them for me."

"To obey you," she responded promptly. "And to enjoy myself."

"Good girl." His forceful kiss, a stroking of tongue and pressing of lips, left her wanting more. "Obey and enjoy. Everything else is to be set aside."

Her body retained the warmth of the bathwater, but the cooler air in the bedroom raised her nipples to hardness. Henry swooped down and breathed heat across them, and she shuddered.

"Too tender, sweet girl?" His mouth hovered above her right breast, lips moving almost against her nipple. She took a deeper breath, lifting her chest, and his tongue flicked out teasingly.

"No . . . just a bit more sensitive tonight, aren't you?"

"Yes, Henry." She'd never had the pain some of her girlfriends had suffered through. She enjoyed the extra sensitivity. The heavy, full feeling in her breasts. But the pain low in her back and belly would return all too quickly. She'd worked herself to orgasm trying to alleviate cramps often enough to name it a stopgap measure. *Got another one for me, Henry?*

"Swollen," he murmured. "Aching. Beautiful."

He cupped her left breast as if he meant to take the weight of it from her even while she lay on her back. His mouth descended on the other.

Henry took his time. Not that there weren't a hundred small differences between the way he touched her and the way Jay did—it was impossible not to compare—but stripped to the base components, the bare wires exposed, the fundamental divide was in their approach. Jay's was eager, sometimes frantic, hopping to and fro. Henry's was patient. Confident. Steady.

Her giggle interrupted the series of soft moans building as he massaged her breasts with tongue and fingers. He lifted his head and then his torso, leaning over her until his mouth brushed her ear.

"Share with me, Alice. Share the thought that makes you laugh so enticingly." He set off on a wandering journey down her body, fingers traveling between her breasts and over her ribs and lower still, past the curve of her stomach. She rocked her hips. "Soon. But you'll share your thought with me first."

"I was thinking . . . about art." She blushed. If there was a god, Henry would leave it at that.

"A particular piece?"

She squeezed her eyes shut. Of course he wouldn't leave it at that. He was an artist, for chrissake.

"Copley Square," she choked out. "The tortoise and the hare."

He'd nuzzled so close his blink grazed her cheek. Silence, into which her heart pounded. And then he laughed. Henry chuckled beside her ear, and her body relaxed. Until his fingers moving across her clitoris made her gasp.

"My delightful girl. I presume I am your tortoise?"

She nodded, cautiously.

"Are you missing your hare tonight?"

"I don't want him to feel lonely. Pushed aside."

"A sentiment I share, dearest." The pressure from Henry's fingers stopped, and her hips strained in an effort to call it back. "But it doesn't answer the question."

"I guess. In theory. So I'd know he's not upset."

"But in practice, you're happy to have a gentler hand? A steadier one? One with less exuberance hopping about?" His voice teased her before it grew deeper. "A hand that understands how heightened your senses are just now, Alice?"

His fingers parted her lips with slow strokes. "How your body is swollen and aching? How the pain serves to make you more aware of those places? Of even the slightest touch?"

A single finger slipped inside her. Not deep, no. Barely there. Circling her entrance. Thrusting and sliding back before she could pull him deeper. But she wanted to. Tried to. Her hips chased his hand until she rocked steadily and he added a second finger, pressing deep. His thumb rolled across her clitoris.

He lay alongside her, curved over her right shoulder, his mouth at her neck.

"Do you feel it, Alice? The slickness? The rush of relief waiting for you? The way arousal banishes your pain? Do you want that, sweet girl?"

"Yes. Yes, I want it." God, did she want it again.

She whimpered when his fingers pushed deep and stayed. Her body contracted around them repeatedly, mimicking his motions.

He kissed her throat, hard, tugging at her skin. His thumb cut the last string of tension holding her back. Firm pressure and rapid movement on her clit had her hips bucking off the bed and her legs trembling as she gave a long, shuddering groan.

Enjoying the almost tickle of his nose sliding up her neck, she labored to catch her breath.

He rumbled low, no louder than a whisper, yet it sounded like thunder in her ear. "You've been waiting for me to fuck you again, haven't you, Alice? Wondering why I haven't?"

She nodded, sharply aware of his erection against her right hip despite the laxity in her muscles, the blissful aftermath of the pleasure he'd given her with his fingers.

"And what did you conclude?"

"That you . . . that you didn't want to." Shame made her stumble, fearing truth and falsity alike. She'd felt him hard for her on every one of their nights together, though he'd done nothing about it.

"I think you know that's untrue." His right arm stretched across her to clutch her left hip, preventing her from sliding away from his forceful thrust against her right side. "You can feel what I have for you, what I want to drive into you with abandon whenever I have you naked in my arms."

"But you haven't," she whispered. Was he going to tonight? Her mouth was dry. *Yes, please.*

"No," he agreed. "I haven't. Because I am able to control myself. Control my urges. Do you believe that, Alice? Do you trust I am able to deny myself and still fulfill your needs?"

He caressed her left side, deceptively lazy, tweaking her nipple when he reached it. She gasped.

"Yes. I trust you. You can control yourself." He could control her, too.

"Good." He kissed her, his tongue coaxing her lips open, sliding along her own in an erotic mimicry of penetration. His hand moved in slow circles over her breast, soothing the pinch of his fingers.

She whimpered when his mouth left hers.

"Then I have properly atoned for taking you so impulsively that first night."

Holy shit. Was that why he hadn't fucked her again? For almost three months? That was some serious self-denial.

"You were punishing yourself?"

"The rules I apply to my own conduct are as rigorous as the ones you and Jay must follow, Alice, if not more so. There is no one to enforce them if I do not."

He rolled away. The zipping rip had to be a condom wrapper opening. Her mind shrieked in silent joy. He grunted. Returned to her, shifting his weight, centering himself atop her.

She shuddered in expectation.

He lowered his mouth to her left ear. "I'm going to fuck you now, Alice. Thoroughly. For the rest of the night. And what are you going to do, my dear?"

"Obey. And enjoy." And come like a fucking river, she mentally added, as the head of his cock slipped over her clitoris. He dropped lower and pressed forward, nudging inside.

He rose on his arms above her, his eyes intent on hers as he pushed. Her body gave way to his, eagerly opening for him. The utter relief and pleasure on his face mesmerized her as he sank until his body rested flush against hers.

Once joined, he seemed in no hurry to move. Was he waiting for her body to adjust? Too close to the edge himself? He'd been right about the sensation. Either that or his words had primed her to feel everything more intensely.

She gave an experimental buck of her hips. Her breath stuttered as the rolling motion, trapped beneath his weight, pressed her clit hard against him.

"Yes, you want this badly, don't you, Alice?" He pulled his hips back.

Her walls contracted, feeling the emptiness, squeezing hard around the tip of his cock. He thrust as if he'd been waiting for it, a fast, unrestrained motion that filled her and dropped sudden weight on her clit. She couldn't control the instinctive thrust in return or the quiver in her thighs as tension raced through them.

He pulled back, always slow as he left her, dragging out the sensation. Shaking, she waited for the faster thrust, the one he was sure to deliver next. He held much of his weight on his elbows, and his gaze had not wavered from her face.

"So do I," he growled. "I want to see your face when you come for me, Alice."

His hips snapped forward, a fierce drive, her whole body attuned to that single movement and desperate to fulfill his desire, to obey his need for her. Orgasm arrived with unexpected suddenness. Left her giddy and boneless and uncaring about anything beyond the press of his body above hers.

A sliver of fear crept into her heart. No toys, no tricks, no third partner, no fingers rubbing furiously over her clit, no imagined scenarios. Nothing. He hadn't used anything but his hard cock and his careful attention to her needs, and he'd made her come from intercourse alone. In the missionary position. A first.

And he was going to do it again, she thought, as he worshipped her face with short kisses and murmured words of comfort and appreciation. Because he was still hard, still thrusting in a more relaxed rhythm now, slow and gentle and not as deep. Maybe waiting for her to come back down to Earth. Something that wasn't going to happen if he kept moving. Tension coiled low in her belly, inside somehow, and his cock didn't thrust so much as rub.

She moaned, her own voice unfamiliar to her ears, a wavering vibrato.

His head dipped to her chest. Closing his mouth over her right breast, he sucked and tugged with the same slow speed his hips had adopted. Her climax grew into a rolling wave that never broke but ebbed and flowed with his motion, as though he commanded her body to provide a continuous fountain of pleasure until he found his own release.

He hadn't been urgent about it by the end. His rhythm hadn't faltered, and he hadn't given a shout. Her body hadn't been merely a means to an end for him. He'd been tender. And silent but for hushed words she couldn't hear as he whispered them to her breasts.

When he lifted his head, she watched him through half-closed eyes. His smile proved impossible to read. He kissed her forehead and her nose and her lips as if she were not a part-time playmate but a beloved partner. He must've known she needed that today, too. The gestures of a lover even if pretend.

"Rest, Alice. I'll be back in a moment, and then we'll begin again."

Chapter 9

"We'll be adding a new dimension to our games this evening, Alice." Henry led her across his bedroom to the second dresser, the one he didn't keep for clothes.

Jay lagged behind, seating himself on the padded bench in the corner. They were all of them still dressed, though Henry had already gone through the ritual questions.

Six toys lay in a neat line across the top of the dresser. Nothing she'd seen before. She sucked in a breath, the sound loud in the silence.

"I am not a sexual sadist, Alice. There is no compulsive gratification in this for me."

Henry stood beside her, but he didn't touch her. The last time she'd been in this room, two weeks ago, he'd fucked her until sunup. Tonight it seemed he had something else in mind.

"Nor am I intending to work out some psychological or emotional trauma on your flesh. This is about testing your limits, allowing you to discover whether the proper application of pain can be a pleasurable experience for you. Do you understand the difference?"

"I think so." Her hands twitched at her sides. She wanted to touch the implements he'd chosen for her before he applied them with force. "You aren't angry, not with me or anyone else. And if I don't like it, you won't keep going just to satisfy yourself. It's for me. To learn what I want."

"Very good." He stepped behind her and lifted her hands in his. "You may touch the toys, my dear. Familiarize yourself with their feel before we begin."

She breathed out, a relieved, near-silent sigh, and picked up the feathers at the far left. They hung at the end of a short whip, soft and silky against her fingers.

Henry stepped away. Vaguely aware of him joining Jay on the bench, she let the toys claim her attention. Down went the feathers. She picked up the next item, a wood-handled hairbrush with a broad head. Stiff bristles. A smooth back, sealed with a finish of some sort. Waxed, from the slight shine.

Third came a paddle with a leather covering on one side and plain wood on the other. She splayed her fingers across the leather. The edges narrowly exceeded her grasp.

Three left. Whips of some sort, all of them. She laid a hand on the first.

Soft. Softer than she'd expected. She rolled an end between two fingers. Suede. It wouldn't be so soft hitting her, not with the added momentum and the force of Henry's swing. But standing here, rubbing her fingers against the material, she shifted her legs and shivered as the seam of her jeans slid over her mons.

Henry's soft rumble formed her name. She half-turned, but his focus stayed with Jay. A chastisement for getting ahead of herself didn't seem to be in the offing.

". . . Alice but also for you, my boy."

She turned back to the dresser. Jay's transition into a scene usually happened before her arrival. She rarely heard Henry give him extensive instructions. Now that she'd heard her name, tuning out their quiet voices was difficult, even if she couldn't catch every word.

". . . need to do . . ."

". . . prove something to is yourself, Jay. But if . . ."

She moved her hand to the second whip. Like the first, it had more than a dozen strips of material extending from a single knot. Unlike the first, the material was hard leather, thick and heavy, with an odd pattern like a bed of tiny pebbles. Her heart beat faster as she stared at the handle, imagining Henry's hand clenched around the leather, picturing the fall.

"... can't help thinking about ..."

"... allow that experience to dominate your ..."

The final whip on the dresser was different. Familiar, in that it was the sort she'd have pictured before playing with Henry and Jay. A woman in leather and thigh-high boots slapping a riding crop across her palm, telling some man he'd been a naughty boy. This whip was long and thin, a bit flexible, with a leather loop at the end. Despite the crop's classic image, its mental association with sex, the thought of Henry wielding it didn't excite her.

She returned to the two multitipped whips, laying a hand on each, stroking. Fantasizing.

"... help Alice out of her clothes, Jay."

She twisted and met two intent stares. The men stood.

Henry smiled. "I do believe she's ready to play this game now."

She put her back to the dresser as they came to her.

Taking her hands, Jay pulled her forward and stepped close to unbutton her shirt. His palms caressed the slope of her breasts and slipped around her waist as he pushed her shirt open.

Henry's voice came from over her shoulder. "You lingered on the floggers, Alice. Why them?"

She should've known he'd pay attention to her reactions, even while sitting with Jay. Her shirt dropped to the floor. She relished the teasing dance of Jay's fingers up her back to the clasp of her bra.

"I don't know."

"But you felt something. Imagined something?"

She wouldn't mistake his low, easy tone for anything other than the demand it was.

Jay tugged her bra down her arms, and it joined her shirt on the floor. He laid his hands at her waist, slipping his fingers into the waistband of her jeans.

"The suede. It was soft. I wanted to feel it ... between my legs." Confusion, not embarrassment, made her hesitate. She didn't know why she wanted these things, but that didn't make them wrong. "And the other, the leather?"

"Buffalo hide, my dear. A heavy leather."

"The buffalo. It . . . it looked right in your hand."

Jay thumbed open the snap on her jeans. The metal zipper ticked as he dragged it down.

"You pictured me using it on you?"

"Yes."

"An arousing image?"

Jay knelt, sliding her jeans down her legs.

She sucked in her lips to wet them. "Very."

Jay lifted her feet clear of her jeans. She stood in nothing but her underwear, a navy-blue pair Henry had given her weeks ago. They matched the bra lying on the floor.

"Good girl. Thank you, Alice."

She trembled, a mix of pleasure at his praise and anticipation as Jay lowered her underwear, his breath puffing against her thighs.

"Thank you, Jay. You've unwrapped a lovely present for us. Waiting pose, please." At Henry's command, Jay sat back on his heels in front of her. "Alice, to the bed, please."

She moved and waited for further instructions, but Henry laid his hands on her instead. She kept her muscles pliant and flowing, allowing him to position her at the foot of the bed as he wished. Her feet spread. Her upper body lying against the comforter. Her arms stretched over her head. He slid a pillow into the gap between the mattress and her hips.

"Are you comfortable, Alice?"

"Yes, Henry."

"I won't bind you this time, but you are not to squirm away from the sensation. Your hands are to remain above your head. Do not attempt to shield yourself from me. You may cause yourself harm that way. I will judge when you have had enough. If you disagree, what are you to do?"

"Say my word."

"And what is your word?"

"Pistachio."

"Good girl." He stroked her back, and she struggled not to press herself into his touch as his palm slid down until it cupped her right buttock. He squeezed. "Your skin is pale cream, Alice. I expect it reddens easily. So many lovely shades."

His hand dropped away. She stood, waiting, her legs parted, her pubic bone grazing the thick pillow beneath her hips as she bent over.

The bed dipped to her right. Jay, naked now too, matched her positioning. Henry's hand lay on his shoulder.

"What are your rules for the evening, Jay?"

"If I want your attention, I have to ask for it."

"Correct. And?"

"If it's too much . . . if I can't . . . I can leave. I don't need permission."

"Correct. And if that happens?"

"I should go to the kitchen, drink a glass of orange juice, sit down and wait for you."

"Good boy."

Henry left them lying alone, side by side. Their eyes met. Jay's showed something like fear. Though she wanted to ask, despite it not being her business, she held her tongue. If Henry wanted her to speak, he would tell her so.

But she shifted her hand, as if she were stretching, letting her arm drift right until her fingers brushed Jay's arm. His eyes softened. His lips twitched in a small smile that quickly disappeared. It was odd to think herself the more confident one, the more trusting one. Excited, anticipatory, she waited for Henry's actions, knowing he wouldn't hurt her beyond what she enjoyed. But Jay trembled as though he might bolt.

She smiled, intending to reassure him, but her smile morphed into a soft sigh, an easy exhalation, as feather tips dragged across the top of her ass from left to right. The light touch, too light, wasn't quite ticklish but something else. Something that focused her attention.

It came again, faster, a wisp, a glide. She shivered, imagining a heavier stroke. Imagining the suede, the buffalo. The feathers danced in a pattern, left and right, high and low, and she arched her back and lifted her heels to press closer.

The feathers stopped.

"How do you feel, Alice? Right now, without thinking about it."

"Focused. Needy."

"In pain?"

"No." Why would she be in pain?

"Highly sensitized?" Something round and cool pressed against her left buttock, and she jumped.

"Y-yes."

"Good?"

"Yes." Her answer was firm this time. She stopped trying to see the end of the bed to speak with Henry.

Jay stared at her with rounded eyes. His teeth gripped his bottom lip. This introduction for her had to be some sort of demonstration for him, too. Maybe he wasn't—

Pain scrambled her brain.

A slap stung the left side of her ass in a broad circle. The sharp crack heralded pain rolling out like ripples in a pond. Rolling still as the pain came again, on the right, now. Her body shifted forward, pressing into the pillow, away from the pain. The hairbrush or the paddle. She couldn't tell and it didn't matter. It was just pain. Twice more, quick, short slaps, and her backside throbbed.

Blinking wetness from her eyes, she pushed down the whimpers rising in her throat. A heated rush of blood rang in her ears. Her pulse, merrily thumping along, surprised her with its presence when the next slap jarred her and pumped her hips deeper into the pillow. Her clitoris rubbed against the soft fabric. She sucked in a breath at the unexpected pleasure, a sensation as powerful as the waves of pain still rolling through her.

No more slaps came.

"Your feelings, Alice? Quickly, now."

"Pain, but . . . good, too."

She forced her eyes to stay open, to look at Jay though it was Henry who spoke.

"How is it good, Alice?"

"A rush . . . my heartbeat . . . my hips, the pillow . . ." God, why couldn't she think? Was she even making sense?

"Not the pain itself, then, not the sting of the paddle?" Henry's question seemed to intensify Jay's stare.

"No, I don't, I don't think so." The sting hadn't aroused her, but it had made her open to feeling the rest. Made it possible.

Henry's hand, familiar warmth and calm and excitement at once, slid between her thighs. He stroked her lips, and she sighed at the comforting touch. He stayed away from her clitoris. Maybe he was checking the level of her arousal. Not much, yet. Damp, but not ready.

She smiled at Jay, a lazy, happy smile, but he seemed too intent on whatever he considered his task tonight to return it.

Henry's fingers went away, and the feathers returned. Teasing caresses on her back. Sweeping strokes pushing aside what had gone before. A palate cleanser. Her breath came faster. Expectation ticked its way down her spine and settled between her legs as the feathers swished across her thighs. What would he choose next?

"Ah!"

Her right thigh burned with a sharp sting. The left as well, a short, snapping pain. Even the forward motion of her hips against the pillow, the soft nap of the fabric against her spread lips, wasn't enough to make the pain pleasurable. The sting came twice more and stopped.

"Your reaction, Alice?"

"No. It's no."

"No, you didn't like the riding crop, did you?"

"The sting is too sharp. It just hurts. I don't . . . I don't want to try it again."

Something in Jay's face relaxed as she spoke. She wanted to ask why he'd stayed when his discomfort had been so obvious.

"Thank you for your honesty, Alice. I'm pleased you don't feel the need to lie in a misguided attempt to please me."

Jay winced. She had to be missing some subtext tonight. Had Jay lied?

The idea horrified her. Henry depended upon their honesty. She trusted him to always be guided by what was in her best interests. She wouldn't make his dominant role more difficult by lying. The machine would only be perfected with accurate data input. Form and function in harmonious motion, striving for a single goal.

"Did you trust that I would stop, Alice? And did I, quickly enough to suit you?"

"Yes, of course. One stroke wouldn't have been a large enough

sample size, but four told you my reaction wasn't likely to change."
Thinking was easier now, when her arousal had ebbed, when she
knew this night was somehow a lesson for Jay. "If you'd kept going, I
would've said my word. But I knew I wouldn't need to."

"And how did you know that?"

"Because you know me. You can read my reactions. You . . . care
about me when I put myself in your hands. You'd never keep going if
you thought you were truly hurting me in a way I didn't like."

Was Jay crying? He blinked, rapidly, and she didn't think he had
something in his eye.

Henry's voice softened. "Jay, you may step outside if you need to,
my boy. But I believe it would be good for you to stay. Perhaps we'll
find something Alice likes. That will be better, hmm?"

Jay nodded, his head rustling against the comforter. "Yes, Henry."
His voice was hoarse, almost silent, with disuse and whatever emo-
tions choked him. A rush of aching compassion tightened her chest.

"Good boy." A pause. Feathers floated across her back. "Shall we
start again, dear one?"

"Yes, please."

The fading sting in her thighs left less of an ache than the paddle
had on her backside. The feathers traveled up, slipping across her
shoulders and pulling her attention away from the lingering memory
of pain. She let her eyes drop shut as the feathers danced.

Oh!

A heavier touch, but still soft, a waterfall of fabric on her left
shoulder. It dragged, and disappeared, and thudded again, on the right
this time, and dragged. The suede, smooth and slow and warm.

She moaned. Her shoulders flexed with the motion. Her nipples
pressed into the comforter, and she arched at the friction as they
hardened. The suede was good. Very good. She lost track of the thudding strikes. Everything was sensation, and sensation was *good*.

The suede's rhythm encompassed her entire back. A solid *thud* on
her shoulder that made her jump. A slow drag downward as she trembled with anticipation. A soft series of back-and-forth slaps across
her backside that set her body rocking, pressing upward to greet the
fall and downward to rub her pubic mound into the pillow, which
seemed an insufficient pressure.

The pattern repeated at different speeds, different strengths, every variation heightening the intensity. The ends delivered a sting on the faster strokes, but it wasn't the painful sting of the crop or the broad sting of the paddle. She welcomed this sting, a sting that sharpened the weight of the straps falling across her skin, a sting soothed by the soft drag of suede.

She basked in the trailing drag, waiting for the fall. The right cheek next. She tilted her hips, eager for suede's sweet kiss. The suede slapped between her legs instead, against lips swollen and flushed and thumping with her heartbeat. She gasped and trembled on the edge of release.

The suede slipped away. She whimpered, a protest, a plea. Her fingers tingled where she gripped the comforter. Her legs tensed, a breath away from shaking.

Henry's fingers pressed inside her, curving forward, rubbing her inner flesh as they thrust. Her eyes flew open as she came, face-to-face with Jay's dilated eyes and panting breaths. Henry drew it out, prolonging her orgasm with his fingers until she slumped against the bed and her knees buckled.

Her eyes slid half shut. Her thighs fluttered with electric shocks, muscle twitches beyond her control. She couldn't quite get her feet under her, and she didn't care. If Henry wanted her to move, he would move her.

Her mind bobbed along, disconnected, floating despite its heaviness. As though she drifted in a dark sea. The rumble of Henry's voice was a pleasant rocking sensation. She may have swayed with it. Or not. It was hard to tell, and she couldn't be bothered.

". . . think she heard you, Henry."

". . . enjoyed herself, hmm?"

Movement. A shadow on her face. Her eyelids twitched open, an uncontrolled jerk.

Jay kissed her, his mouth grazing her forehead, her cheeks, her lips.

Her eyes drifted shut.

". . . still not here with us . . ."

". . . fine. Let her bask . . . steady . . . left a few marks." A hand traced the outside of her left thigh.

Her arms and legs moved, though she didn't think she'd caused it. Probably not. Could she make them move? She couldn't recall how. Her body lifted, weightless. Her head came down on a pillow.

". . . crash soon. Stay with her, Jay. I'll be . . ."

She burrowed deeper into her cocoon, her mind insulated from the noise, her body welcoming the warm press of another.

Jay, murmuring in her ear. ". . . amazing. I'm glad I stayed. You were beautiful, Alice. Happy. Trusting. I hope I can get there again. You're floating, right? Like there's this bubble around your mind and nothing can touch you. No worries. No pain. Just peace."

She mmmphed in agreement, wiggling to press her face to his. He stroked her hair and kissed her cheeks. She rocked as the bed dipped to her other side, her eyes opening.

Jay gave her mouth a final kiss before his head moved away. "She's a little more aware, I think, but still pretty out of it."

A hand rested on the center of her back, over her spine, where the toys had never touched her. Henry's hand, warm and reassuring.

"Alice, sweet? I need for you to answer me in words, dear one. Are you well?"

She fought to find her voice, to recall how to use it, to respond to the gentle demand in his tone. "M'good."

"I want you to have a sip of juice, Alice. Jay?"

Her body rolled and turned, until her head lay in the cradle of Jay's neck. Henry's intent stare made her giggle, thinking it a reversal of earlier, when Henry had been behind her and Jay had watched so intently.

Henry smiled. His hand insistently raised a glass to her lips. "Drink, Alice."

The juice tasted sweet and just a bit tart. Pineapple? The chill spread all the way down as she swallowed, and she shivered. "S'cold."

"It's the crash, dear girl. The euphoric state only lasts so long."

He made her drink again, while his other hand rested against the side of her neck. He'd undressed. When had that happened? He set the glass on the nightstand and pulled her toward him, chest to chest, leaving her back exposed to the air. He slid down until they lay on the bed, her body draped over his.

His right arm wrapped around her back with care. Clasped above her waist, between the areas on her shoulders and her bottom where aches were just making themselves known. His left arm rotated below her. Outward. He leaned left, tilting her with him, though his right hand held her steady. Where was Henry going?

Jay's breath washed over her shoulder, his face inches away as he rolled toward them. Oh. Not going. Just pulling Jay against his side. Tucking him into the circle of his arm.

She reached for Jay's hand and brought it back with hers, curling them both between her breasts, above Henry's steady heartbeat.

The three of them lay in silence. Henry would eventually want to talk. Want to analyze their reactions. She wasn't there yet. She was hardly even at thinking. He seemed to know it, had probably expected it.

And Jay. Jesus. She had no idea what had prompted his reactions. She squeezed his hand, and he nestled closer, jostling Henry.

Her eyes blinked open. Jay's head rested against Henry's shoulder, nearly touching her own on his chest. Did Henry mind being used as a mattress for them both? A careful stretch let her kiss Jay's forehead and then Henry's jaw.

"Thank you. Both of you."

Henry clasped her more tightly. Jay squeezed her fingers.

Henry's chest rumbled beneath her ear when he spoke. "All right now, Alice? Feeling more yourself?"

She nodded. He was too polite to hint, but she was probably getting heavy. Monopolizing his chest. And his attention. How long had she been lying on him, cuddling up to him like he was her personal sleep aid? "Yes, Henry. My brain's working again. It wasn't for a while there."

"Did you enjoy that feeling? The silence in your mind?"

"I . . . yeah." She wouldn't lie to Henry, but saying the words made her uncomfortable. There was something not right about wanting that. Wanting to not be herself. Her thoughts made her who she was. Made her a unique person, one in charge of her own life. Gave her control. A way to organize and categorize her life.

Why would she want to get away from that? And why would pain give her that? Why would it make her feel good? She shifted, restless, her feet rubbing against Henry's.

"Jay." Henry commanded immediate attention. "Go and fetch a washcloth, please, and the arnica cream I set out on the counter."

"Yes, Henry." Jay kissed Henry's shoulder and Alice's cheek before he rolled away and off the bed.

She pushed, gently, against Henry's chest, and he let her go, though not far. She pulled the sheet up and lay on her stomach, flinching when the fabric settled on sensitive skin.

He rolled onto his side and dipped his head to catch her eyes. "Tell me why it disturbs you, sweet girl."

"I liked it. I did." She didn't want him to think she hadn't. That she wouldn't have told him to stop if she'd needed him to. That he couldn't trust her. "But . . . why do I like it when it's so wrong?"

"Did you ask that of your previous partners, Alice?"

"No, of course not. They never—we didn't play these games. You know that." He'd seen the extent of her experience from her contract answers. He'd interrogated her about them for hours.

"And if we weren't playing these games, if Jay and I had simply told you we enjoy engaging in sex with men as well as women, would you have asked why we like it when it's so wrong?"

"God no, that's not—Jesus, Henry. There's nothing wrong with having same-sex partners."

He laughed, quietly, and squeezed her hand. "You're very young, Alice. The decade between us is a significant one in this case. I assure you, when I reached puberty and discovered my interests were not limited by gender considerations, the majority of people did, in fact, believe there was something wrong with homosexuality."

"Were you bullied?" She squeezed back. Was that why he enjoyed being in charge? Because he'd been victimized before?

He shook his head, a small smile on his lips. "No, Alice. You're seeking a reason, an explanation for where things have gone wrong. Have you considered such a rationale doesn't exist?"

"Well . . . it's not normal, is it? What we're doing? I mean, I liked it. Tonight. But it was painful. I shouldn't like that. So why . . ." She shrugged. "Just why?"

"Why do we do it, you mean?" Henry's tone was light. "What damage must we carry that makes us react to such stimuli in a sexual fashion?"

She turned on her side and curled her body into a ball, tucking her legs to her chest. The movement stretched her back, pulling at the places where he'd flogged her. She was sore now, but the game had felt good in the moment. Amazingly good.

"Yeah, that, I guess. I don't feel like I had a damaged childhood or something, but . . ."

"But mainstream psychology and social mores about sexuality have given you the impression that what you desire is something forbidden and therefore something must be wrong with you."

"Aww, man, you're giving her the psych talk, Henry? And I'm missing it? Did I miss the good bits?"

She craned her head over her shoulder to watch Jay saunter into the bedroom, naked as a jaybird.

"What, you got this talk, too? I would've figured psychology was way over your head."

"Ha-ha. You're a comedian. Guess who won't be getting this soothing cream rubbed into her aching backside?" He waggled a small jar held delicately in one hand, a washcloth in the other.

"Like you could resist putting your hands on my ass." She smirked at him, sticking her tongue out for emphasis.

"Oh, I'll put hands on your ass, all right." Jay hopped onto the bed, dropping the jar to the pillow, and yanked at the sheets. She held on tight and rolled toward Henry. The move overbalanced Jay, sending him sprawling across her back.

"Ow. Ow, ow, ow," Alice yelped.

Jay propelled himself backward so quickly that he tumbled off the end of the bed.

"Owww. That hurt." Jay rested his chin on the bed, one hand rubbing his head.

Henry sighed.

"Now that you've gone and hurt yourselves, if you two children are done teasing each other . . ." Despite his dry tone, his smile was tolerant, amused. He wouldn't be so if they'd truly hurt each other, but he otherwise seemed fond of their exuberance.

She pulled herself forward on her elbows and kissed his cheek.

"That's why we leave you in charge of playtime. Jay and I would make a mess of things."

A delicate dip in the mattress and fingertips ghosting across her ankle marked Jay's silent return.

Henry's gaze flashed past her shoulder. He nodded once before returning his attention to her. "Ah, you see, Alice? You do know what's 'wrong' with you. You're playful, inexperienced and overeager. It's a recipe for disaster. Thank heavens we found you when we did. Who knows what trouble you might have gotten into otherwise."

"You're teasing me." She gasped. Jay had chosen the right moment to press the washcloth to her sex.

Henry's smile turned sly. "It *is* part of my contractual obligations to you, dearest."

"Not verbally, it isn't." Her legs relaxed. Jay's gentle strokes seemed almost an apology for his earlier tumble.

"Don't be ridiculous, Alice. Of course it is." Henry arched his right eyebrow. "Or would you deny that you come so sweetly when I speak to you of all the ways in which Jay and I shall debauch you?"

She flushed red, and the heated welts across her ass and thighs throbbed. The washcloth went away.

"You know I won't deny that. I promised I wouldn't lie to you. That's part of *my* contract."

"Mmm. For your own safety and enjoyment, dear one."

She hissed and burrowed into the mattress at the first touch of cold on her backside. Jay's hands, spreading the soothing cream over her welts.

"So you're saying nothing's wrong with me."

"I'm saying there isn't necessarily anything 'wrong' in your past that has somehow caused you to accept aberrant or deviant sexual practices as normal, Alice. You may simply like these things, as I do. That's not to say you won't meet some for whom the impetus is different. Some who struggle with self-loathing. Some who have suffered abuse. Some whose sexual responses have been negatively influenced by life events."

Henry reached out and cupped her face, his fingers warm and gentle, pushing her hair behind her ear before moving off.

"I was neither neglected nor abused, Alice. And if I am a disappointment to my mother, it is only because I have not given her grandchildren, a situation I feel my older brother has well in hand. That I enjoy planning scenes, providing a safe outlet for healthy sexual desires and lavishing attention and affection on you and Jay might indicate that I am an analytical, obsessive caretaker, nothing more."

She crossed her arms under her head, enjoying the comfort brought both by Jay's hands and Henry's words. "And me?" She crooked an eyebrow. "And Jay?"

"Jay's story is his to tell, if he chooses. As for you, my dear, I'm still tunneling into the depths of your thoughts. I would say, thus far, that you enjoy pleasing others and a firm hand, that you are generous and inventive, and that you dislike disharmony and distance." Henry slid closer, until his warm bulk lay beside her, and he kissed the tip of her nose. "You're a cuddler."

Jay's hands slipped away from her thighs. The slight *clunk* to her right had to be him setting the jar on the nightstand before lying beside her. Mirroring Henry's pose, from the heat along her right side. He was warmer than Henry, pressing in close like an overgrown puppy and nuzzling her neck.

"Plus, you taste great. I can confirm that a thousand times over. I can't believe you didn't mention that, Henry. It's a tragic omission."

She laughed, happy and content lying between the two men in her life. But Jay's avoidance hadn't escaped her. Pressing her head back, she pushed at his teasingly. "You gonna share?"

"Who, me?" His words came mumbled between kisses to her neck. "What, are you hungry for more so soon? I thought Henry had you pretty wiped out."

"Not that, you horndog. Your story." She affected a cultured, literary tone, an imitation of one of her college professors. "Why you *are* the way you *are*, darling boy." She returned to her normal voice and rolled her head to face Jay. "Or at least how you met Henry. It's a love story, right? I bet it's hugely romantic."

Jay's kisses stopped. "It's . . . I . . . I made a pile of bad choices."

Shit. She'd just totally stepped in it.

"But then I met Henry. Now I let him make all the choices." Jay nipped at her ear, his playful mood, or the veneer of it, restored. "And that works so much better."

She couldn't disagree. Everything worked so much better with Henry in charge of it. If Jay didn't want to talk about his bad choices, it wasn't her place to make him. She wasn't his lover. She was probably here to entertain him. To teach him something? Was that what Henry had been doing tonight? Was the lesson related to Jay's bad choices? Even if it was, she wouldn't get answers tonight.

Chapter 10

Alice woke at her normal time Friday morning even though she didn't have to. The company had given everyone off for the Thanksgiving holiday. Which was fine. Nice.

Except she didn't have Christmas shopping to do, and she didn't have leftover turkey to stuff her face with. And Henry's car still wasn't back in its space.

She knew from her Tuesday lunch with Jay that they were visiting family. He'd said something about driving up to New Hampshire on Wednesday night, and she hadn't seen Henry's car since. But Jay hadn't said anything about skipping their Friday. In fact, he'd made a point of saying he'd be sure he was back by Friday night.

She stood in her bathrobe at eight in the morning, looking out her window and waiting for that space to fill up. Eleven hours.

"I am not going to sit at home all day and wait for sex." She said it cautiously, testing the words. They sounded right.

Even if sex was what she wanted. A shower by herself was not bad, but a shower with the memory of Henry's marathon night of sex four weeks ago was—good God, that man could fuck. He hadn't let her leave until after breakfast the next morning. Insisted if he was going to keep her awake all night burning calories he was going to replenish them, too.

But she hadn't seen Jay at all that time, and neither of them had fucked her two weeks ago after her flogging. Henry had insisted she stay overnight again, so he could be certain she'd taken no lasting harm from what he'd called impact play. Jay had seemed too rattled for sex, and Henry hadn't asked either of them for anything. He'd cuddled them close and talked until they'd fallen asleep.

She'd been reluctant to let sleep take hold, wanting to listen a little longer as he described the slick, rocky shoreline he'd explored as a child. Watching sailboats bobbing in the bay, their triangular sails falling slack or snapping tight as the wind's moods demanded. Listening to the scratch of his mother's charcoal pencils as she sketched. He'd been seven that summer, and he'd filled his first sketchbook with drawings of the bay and the boats and his mother.

"It's important to capture such moments before they pass us by," he'd murmured as Alice's eyelids fell and refused to rise again. "To let every stroke, every line, carry the weight of the love one has for the beauty in the subject."

She'd dreamed of child-Henry that night, his green eyes flashing like the sunlight off the waves. That and the painting hanging in the hallway, the one of Jay's naked back from the tops of his shoulders to the curve of his spine just above his beautiful ass. Was that Henry's love, on display, where Jay could see it every time he passed?

If romantic love existed, truly existed, not convenience or polite fictions, it had to be what Henry and Jay shared.

"And even then, they still fuck other people sometimes." She leaned her right shoulder against the window frame. "Like me. So how great could love be, if it still isn't enough?"

Six weeks without having Jay inside her. Not since his final exam. She smirked. No wonder he'd been eager to promise he'd be back in time for tonight. Hell, she was equally eager.

She'd never been so obsessed with sex before. Even when she and Adam had been fucking like rabbits those two years at college, she hadn't replayed their fuckfests in her head as fantasy fuel. Hadn't woken up with his name on her lips. Hadn't been desperate for Friday night to arrive so she could get him inside her again.

The pre-Henry-and-Jay era of her sex life was looking even more awkward and unsatisfying than she'd already deemed it. Pathetic.

Maybe if she met an interesting guy Henry would be willing to vet him. Give him some prep work. Because Henry knew what to do, and he wasn't shy about telling *her* what to do.

"Random Stranger, meet Henry, my fucking coach. Henry, please teach Random Stranger how to touch me properly." She shed her bathrobe and gathered her clothes.

Henry, of course, would be unfailingly polite. "Certainly. It's a pleasure to meet you, Random Stranger. Tell me, how did you and Alice meet? If you'd just remove your clothing, we'll begin. Have you touched many women before?"

Dropping to the futon, she rolled with laughter. "Oh God. That's too perfect." She gasped for breath. "Shit, Henry, how the fuck am I ever gonna meet a man who measures up?"

Maybe he considered his attentiveness normal behavior. The appropriate courtesy for sexual partners. He'd probably die before he left one unsatisfied. His parents had probably sat him down for The Talk and handed him a book.

"*Sexual Etiquette for All Occasions*, that's just the thing, Henry, dear. Do come to us if you have any questions." She giggled. Every guy should have a copy of Henry's guidebook.

But if their last night fucking each other was Henry's basic repertoire—the comforting bath, the tender touching, the snuggling and caressing, the three rounds of fucking and the hearty breakfast afterward—and if the flogging that had sent her brain to a happy, happy place was the intermediate course . . .

She sighed, half-dressed, staring at her ceiling while her legs hung off the side of her futon.

"Jay, you are one lucky fucking bastard." By extension, so was she. For now.

Odd to be excited not only by the sex but also by the promise of more of it. Especially after four months.

From the third of August, when Henry had bent her over his dining room table and fucked her while dinner waited on them, to today, the day after Thanksgiving, when she had no idea of his plans and couldn't wait for seven o'clock to arrive.

"Almost four months, and I'm not bored with them."

Only two of her real relationships had lasted this long. Maybe

Henry had the right idea, with his contracts and his every-two-weeks model. The sex meant more when she had to wait for it and she didn't feel pressure to perform at the drop of a hat.

He wouldn't text her at one in the morning on a Tuesday because he was drunk and horny, and he wouldn't expect her to run right over and blow him. He hadn't expected a blowjob at all yet. He didn't treat her like a convenience.

He respected her, because they had a piece of paper. Okay, several pieces of paper. He'd signed them as a promise that he would. She didn't expect Henry broke many promises. He just made her wait. And waiting built her sex drive in a frenzy of anticipation no matter how many times she got herself off during the time between.

If Jay was a lucky bastard, then Henry was a clever one. He'd held her attention for four months, and he'd only fucked her twice the entire time.

"You're an evil fucking genius, Henry."

She finished dressing and hurried out the door. Not needing to shop wouldn't bar her from spending the day people-watching. Faneuil Hall was bound to be packed. She'd wander for a few hours. Keep an eye out for hot guys who wouldn't mind getting sex lessons in how to please her from Henry.

What, you mean guys like Jay?

"Shut up, brain." She headed for the Longwood Station to catch the D train. "If we weren't friends and the sex wasn't so hot, I'd have already said 'so long' by now. I don't need all that relationship drama. Henry's just good at making everything . . . easy."

She spent most of the day thinking about Henry and Jay and their nights together anyway. Or, more to the point, their mornings together. Three, now. True, the contract had the option. She wasn't arguing with Henry's choices, not when they turned out so satisfying for her own libido. But three. In a row. Their time together was expanding. Was that good? Or did it mean they were rushing toward an end?

What did it mean if she wasn't ready for that? She'd never had trouble closing the door on a sex partner before. Even with Adam, after two years, she hadn't felt conflicted about turning him down. When things were over, they were over.

But when she took the train home at five thirty and discovered Henry's note waiting, the thrill still rushed through her. The jump in her pulse and the desperate need to see what instructions he'd left.

She pulled the envelope from the wood and took it inside.

"It's okay," she murmured as she opened the flap. "It's just a temporary addiction."

No special instructions tonight. Which meant what she wore didn't matter, because she wouldn't be wearing it long.

Shedding her clothes, she stepped into the shower. She resisted the urge to touch herself beyond what was necessary for cleanliness, though the arousal that had simmered in the back of her mind all day was nearing a boil. Touching herself now would be disrespectful to Henry. As if she were telling him he couldn't get the job done, even if he'd never know.

She would know.

She put on the slate-gray underwear from a set he'd given her and a deep green dress, darker than his eyes, that floated above her knees and bared her back. Flat sandals, because they were easier to slip off at the door. She'd better hope they weren't playing strip poker tonight. Once her shoes were off, she'd only last two hands.

Jay answered her knock at seven. Her body brushed his as she entered the apartment, his dress shirt crisp against her arm. He swayed toward her before he remembered himself and closed the door.

Eyeing him, she toed off her sandals to match his own bare feet. He resembled an elegant party favor, in sharp black slacks and a deep bronze shirt with a tie design she recognized, though she'd never seen Jay wear it. Confetti and balloon glass on a deep red background. A Frank Lloyd Wright design.

She smiled, and he grasped her hands and kissed her cheeks. "Ready, Alice?"

"Boy howdy am I," she teased.

He smirked. "Can't wait to see him, can you?" His voice lowered to a whisper. "I get that feeling every day on my ride home from work."

She almost missed the rhythm of the conversation, fumbling not to blurt something stupid about how she didn't have that option. Henry wasn't waiting for her at the end of every day. But she wouldn't want him to anyway. Too much pressure. Right. Right?

She dug deep for a smirk of her own. "That's because you're a horny devil."

"Nope." He led her down the hall toward Henry's bedroom. "I am, but that's not why."

He ushered her into the doorway ahead of him. They both stopped a step over the threshold, Jay's right hand resting on her right hip.

Henry stood at his dresser with his back to them. He wore black pants and a dress shirt similar to Jay's, but in a creamy white. Surely he'd heard them coming down the hall. His shoulders flexed as he straightened.

Alice and Jay inhaled as one breath.

"That's why," Jay murmured. "I love that feeling."

If what Jay felt was anything like what she felt, it was an exquisite mix of comfort and desire, of the certainty that her entire being rested securely in Henry's hands.

When Henry turned, he held three half-filled glasses of wine. "Come here, my dears."

Though she wanted to scamper to his side, she held herself to a slow walk.

Henry's tie matched Jay's, the same Frank Lloyd Wright confetti and balloon design but on a cornflower blue background. Festive. Playful, within a structured pattern. *Like me? Us?* Her fingers rose on instinct, hovering in front of his tie as he handed a wineglass to Jay and pecked his lips.

Henry drew her attention from the tie with a tip of his head. "It's all right to touch, Alice. You like the ties, I take it?"

She ran her fingers down the center. Soft. Silky. She nodded.

"Wonderful. They reminded me of you, dearest. It seemed an appropriate choice for such a festive occasion."

Were they celebrating? Treating Thanksgiving as if it were a New Year's party seemed strange.

Henry handed her a glass. The wine held a strong golden color, a shade lighter than her hair. It smelled of Christmas, a sweet and spicy mix of nutmeg and citrus and candied apricots. Henry nudged her chin up with his free hand and gently claimed her mouth. His fingers brushed her hair back when he let her go.

"A toast to the birthday girl, hmm?" Henry lifted his glass.

"You remembered." Her pleasure was obvious in her voice. In four days, she'd turn twenty-eight. His remembering didn't surprise her, but his mentioning her birthday tonight did. It seemed to belong in the friend sphere.

"And would have done so last year, had you been so kind as to inform us before rather than after the happy occasion." Henry smiled as he chided her, and she looked away.

He and Jay had taken her to dinner last January upon learning they'd missed her birthday. Henry had seemed to consider it a personal failure that he hadn't asked sooner. Of course, she'd been dating Brandon in January, and he hadn't been thrilled about her going out with two male friends. His reaction had precipitated their breakup. Too territorial. God forbid she let him hang around through Valentine's.

"But it's no matter now, Alice. We'll simply make this birthday a more memorable one." He tilted his glass, and she and Jay raised theirs. "To a life filled with many memorable birthdays for our dear girl."

The glasses chimed as they touched. The wine was deliciously sweet, a dessert in itself, like pears or peaches coated with honey.

"Good enough to taste again," Henry said, his voice low and rolling.

His tongue swept across her lips and inside as though he chased the flavor. The kiss hardened her nipples and made her thighs clench.

He urged her to take another sip. "Jay ought to have a taste. It's traditional to kiss the birthday girl."

She took another sip of wine, the flavor intensified by the knowledge of what would come after. Jay lapped at her lips before he deepened their kiss. Her body ached with want by the time his taste ended.

Henry handed off the glasses to Jay and took her hands in his. He rubbed his thumbs across her knuckles.

"We've a long night of traditions ahead of us. Let's begin with this one, shall we?" He squeezed her hands. "Tell me your safeword, Alice."

"Pistachio."

"Excellent. And when will you use your word?"

"When I'm feeling too unsure to continue." Henry was scrupulous about ensuring she never reached that point, though.

"Lovely. And will you hesitate if that moment comes?"

"No, Henry." She shook her head. "I'll tell you the truth and trust you to understand."

"My beautiful girl. You learn so well."

Henry embraced her, his hands stroking her bare back. Jay placed the glasses on the dresser.

"Thank you, my boy."

Henry stepped back to stand beside Jay, the two of them studying her in silence. Henry was appraising her, perhaps, assessing the drape of her dress or the play of light across it. Jay stared with a hunger she felt herself.

"There's a rhythm, Alice, to birthday parties." Henry circled her, closing in until his nearness warmed her back. "A sense of give and take."

His hands spanned her back, palms splayed, and his fingers slipped under the sides of her dress. She forced herself to stillness, but it was hard, so very hard when she wanted to beg him to take her. He stroked upward. His fingers lifted and spread the straps of her dress, dropping them to her arms, where they shifted and slid as she breathed.

Two feet in front of her, Jay pined for her breasts, undoubtedly waiting for the breath that would send the fabric cascading past her nipples and bare her to his view. For a gayboy, he was quite the breast man. She smothered a giggle.

Henry's lips grazed the left side of her neck, and a small gasp escaped as she tilted her head to give him more access.

"We'll start with a bit of unwrapping, hmm?" He rubbed her upper arms as if he sought to warm her, dislodging her dress. Her hips were all that held it up.

Jay half stepped forward before he stopped himself, his gaze fixed on her breasts.

Henry's voice lowered to a whisper. "Jay's rather fond of the unwrapping. And it's only fitting for the birthday girl to be in her birthday suit."

Closing her eyes, she shivered at the promise in his tone. He took his time lowering his hands, avoiding her breasts and holding his body away from hers. Close enough for heat but not touch. He did seem to love making her wait.

He paused with his hands embracing her hips, fingertips beneath her dress, poised to push. His cheek rubbed hers. His breath tickled her neck.

He looked straight down, and her eyes followed. Bare breasts. His hands on her hips. Flowing green fabric ready to fall. He growled, a vibration against her skin. His fingers tightened around her hips. "You'll grow accustomed to the feel of my hands here tonight, Alice."

A shudder rolled through her, and slickness clung to her thighs. Her panties had to be drenched. He didn't have to take his time. Now was good. Better than good. She'd bend over and brace her hands on the floor if he said the word.

He didn't say the word. But he did give her dress a final push. It fell. His fingers traced the top edge of her panties.

"Jay. The birthday girl is handing out party favors. A brief taste, my boy."

Jay stepped forward and dropped to his knees, a motion he made look smooth despite his haste. Henry held her still as Jay sucked her panties into his mouth and pressed his nose hard into her clit.

Jesus, fuck, Jay.

Her body burned with the need to move, to thrust toward his face as he practically wrung her panties dry. No danger of that, since his eager nudges replenished the source.

Her chin touched her chest as she stared at the mop of black hair hiding the teeth tugging, the lips pulling at her. He wasn't using his tongue so much as his whole mouth, making her labia slide across each other behind the silk of her panties. His nose bumped rhythmically against her clitoris as he sucked, again and again, until she trembled on the edge, her body desperate for release.

Henry dipped his fingers under the top edge of her panties, one on each side, still stroking. She whined, a soft plea, unable to prevent it from emerging from her throat, unsure whether he'd stop and make her wait.

But his nose nudged her ear with the same rhythm Jay was using, and his low, encouraging voice was every bit as stimulating as Jay's mouth. "My good girl. I've got you. It's all right to let go, dearest."

Finally, finally, he closed the gap between them. The crispness of his shirt contrasted with the silk of his tie on her upper spine, and the lightweight wool brushing against her from waist to ankles contrasted with the hard press of his erection against her lower spine.

"So beautiful in your need, your skin flushed, your breath uneven . . . you're so close." Gripping her hips, he gave a short, sharp thrust. *She* had done that. Her body, her responses, her interaction with Jay had fueled Henry's desire. "Won't you let us give you this, sweet girl?"

He thrust again, and a strangled moan left her as she crashed through the last barrier and tumbled into orgasm. His hands kept her hips still, though the feel of it, the burning fire of the fall, rushed through her and shook her with its force.

All the while, Henry murmured in her ear. "That's it, my magnificent girl. You feel the rush. Let it take you, my wonderfully responsive Alice."

He kissed her, a light kiss, in front of her left ear. His voice grew louder. "Jay."

Jay licked his lips as he tipped his face toward them. His eyes gleamed.

"Excellent work, my boy. Truly a joy to witness. I feel confident in speaking for Alice when I say it was a joy to experience as well. Isn't that so, Alice?"

She smiled. He didn't need to prod her to praise Jay. She knew Jay loved praise. And deserved it. Henry's prompt told her she was allowed to share her praise now.

"It was wonderful. The best birthday gift I've had in years. Jay's very thoughtful to make sure I'd enjoy it so much."

Jay's grin lit up his face.

Henry chuckled. "It's lovely to hear that, my dear, as you've many more gifts to come."

Oh God. Was Henry taking it as a challenge? How many times the two of them together could make her climax? She shivered, an aftershock buzzing along her nerves.

Henry pushed the top of her panties away from her skin. "Go on, Jay. Finish the unwrapping, please."

Jay hooked his fingers in her panties and pulled them down, easing them around her feet, which weren't too steady.

"Help me set the table, Jay."

Standing, Jay took her hands and led her forward. Henry kept pace, a firm bulwark at her back. Set the table?

They turned her together, and lifted together, and she found herself lying on the bed, sprawled on her back, nude, uncertain how she'd arrived there. Her boys sat on the edge, one on either side of her. With knees turned inward toward her, they raised hands to their throats in unison and loosened their ties.

"It's tradition, Alice." Henry's tie sung, a quick zipping sound as he whisked it out from under his collar with one hand and opened a button with the other. Jay followed suit mere seconds behind.

Henry gave a brief nod, the barest tip of his head, not to her but to Jay. The men knelt on the bed and shifted forward, each taking one of her hands in theirs. The silk of their ties slid over her wrists. A rush of excitement penetrated her dazed, post-orgasmic relaxation.

The knots took shape, what she thought would be a slipknot before Henry made a loop of one side and pulled a second loop through it. Jay copied his movements exactly, his lips in silent motion as he worked. He must've practiced. Learned this knot for her, like an extra birthday gift, because he wanted to participate and Henry was serious about safety.

They raised her arms to the headboard. Tipping her head back didn't reveal the knots they used there, but Henry gave a satisfied nod. "Well done, my boy."

They leaned over her, heads mingling above hers, chests teasingly out of her reach. Henry kissed Jay, a commanding kiss Jay seemed to relish. When they separated, Henry's left hand came to rest at the base of her throat. His thumb traced her collarbone.

"Are you comfortable, Alice?"

"Yes, Henry." Comfortable and excited.

"No unusual tingling in your fingers? Wiggle them for me, please."

She wiggled her fingers and smirked at him. "Nothing but tingles of excitement."

"Good girl." His answering smirk made her pulse jump between her legs. "And you're still able to tell me your safeword, hmm?"

"Pistachio. But I don't want to stop."

"No, you're my fearless adventurer, Alice." His left hand traveled down, between her breasts, across her stomach, until it rested atop her sex. "Always eager for new experiences. And Jay and I are happy to share in them."

He nodded to Jay. "The table is set, my boy. Let's not stand on ceremony, shall we? Go ahead."

Jay's mouth closed over her right nipple in a flash. Her spine arched, pushing her breast farther into his mouth and sending silk sliding across her bound wrists.

Henry settled in beside her on her left, his eyes on hers.

"Tradition, as I said, Alice. The birthday girl is called upon to provide a feast for her revelers. Cake. Ice cream. The specifics are unimportant, so long as she offers . . . something sweet."

He claimed her mouth, and her mind, for all its insistence upon structure and categorization, grew lost and dizzy as hands and mouths moved over her. A line of soft kisses up her arm. A fierce kiss to her throat. No, two, both sides at once. She fleetingly worried she'd have matching hickeys. Her hips surged at the thought.

Hands stroked her sides and cupped her breasts. Fingers teased and pinched her nipples. Their bodies danced over hers, but she couldn't touch them in return. The ties around her wrists made certain of it. She could only submit, and enjoy, and anticipate. Henry had called it a sweet feast. Surely he'd allow Jay's head between her thighs again.

But Jay was kissing her mouth, hard and penetrating, a mimicry of the way Henry kissed *him*, when the warm swipe of a tongue fell between her legs. Which meant . . . oh sweet fuck.

Her hips bucked, and two hands clamped down on them. *He said I'd get accustomed . . .*

Her orgasm rolled over her like a wave while Henry sucked at her clit, popping it in and out of his lips. She gasped for air when Jay released her mouth. He peppered her face with light kisses.

Henry let go of her clit as her shivers subsided, but he didn't move away. His tongue dropped lower and lapped slowly, steadily, at the outside of her labia, catching what would otherwise soak the sheets. Her sweet climax. His feast.

Had she thought Jay a master of this art? Here was his teacher.

Henry traced the seam of her lips with his tongue before he probed deeper, parting her. His mouth swiftly opened as an enthusiastic squeeze of her muscles brought him a slick flood. He moaned, and she returned his appreciation with a happy whimper.

Jay's head bent to her breasts, his worship of them a constant stimulant, an enticement that grew when Henry stiffened his tongue and entered her. His hands never left her hips. The rolling rhythm her body sought became an internal ripple rather than an external shudder and repeated itself into what seemed infinity.

She couldn't count how often they brought her to climax. Wasn't certain when Jay's mouth left her breasts and joined Henry's between her legs, one tongue thrusting inside her while the other swirled around her clit and sucked at her. But at some point, her eyes clenched shut as her body arched, and she saw a sharp strike of lightning, her whole body electrified. She sagged against the mattress, mumbling indecipherable praise.

Henry said something she couldn't hear, his head a fuzzy shape rising from between her legs as she blinked, and Jay left the bed. Hands tugged at her wrists, one at a time. The ties loosened and slipped away. Kisses pressed where fabric had been.

". . . provided us with quite a feast, dear girl. Beyond all expectations. But you've neglected to indulge yourself." Henry kissed her mouth, and she tasted her own honeyed musk on his lips and tongue. He lifted her, settling her on his lap as he rested against the headboard. "You'll need a bit of fortification before going on, I expect."

Going on? More pleasure was likely to kill her.

His head turned, and hers followed. Jay carried a plate and glass through the doorway with a waiter's poise.

"Wonderful, Jay, thank you. We want to keep our birthday girl in tip-top shape, don't we?"

Jay nodded as he handed Henry the glass and settled beside them on the bed. "She's special. It's important to take good care of Alice."

He wasn't parroting something Henry had told him, not with such an earnest, assertive delivery. Boyish Jay protecting a cherished toy. Maybe he thought of her as a teddy bear, albeit a sexy teddy bear with breasts. She giggled, and Henry kissed her left temple.

"Very good care," he agreed.

He raised the glass to her lips, and she drank. Pineapple juice. The same thing he'd given her after her flogging, when she'd been so drained and satisfied.

Jay held something to her lips after she'd swallowed, and she took it without bothering to note what it was. *Mmm.* Apple slice. With peanut butter. He fed one to Henry, too, and then himself.

"After-school snack," she mumbled, and Henry laughed, his left arm tightening around her.

"You and Jay do put forth excellent efforts at your lessons. It's only right you be rewarded for it."

She let Jay feed her another slice and a few almonds. Sipped when Henry offered her the glass. He and Jay finished it between them before Henry picked up her hands in his and rubbed her fingers as Jay set the dishes on the nightstand.

"Feeling a bit more energized, my dear?"

She nodded. "Yes, Henry."

She'd regained her sense of self, at least. Relaxation no longer interfered with recognizing the touch of his fingers on hers and the occasional nudge of his cock against her ass, and they sure as hell weren't making her sleepy.

Knowing he hadn't come yet tonight didn't make her feel guilty or inadequate anymore. She wasn't responsible for Henry's orgasms. He was responsible for hers. He'd make sure she came, and Jay, too, and he'd decide when and how they did.

And when he wanted to come, he would make that happen, too. He liked waiting. Seeing their satisfaction made the wait, and the act, more meaningful to him, maybe. *I'm starting to understand you, Henry.*

"Perhaps you'd like to unwrap a present yourself?" Henry guided her hands to Jay's shirt, pressing her fingers to the top button. "Now that your guests have taken their repast, it's only fair they give you something in return."

Henry caressed her arms while her fingers worked, and she stroked Jay's chest as she revealed him.

He leaned into her touch, a pet seeking affection, and she gave it in spades. Fingers, knuckles, palms. She used them all, spreading his shirt open and rubbing his chest until his nipples tightened and his breathing deepened. Trailing her fingers down his abdomen, she reached his waistband and dipped under to tease out the shirttails.

Jay whimpered.

Henry's hands rolled over her shoulders and down her ribs. "Alice was the birthday girl who peeled the tape away and refused to tear the pretty paper, isn't that so, Alice?"

She nodded, holding her breath, wishing. Her whimper echoed Jay's at a higher pitch as Henry cupped her breasts, taking their weight and teasing her nipples between thumb and index fingers.

"Good girl. Honesty deserves rewards." He brushed his lips across her left shoulder. "Go ahead and rid Jay of his shirt. We want to see his beautiful chest, don't we, Alice?"

Her fingers had grasped the collar and begun to push it down Jay's back before Henry finished speaking. "Yes, Henry. He's a beautiful gift."

"Mmm." Henry kissed her right shoulder. "A beautiful gift for a beautiful girl. And you'll be beautiful together in a moment."

She shivered. The shirt sailed from her hands, over the side of the bed, and fluttered to the floor.

"Pants next, my dear. You want to see all of your gift, don't you?"

"Very much," she murmured. Her right hand skimmed the edge of Jay's waistband, teasing him the way Henry had done to her earlier. Jay's stomach flinched as he gasped.

Her left hand made him moan when she palmed his cock through his pants and squeezed. Payback. He'd made her come in her panties. If she weren't so eager to have him inside her, she might've . . .

Henry pinched her nipples, and she jumped. "Such a naughty girl, playing with your present before you've unwrapped it. But we'll take you to task for it later, hmm? Go on, now. Jay's been a very patient boy, but he wants to give the birthday girl his present."

"And I want to receive it." She smiled at Jay, an apology for teasing, and he smirked.

She took care opening the clasp on his pants and drawing the zipper down. Damaging her present would ruin the night for both of them. But she giggled at his boxers. A match to his tie. "Festive shorts. I like it."

Henry clasped her elbows and pulled her hands back. "I'm afraid they'll have to go, my dear. But perhaps Jay will model them for you at length at a later date."

He nodded. A sign Jay had been waiting for, by the way he shimmied out of his clothes in seconds. Henry barely had time to kiss her hands before Jay presented himself, his cock almost brushing his stomach. Jay might get a chance to work off some energy on top of her.

But Jay's eagerness didn't speed Henry along. In silence, he slid his hands across her forearms and held her hands up, fingers spreading hers. He bent his head over her shoulder and sucked her fingers into his mouth one at a time. His tongue teased, and her muscles clenched as she recalled the feel of him between her thighs.

Panic flashed on Jay's face. He dropped into his waiting pose in front of them, vibrating with arousal and something else. Nervous energy. A performer waiting to take the stage for the first time. Something new? For her?

She shivered as Henry shifted his attention to her neck, his head nudging hers. He delivered hushed words between kisses.

"Timing is a delicate art, my dears. Alice understands how delicate, I'm certain. She balances timing and tools and stressors in her designs. Seeks the optimum combination to avoid fracture. To create harmony."

Henry's teeth tugged at her earlobe, and she moaned. Jay had his eyes closed, his head bowed. He breathed as though calming himself. Had she thrown off his timing with her eager grab for his cock?

"But Alice herself is a delicate creature, a wondrous harmony of elements. Her pleasure depends on optimum timing, more so than ours, my boy."

Henry's hands, still clasping hers, covered her breasts, molding their hands together. Her nipples hardened against her palms, the soft skin surrounding them puckering, rising. Henry ran his tongue along the side of her neck, ending in a gentle bite where the slope began its run toward her shoulder.

"Her satisfaction is a feast for the senses, beautiful to behold, but it is not inevitable. Alice requires our patience. Our focus."

Our. Whatever Henry had planned, he and Jay would be working together. She sucked in a breath through her teeth. Her hips rocked in Henry's lap, a movement she hadn't intended and couldn't stop. Henry's hands dropped from her breasts and stilled her hips in an instant.

"Alice is ready for you, Jay. Are you ready to focus for her? To work in harmony? To remember your timing?"

To remember his . . . she'd been right to call Jay a performer. He'd worked on this gift with Henry, and he was nervous. Her pulse felt like a drumbeat, her clit thumping hard, her slick walls clenching around emptiness. How much of their private, noncontract time had the two of them spent thinking of her? Of her needs?

That was a gift. She'd never fake an orgasm, never disrespect Henry that way, and didn't expect she'd have to, because he'd make certain of it . . . but even if Jay's timing stuttered, if he couldn't quite manage the gift she waited for now, she'd fucking praise him until she was blue in the face. Because he'd worked so goddamn hard on it. On her. On his own time, because he wanted to. Because she mattered to him.

Christ, he'd better be ready, because she'd come just from thinking if she wasn't careful.

Jay raised his head, his eyes clear and intent on hers, his face calm. He nodded, once. "I'm ready, Henry."

"You are," Henry agreed. "Lie back, Jay."

He lay on his back, legs together, arms resting beside his head.

Henry grasped Alice's waist and lifted. She bent her knees, recognizing what he wanted as he shifted forward and settled her across Jay's thighs.

"A moment, Alice. Be still, please."

No disrupting his timing, he meant. She'd be riding tonight. In control? Jay wouldn't have to worry about his timing then, but she'd better start thinking about her energy level. The longer she held herself still, straddling Jay's thighs, the more her anxiety grew. What if she was the one who couldn't perform to Henry's expectations?

The snack had helped, but her legs were bound to falter fast after they'd already been pushed so hard. Her teeth worried at her lower lip. She didn't want to disappoint Jay after he'd worked so hard and waited so patiently. She'd be devastated if she disappointed Henry, for reasons she couldn't define.

She looked into Jay's face and found him confident. Determined. He squinted up at her and cleared his throat.

Henry shifted in an instant and dropped the silk ties and a condom on Jay's stomach. His hand touched Alice's chin, turning her face toward him. He studied her in silence until she lowered her eyes. God forbid he see her nerves.

"Thank you, Jay," he murmured. "You're thinking too much, Alice. Trust I wouldn't demand more than you're able to give, hmm?"

She blushed. "Yes, Henry."

"There's always your safeword, if you find you've reached your limits. Don't be afraid to use it if you need it."

She shook her head. "I don't need to. I'm just . . . I want this to be good for Jay." Jay, who smiled up at her, his head shaking as he reached for the ties on his stomach. "I don't know if I have the energy . . ."

"I think you will, dearest." Henry kissed her cheeks. "Trust me a moment longer."

"I do," she murmured.

She fell silent as Henry guided her hands forward. He pressed them together once her arms were extended. A command for her to remain in place? He dropped his hands, one to her left thigh and one to her back, lightly massaging.

"Good girl."

Jay bound her wrists with a different knot, his lips moving while he worked, though no words emerged. Henry stayed silent, and she followed his lead. If he wanted Jay to focus, she needed to let him focus. The second tie was knotted around the first, between her wrists, until Jay had . . . a leash.

"Excellent work, Jay." Henry leaned down and kissed him, a thorough, deep kiss that made Jay's cock bob scant inches in front of her.

She understood the impulse. If she'd had a cock, it would've been bobbing, too. With her hands bound, and the leash in Jay's hands, she'd have little balance and less control.

She wanted to be on his cock, to feel filled as she hadn't been in weeks. Her thighs might not lift her much, but they would lift her enough. Henry wouldn't let her fail. He'd already considered her fears. Of course he had.

If Jay had spent so much time perfecting knots and timing, it was at Henry's direction. She might be the one tied, but even Henry's *silence* had been a sharp reminder to Jay. Henry controlled him in ways she couldn't fathom yet. Years of practice, maybe. Conditioning. Maybe someday . . .

Her mind shied from completing the thought, and she focused on Henry's hands, unrolling a condom over Jay's cock with a light touch. Not wanting to stimulate him too much, she assumed. She waited, expecting Henry's command to shuffle forward at any second.

He'd have to make it verbal. She couldn't read his silent cues the way Jay did. The waiting made her eager, trembling, when Henry leaned in and kissed her as he had Jay. Firm lips, his tongue stroking hers, a familiar sensation that relaxed her. Reminded her of every time he'd made it good.

"Soon," he whispered.

He moved down the bed, out of her sight. Settled at her back, his legs thick and warm around her own, the soft wool of his pants rubbing against her. An odd mix of excitement and panic stole her breath.

"Shhh. Easy, Alice. Easy." The breadth of Henry's chest pressed to her back, his hands coming around to the center of her own, not atop her breasts so much as her heart as he clasped her. "No surprises, my sweet girl. Just Jay, your next present, waiting so patiently, and a bit of help for your trembling legs."

She nodded, tiny movements repeated unthinkingly. She didn't know what had frightened her, or why fear added to her arousal. She took a deep breath. This was nothing more than a birthday gift. A special day. That's why they'd put so much effort into it. But a smaller voice whispered in the back of her mind. *So you'll enjoy it. Which wouldn't matter to them if you didn't matter to them.*

Henry lowered his hands to her waist and raised her up. He urged her forward, supported by his body. His right hand traveled between her thighs, his fingers opening her labia and spreading them, dragging through her wetness. A single finger parted her with ease, slipping inside.

Her sigh emerged as a whine. She needed more.

"Good girl, Alice. You're ready for your present, aren't you?"

"Yes . . . yes, Henry." She hardly dared to breathe as Henry lowered her onto Jay's cock. She sank until their bodies rested flush. They groaned, both of them, and Henry chuckled.

Neither she nor Jay moved. Henry laid his hands on her hips. A tight hold. Secure. Commanding. Jay showed no signs of impatience, none of the boyish need for attention and constant fidgeting she associated with him outside this room. He waited with an intent stare over her shoulder. Jay might hold the leash, but Henry controlled the action here.

Jay tugged the silk tie in his hands, though she'd neither heard nor seen a prompt. She rocked forward, her weight shifting, tipping her toward Jay's chest and flattening her clitoris against his pubic bone. His body gave her a hard surface, and her own weight provided the pressure. She inhaled deeply. This game could be fun. Very fun. For her, at least. But would rocking be enough for Jay?

Sensitive skin dragged across Jay's wiry curls when Henry's hands on her hips pulled her back. His clothes seemed a delicious sin against her bare skin, hers and Jay's.

Jay tugged her forward. Henry pulled her back. They were both silent, intent on their tasks, and the concentration surrounding them buzzed like the aura off a high-tension wire. They'd started slowly, but they'd found a faster rhythm, the pressure and teasing relief alternating against her clit.

Oh holy fuck. Had she expected to have control in this position? Any at all? A ridiculous notion. But having no control . . . how was . . . why did . . . what made it so good? How did Henry do that?

She shuddered. Henry clamped down hard on her hips, raising her up and dropping her on Jay's cock. Her breath whooshed out in a groan.

"Again," she begged, recognizing the plea too late to force it back.

"Oh, *very* good, Alice." Henry lifted her again. And waited.

Alice panted, wishing he would drop her, why wouldn't he just . . . oh. "Please."

Henry's hands forced her down, and Jay's hips thrust to meet her as she moaned. She'd pleased Henry by asking. Verbalizing a desire. He'd added the new motion to the rhythm to reward her.

Jay tugged on the tie. Henry pulled her back, raised her up, dropped her down as Jay thrust. Again. And again.

Two actors, utterly dependent on Henry. Without his direction of Jay's timing and her movement, neither of them would be able to strive toward the need coiling in her now. Despite his unexpected silence in this game, he had complete control. Henry's knowledge of their needs, his understanding, would bring them to climax or not.

She whimpered, a sound of surrender, an acknowledgement that here, now, he would make the decisions and she would submit to them. His fingers squeezed her hips as he increased the pace.

Henry dropped her again, and this time when Jay tugged her forward, Henry teased her clitoris with darting fingers between her legs. He repeated it, a new beat in the rhythm, an addition that maybe . . . signaled his pleasure at her surrender? He'd added to the rhythm when she voiced her desire. And now he'd done it again when she voiced her acceptance of his control.

He wanted those things from her. In these hours, he demanded them of her. The intensity of the emotion that washed through her then was beyond her understanding.

She gave voice to a desperate whimper Jay matched, the two of them crying out as Henry urged them faster, his fingers tapping hard against her clit the final push she needed. Her hips moved on their own, uncontrollably, and she gasped for breath as Jay cried her name and Henry's when she took him with her.

Henry's pleased growl rumbled in her ear. Because his timing had worked, because she and Jay had found their release together at his direction? Because Jay had called her name *and* his? She'd lacked the breath to fill her lungs as her body seized with pleasure, but Jay had seemed desperate to feel that connection.

She lay back against Henry, just breathing, wanting to ask Jay why. What had prompted his call. But this was Henry's show. Asking now wasn't appropriate. Trying to ask Jay during their lunch on Tuesday would earn her a vague answer or a panicked look and a subject change.

Their Fridays didn't exist on Tuesdays, and their Tuesdays didn't exist on Fridays. Friends. Sex partners. Two separate roles.

Except her birthday would be Tuesday, and they were celebrating it as a Friday. As sex partners.

And Henry and Jay had put special effort into tonight, a Friday, as friends.

Wasn't the contract designed to prevent this blurring of lines? Maybe she needed to expand her understanding of the terms. It wasn't as if she confined her sexual thoughts about them to contract hours. Hell, she'd imagined having them in her bed almost a year before anything sexual had happened.

Sitting atop Jay in the aftermath of such a powerful climax that she still tightened around him at odd intervals, she almost believed she belonged there permanently. Resting in Henry's arms. Seeing Jay's blissful smile.

"Well done, my dears," Henry murmured.

She shivered with joy.

She might be a temporary partner, but she was a valued one. A good friend. Tonight had shown her that. She was someone they trusted enough to bring into their bed, a fun challenge for their skills, maybe. A chance for Henry to demonstrate his prowess and Jay to expand his. Someone they trusted to accept their affection and their arousal and to let it go when things came to their conclusion. When they were ready to go back to being just the two of them.

But for now, for now, she could enjoy what she had. What Henry gave her.

She twisted, trying to look back at him, to thank him for this. Whatever it was. Tonight. All of the nights, and the mornings, too, and the way he and Jay allowed her to feel part of something special.

"Thank you," she blurted, as Henry's face tipped toward hers. She repeated it, because once didn't feel like enough, and she couldn't stop saying it, the words tumbling too fast and overlapping until Jay was laughing beneath her and Henry's lips came down on hers. Soft. Warm. Slow and calming.

She sighed against his mouth, a sound that morphed into a giggle when he kissed the tip of her nose as well.

"Sorry. I don't usually . . . I mean, I'm not . . ."

Henry chuckled. His arms tightened from a light clasp into a true hug.

"Jay, I believe what our girl is trying so very hard to say is that she's quite satisfied with your performance. Shall we take her incoherence as a compliment of the highest order?"

Jay smirked. "Yes, Henry."

"You were amazing," she agreed. Sharing seemed easier, somehow, once Henry had spoken first. "I can't believe how synchronized you were."

Jay's grip on the tie had slackened enough to let her lower her bound hands and scratch his belly. "It was a wonderful gift. You followed commands from Henry so well I couldn't even tell he was giving them."

He stretched beneath her, arching into her fingers, and his beaming smile lit up his whole face.

"Yes, Jay has done exceptional work this evening." Henry's breath warmed her ear. "Go on and untie Alice, my boy, and we'll have a bit of leisure time."

Leisure time. Free play, so long as nothing between Alice and Jay got more sexual than a twelve-year-old's first date. Henry's way of telling them they could move freely, talk freely. A chance to use the bathroom or get a drink without gaining his permission, because they wouldn't be interrupting a scene.

She supposed Jay needed it. No, they both did after being so strictly controlled tonight. Time to feel the pressure was off, to bask in the contentment they'd created. And when leisure time was over?

She held back a shiver.

Henry didn't have to fuck her, of course, but she thought he planned to tonight. He was just making her wait for it. Time for her legs to recover. She stifled a laugh.

Jay's nimble fingers freed her wrists. She rotated them, wiggling her fingers before Henry asked.

"All's well, Alice?" Henry raised his hands to hers. "No tenderness?"

His touch was tender, but her health was fine.

"Nope. Everything's in good working order." Not that she'd expected otherwise. Henry was so careful about—*wait, back up.* Henry had let Jay tie the knots. With supervision. First time? "Jay must've done a great job on those knots. My wrists don't hurt at all."

"Wonderful." Henry had to be smiling, given how Jay wiggled like an eager puppy greeting its owner. "Jay?"

Henry's voice was prompting, and Jay's right hand slipped between her body and his where they joined. He smirked. "Ready for liftoff."

Alice giggled as Henry helped her to her knees and toppled her beside Jay, who held his condom in place with no hint of self-consciousness. Her adorable playmate.

She rolled onto her side and called his name. Jay swung toward her, his expression open and eager to please.

She leaned into deliver sweet kisses, mouth and forehead both.

"Thank you, Jay."

"It was good?"

"*You* were good."

"You're happy?"

"*Very* happy."

Jay heaved an exaggerated sigh of relief and wiped imaginary sweat from his brow with one arm.

Alice laughed.

Henry smiled, his right hand stroking Jay's left thigh. "All right, my little comedians."

Rising to stand alongside the bed, Henry sported rumpled clothes, not so crisp as when she'd first seen him tonight, formal and dignified. The sight of Henry mussed, his collar open and askew, his shirt crinkled, sent the same thrill humming through her veins. *Yum.*

"We've more juice and snack in the kitchen, and I want to see you both make use of it. Alice, please bring the plate and glass with you. It seems Jay has his hands full."

Jay did, indeed, have his hands full, holding the condom against his softening cock as he rolled off the bed. She struggled not to laugh again. "Yes, Henry."

She hummed to herself as the boys left the room. Jay to the bathroom, she assumed, and Henry to the kitchen. Lounging in their bed without them felt decadent, like the morning she'd awakened in time to witness Jay's devoted attention to Henry's cock. She stretched, gleeful, giggly, wondering if Henry would ever offer her the same opportunity.

As she closed her eyes, she caught the faintest murmur of masculine voices. For a moment it seemed a trick of memory, but Jay's quiet laugh broke the spell. Henry. Aftercare. Should she wait here? No, he'd asked her to bring the dishes, so he must have meant for her to go to the kitchen. She lay still a moment longer, indulging herself. *Don't get too comfortable, Alice. It's not your bed.*

Her eyes popped open to the sight of Henry passing the doorway on his way to the kitchen. But if she took a deep breath of the pillow as she rolled to stand up, well, no one was there to witness it but her. And if the voice in her head had something to say about it ... *stuff it. I can indulge on my birthday.*

She carried the plate and glass to the kitchen, where Henry was setting out another plate of sliced fruit. Apples, bananas, oranges. Bowls of honey and peanut butter for dipping.

Three glasses of juice stood on the counter. She put the used dishes in the sink and snaked an arm under Henry's to pop a banana slice in her mouth. He pushed a glass closer to her hand, and she drank. They shared the snack in silence.

Henry looked past her shoulder. "Ah, thank you, Jay."

She started to turn and gave an ungraceful yelp as Henry grasped her waist and lifted her to the counter, setting her down near the edge. He nipped her ear.

"You didn't think I'd neglect you, did you, Alice?" His hip nudged her thigh. "Open your legs for me, dearest."

She leaned back on her hands and let her legs fall open, unquestioning.

Jay laid a washcloth across Henry's open hand before he came around the counter and fell upon the snack with the appetite of a teenage boy.

Henry hummed as he bathed her thighs and sex, a melody she didn't recognize, for all that she found the music as soothing as the gentle motions of his hand. He hadn't said what would come after leisure time. He might dress her and send her home.

Her fingers twitched with the urge to tousle his hair as he bent his head. She wouldn't have resisted with Jay. But how Henry would take such playful behavior directed at *him*, on his time, was a mystery, even if they were at leisure right now. She pursed her lips, considering.

Jay slid his hand across the counter and squeezed hers. "Don't look so sad. Your night isn't over yet." He smiled at her, not childlike or teasing but seriously. What she assumed he meant to be reassuring, though a hint of nerves seemed to tug at the edges.

Henry stopped humming and raised his head. He studied her face. "Jay's correct, Alice." His voice was soft. Coaxing. "There's a tradition we haven't indulged yet. The birthday spanking. One for each year and one to grow on."

She stopped breathing. Stared at Henry. *That's why Jay's nervous. But I'm . . . not. Not exactly.* Her lungs sucked in air on their own, making her jump.

"Twenty-nine," she whispered, equal parts terrified and thrilled. She'd turn twenty-eight on Tuesday, which meant twenty-nine spanks.

"Plus one, Alice," Henry added in a mild tone. "To remind you not to tease your gifts before unwrapping them. Thirty, altogether."

Jay's fingers tightened around hers, and she rubbed her thumb against his in an automatic attempt to soothe.

She wanted to argue that Jay had gotten to play with her before unwrapping her. But one extra spank wasn't a terrible punishment. Jay'd had Henry's explicit permission. And she wanted her spanking.

Her mind raced to picture where he'd position her. Wondered how spanking would compare to the flogging he'd given her two weeks before and if she'd reach that odd floaty feeling where she couldn't quite hold a single thought. Thirty. Surely that was so much more. What if she disappointed him?

He leaned in and nuzzled her cheek. "You're quite capable of taking it, Alice. Think of the flogger, hmm? Perhaps you lost count of how many times you enjoyed its touch." His hand stroked down her back, following the path where he'd dragged the suede over her skin. "Not to worry. I'll keep the count. You need only enjoy it. This is simply . . . more personal."

His hand moved again, clasping hers and Jay's together on the counter. "The touch of my hand. And if at any time you feel you are not as capable as I believe you to be, you have your word. Say it now, Alice, so I know you remember it."

"Pistachio." The word popped to her lips on instinct. Maybe he'd been right about that training thing.

"Jay?"

"Tilt-A-Whirl." His voice was steadier than she'd expected, but the touch of Henry's hand might be enough to calm his nerves, too.

"Lovely, both of you." Henry smiled at them as he released their hands and returned to a less intimate distance. "Have you finished your snack, Alice?" A loaded question, a question that asked if she was ready for her spanking.

"Yes, Henry." She couldn't eliminate the trepidation, or the excitement, from her tone. Henry's eyes and smile told her he'd heard both.

He lowered her feet to the floor, kissed her cheek and handed her the washcloth. "Go on and take this to the bathroom. Five minutes, no more, and then I want you waiting for me at the foot of the bed. Just stand quietly and wait, dearest."

She left the kitchen with a single glance back. Would Jay get special instructions? He'd been so nervous and upset last time, with the flogging toys, and she still didn't know why. Would Henry's hand make it easier or more difficult for him to watch? Or would he not watch at all?

Her mind flitted from question to question as she hung the washcloth. Used the bathroom. Washed her hands and stared at herself in the mirror.

"Henry wouldn't offer it as a birthday gift if he didn't think I'd enjoy it. He was careful with Jay last time. He has everything under control. All I have to do is . . . surrender. Trust." She breathed slowly, in and out. "Trust Henry."

Turning off the light, she left the bathroom behind, and her confusion and fear with it. If there was pain, it would be good pain. If she needed Henry to stop, Henry would stop. And if not . . . if not, it would be amazing.

She walked to the foot of the bed and waited, naked, hands clasped behind her back, feet spread, head bowed. Closing her eyes, she imagined the smack of Henry's hand. Silently counted to thirty, welcoming the growing wetness as her body responded, resisting the urge to press her thighs together to ease the ache. She breathed in the scent of her own arousal, heavy in the air around her.

"Lovely." Henry's voice, soft, pleased. He stood in the doorway at the edge of her field of vision, Jay behind him. "My beautiful birthday girl, ready and waiting for me."

Henry crossed the room and Jay followed, a pace behind Henry's right shoulder. A commanding pair. Even Jay had his shoulders squared, his back straight. Imitating Henry, and standing so close that the aura of Henry's authority washed over him, too. This wasn't play. This was serious business. She ducked her head and gazed at the bedspread, her lips parting as she breathed.

A quiet hum of approval came from behind her. A hand rested between her shoulder blades, at the edge of her hair.

"Such delightful instincts." Henry slipped his fingers under her hair and stroked the back of her neck. "Do you know why you bowed your head, Alice?"

"It felt right. Respectful." He hadn't told her to move, but he didn't seem displeased, either.

"Good girl." He was silent a moment, his face beside hers, close enough to feel the warmth of his cheek but not the touch of his skin. "Tell me what you're visualizing right now, Alice."

"Our last Friday." The thud of the flogger against her ass and shoulders. The drag of the suede down her back. Her thighs twitched.

The hand on her neck trailed down her spine and lower still, until it covered the right side of her ass, lifting and massaging.

"You enjoyed it when I bent you over this bed and flogged you, didn't you, Alice? You're anticipating something like that again?"

"Yes, Henry." God yes. She'd never been in that place before, where even the simplest thought was too much to hold. Where not only her body but her mind had been satisfied and silent.

"A birthday deserves something more personal, more intimate, wouldn't you agree?"

She agreed it did. With his breath washing over her ear and his hand rubbing circles on her ass, she'd agree to almost anything.

Henry turned his head. A signal to Jay, from the rustling on the carpet behind her.

"Flogging is a lovely bit of fun, but it allows a distance, and I'll not have that space between us on this night." His right hand slid up from her ass and around to her hip, and his left hand matched it. He stepped in closer. The soft wool of his pants teased her skin.

"Though I'll allow *this* space, for now."

His hips swayed. She shivered as the fabric moved.

"Because you enjoy it, don't you, Alice? You have since the first night I touched you." His hands tightened on her hips. "Facedown across the dinner table, your beautiful hips rattling dishes when you came."

She moaned, remembering that first thrust. The first time she'd had confidence a lover could give what he'd promised, the pleasure she'd always had to find herself.

"Tell me, Alice. Tell me what it is about the pants that you enjoy so well."

"You're dressed. And I'm . . . exposed. Vulnerable." More than that, but she couldn't put into words what it did to her insides to be naked and at his mercy while he was buttoned up, hidden away, so thoroughly in charge.

"And do you like feeling exposed? Vulnerable?"

"I . . . not before."

"Before?" His right hand moved to her stomach, fingers stroking the curls above her sex.

"Not before . . . you."

"And now?"

"It scares me. But . . ." Was it wrong to want that excitement? The false sense of danger?

"But you like this fear? You enjoy it, crave it? Perhaps it heightens the experience for you?"

"Yes." No hesitation, and Henry's fingers dipped lower, brushing her labia. A reward for her honesty? "It's a good fear. I know you're in control. I'm safe."

"All this from the brush of my clothes on your skin, sweet girl?"

"Yes."

His fingers stroked her. His hips swayed, and she shuddered.

"Such beautiful thoughts deserve a reward, Alice. And that's why I'll allow you this space, this thin layer of wool. Because it isn't a distance in your mind." His lips grazed her ear. "It brings you closer to me."

She wanted to beg him to be closer still, to forget the spanking and fuck her now. No, to fuck her now and spank her afterward and fuck her again. Yes. That might be enough to sate the desire she had for him, the tugging, thumping riot of need between her legs.

Withdrawing his hands to her hips, he turned the two of them to face the room rather than the bed. Jay, whose presence she'd forgotten as Henry's voice wrapped around her, had kept busy. The bench, the one Henry had against the wall, had been moved into the middle of the open space. Room for two, three if they were exceptionally close. On one end lay Henry's silk tie. Jay placed a few condoms beside it.

"Thank you, my boy. Well done. Come here, please." Henry's hand rose from her right hip, and his left stroked over her skin. He guided Jay to them, drawing him in until she stood snuggled between the men, her nipples brushing Jay's chest.

Henry raised his hand to Jay's cheek and kissed him. Their lips moved together inches from her own, Henry's soft murmur and Jay's groan rising in the air. Henry ended the kiss with a tug at Jay's lower lip. "Share with Alice, my boy, and then you may make your choice."

A choice? What choice was Jay—

He kissed her, firm and determined, and she committed herself to returning the kiss with equal attention. She let him end it. Jay stared into her eyes before turning away. A close study revealed no choice she could discern. He went to the end of the bench and knelt in his waiting pose, a motion he never failed to make graceful.

"Thank you, Jay." Henry's voice was soft. Tender. Loving.

Jay looked at them both with a calm, serious expression, though his fingers rubbed repeatedly against the tops of his knees.

His head was a short distance from the tie, the cornflower-blue tie with its festive confetti and balloon pattern, and the smattering of condoms. The square packets stood out like a promise, a guarantee, that Henry would be inside her soon. The tie fed her fantasies. Would he bind her wrists again? Drape her across the bench and spank her while she couldn't use her hands to protect herself? She curled her toes and resisted the eager whine in her throat.

She jumped when Henry pinched her nipples. He soothed them after, laid his fingers flat and circled her skin. Jay fixated on her breasts, his lips parting.

"You're giving Jay a beautiful view, Alice." She tilted her head toward Henry's voice in her left ear, and he traced the outer curve with his nose. His fingers never stopped their teasing, rolling across her nipples. "Your breasts fascinate him. The way they bounce when you ride him. The way they swell in his mouth. He cannot look without desiring you, dearest."

What suffused her was neither shame nor embarrassment but the hope he'd see whatever he needed in her. She watched Jay watching her until he raised his eyes and met her gaze. Lustful. Tender? Hopeful? Desire and something else, though she knew not what.

Henry surprised her, stepping away, his hands leaving her breasts. Drawing her forward, he seated himself on the bench and left her to stand before him, her legs between his knees.

"You see desire in his eyes when he looks at you, don't you, Alice? Feel it in his stare?"

"Yes, Henry." Jay made his desire obvious on their Fridays, usually from the moment she walked in the door. He was either incapable of or uninterested in concealment. The same way he was about most things. What he felt or thought always visible on the surface.

Henry caressed her sides, his hands sweeping up from her thighs, slipping toward her back as they reached breast height.

"You believe, perhaps, that I am not so taken, because you cannot always see my desire."

Alice shifted her weight, uneasy as a scolded child despite his forgiving tone. "Yes."

He lunged forward and locked his mouth around her right breast. Sucked hard, almost painfully, and she whimpered. Her legs trembled. He bit her gently before he let go.

"Sit." A demand, his hands tugging her into his lap without pause.

She found herself sitting on his right thigh, soft wool beneath her ass. The command in his voice replayed in her ears, and a flood of wetness between her thighs waited for his entrance.

Henry picked up the tie. "Jay showed exceptional focus tonight, Alice, and I believe you are capable of the same. I want you listening to my voice. Feel my touch and listen to my voice. Nothing else. Do you understand?"

"Yes, Henry." Her eyes remained fixed on the tie. Her hands rested on her knees, awaiting a request to present them.

"I'm going to help you with your focus, my dear."

He moved the tie closer, but not to her hands. The darkness as he bound her eyes wasn't complete, not like it had been the night of their concert in the "park" of his living room. But she could no longer see Jay, kneeling beside the bench, or Henry's eyes, intent on hers. She could, if she strained, glimpse her own stomach and thighs while looking almost cross-eyed down the side of her nose.

"Not too tight?"

"No, Henry."

"Good. I can look my fill now, but you won't see my desire. Does that negate its very existence?" Her left hand was lifted, pulled toward him and pressed against soft wool and . . . She squirmed on his thigh, her hand surrounded by his, both squeezing his hard cock. "You cannot see, but you can feel, can you not?"

She nodded, her answer a whispered yes, her throat choked with need and anticipation.

"Then listen, and feel, and understand I *will* fuck you before the night is over, my lovely girl."

Every nerve in her body tingled at the thought. *Yes. Yes yes yes.*

She let herself be guided by his hands as Henry lowered her across his lap. His right leg pressed against the backs of her thighs, and he ordered her hands to the floor. His left arm lay atop her back like a weighted saddle pad. But his right hand received the lion's share of her attention. The hand circling the top of her ass and sliding down to caress her cheeks.

His hand left her skin. The stillness of his legs made the trembling of hers more obvious.

"Tell me what you're feeling, Alice."

"Fear. Anticipation. Desire."

His hand came down before she'd finished, and her words became a hiss of air. He rubbed a circle over the chosen cheek, the right side, afterward.

"And now?"

"A fading sting. Warmth."

His hand lifted. Her body tensed, waiting.

"You have beautiful lines, Alice. So many slopes and curves where shadows cling. Your body a map of rolling hills. The sort of places that invite curiosity and exploration, where adventurers are sure to find excitement and riches."

His voice relaxed her, rising and falling in a gentle wave akin to the hills he—

"Ahh."

She panted as the sting registered, the fall of his hand on her left again followed by the soothing rubbing of his palm on her skin.

"Good girl." His hand moved away, and she listened, determined not to be caught off guard.

The fall was immediate. Forceful, enough to push her into his left thigh and make her groan at the pressure. A finger between her legs swiftly followed, opening her lips and sinking inside. Her hips rocked a second time.

"Quickly, my girl, tell me what you feel."

"Hot," she mumbled. His finger, thrusting, occupied her mind as much as it did her pussy. "Tingling. Wanting."

Henry's hand withdrew.

"As am I, Alice, with you draped so sweetly across my lap. Your heat warms me, as well. The delights"—a sucking sound as he surely tasted her from his finger—"that flow so freely from you harden my cock until I ache to take you."

His hand came down in a rolling smack that lifted her cheek and sent her forward. He rubbed away the sting, transforming it into a pleasurable burn. His fingers stroked her outer lips without entering. She whimpered.

"You want more, Alice?"

"Yes, Henry."

"More spanking, or only more touching?" His voice gave no hint of whether her answer would change the outcome.

She responded without stopping to think beyond the clenching emptiness between her legs, an ache that left her entire body hollow and needy. "Both. I need both, please."

He spanked her twice in rapid succession and plunged a finger inside her before the sting had begun to fade. She cried out, an eager affirmation if not a recognizable word, and her hips surged against his thigh.

"Do you want to come for me, Alice? Caught here, pinned between my legs, helpless? Is that what you want?"

"Yes. Yes, Henry, please, I want it."

Two more times his hand come down. His finger, no, thicker now, two fingers, thrust. Hot and burning, her body pulsed from its center outward, the tension building in her.

"And I want it for you, dearest, to hear the joy in your cries, to breathe in the heavy scent of your need. To see the flush on your skin, to feel the heat of you around me, to taste . . ." She moaned with the loss when he pulled his fingers out, her voice mingling with his appreciative *mmm* and the sound of suction.

"Do you doubt my words, Alice? My desire?" He thrust his hips, rocking her body in his lap, and she hungered for his cock inside her, where it belonged.

"No," she gasped. "No, Henry."

A series of hard spanks, alternating sides. She lost count as the burning spread and her need grew.

"Good girl," he crooned to her, his fingers thrusting, her hips rocking faster against his thigh.

Her hips rocked even when his fingers left her, soft wool rubbing against swollen lips, pressure building against her clit. Two spanks, hard, quick, Henry's hand lifting her ass and pushing it upward. The burn was still forming as his fingers penetrated her again, solid and thick. The start of her orgasm, her body clamping around him, denied him the chance to pull back while she cried out and shook, her fingers digging into the carpet.

"That's it, my beautiful Alice, you're safe in my hands." His gentle singsong whispered above the white noise in her ears. Her head felt heavy, her legs light.

She lost all sense of balance when his fingers pulled free and the weight on her back shifted to her chest. A swift rise brought her to a seated position. An arm held her close to Henry's body, his musky leather-and-citrus scent a familiar reminder of comfort despite her disorientation, and alongside it the tantalizing scent of her own arousal. A suction-pop sounded to her left.

"Yes. Taste." A command.

Henry's mouth covered hers. She opened to him, tasting herself on his tongue. He controlled the kiss, the pressure, the speed, his hand firm on the nape of her neck, cradling her head. His other arm tightened around her back. The pressure of his leg against the front of hers moved away, replaced by a light tickling against her stomach and—*oh God yes.*

She moaned, the wavering sound resonating as Henry released her mouth.

Jay. Henry's command must've been for them both. That had to be Jay's tongue pressed flat to her sex. His hair brushed her stomach. The hand at her neck dropped away, and then it, too, touched her stomach. Knuckles, she thought. Henry stroking Jay's hair while Jay bathed her with his tongue.

The licking stopped. Henry's hand and Jay's head, both gone. She trembled, unable to see what was happening, what was coming next. Reveled in the burn of her ass resting on Henry's thigh.

"Satisfied, my dears?" Henry's voice, a mixture of tenderness and teasing.

No lying, she reminded herself.

"No," she said, her voice overlapping with Jay's surprised, "yes."

Henry chuckled. "Just the answers I was hoping to hear. Tell me, Alice, you're certain you wish to go on?"

"Yes, Henry." He'd promised to fuck her, and he wouldn't lie.

"Truly? You're halfway there. Fifteen. There's no shame in stopping if you can't go on."

"No. Please, Henry."

"Hmm. You're the birthday girl, my dear. If you say you want another fifteen . . ."

Was that the game? To make her beg for it? With anyone else, the idea would infuriate her. With Henry, her head nodded before she'd completed the thought. "Yes, I want it. You promised thirty. I want them all."

"Do you hear our girl, Jay? Such a demanding little thing, isn't she? So adamant she wants this. Does she deserve to receive what she wants, my boy? When she wants it enough to ask for it?"

Her panting reverberated in the silence. She was ready to bend *herself* over Henry's thigh, blindfolded or not. Faith in him was all that held her back.

"Yes, Henry." Jay's voice, steady and clear. "She wants it because it makes her happy. And you want to make her happy."

Henry wanted to satisfy her. Happiness and satisfaction might overlap, but they weren't the same. Still. For a sex partner, wanting to satisfy marked the pinnacle of her experience, even if he meant to satisfy his own ego as well.

Her body tipped forward into a waiting hand as Henry repositioned her across his lap.

"You're correct, Alice." The weight of an arm across her back. The brush of fingers against her ass cheeks, the skin warm and sensitive now. "I promised you thirty, and I won't break my promises to you."

The *smack* rang in her ears after his hand came down. He rubbed and soothed her cheek and stroked her labia. Again and again, coming faster, an alternating pattern, high and low on each side, and she cried out in pain and pleasure both each time he touched her.

"You color brilliantly, sweet girl, quick to blush under my palm."

She tilted her hips, desperate to push into his hand, a silent encouragement to slide his fingers inside, but he rubbed her outer lips with teasing lightness. The contrast drove her crazy. The heavy slap forced her body forward against his leg. Firm circles turned the sting into heat. The soft touch, the light stroke across her lips, taunted her with the promise of more.

"So close now to the end, my lovely little masterpiece."

She whined, a denial. *Can't be. Need more. Need Henry.*

"No? Not the end?" His hand fell, and she groaned and pushed back against him. "You want more?"

"Need more," she panted, her mouth dry.

He gave her what she wanted, what she needed, his hand falling harder. His fingers drove into her until she climbed beyond thought or speech, attuned to his hand and his voice alone.

"A substitute only, Alice." His fingers thrust deep. The heel of his hand ground against her lips, a wet smack sounding when he moved. "Soon you'll have all of me here, harder than this. Deeper than this."

His voice dropped to a low growl. "Twentyeight, Alice."

His hand landed high on her left. No rubbing now, just the plunge of his fingers following.

"Happy birthday, dearest."

Fingers gone. *Smack.*

"Twenty-nine." High, on the right. Plunge.

"Will you come for me again before I fuck you, dear girl? So tight and wet, eager and moaning."

His hand pulled back. She held her breath, trembling, toes curled, fingers grasping, heart pumping at breakneck speed.

"Thirty."

Low, and hard, across the center of her ass, and she was coming even before his fingers dipped inside her. Her climax blazed like fire, overwhelming her senses, her mind floating in the smoke and leaving her body to burn.

She barely registered his fingers leaving or her body shifting or the soft nap of the padded bench on her breasts. Such things seemed wholly disconnected from *Alice*, who existed in a haze so deep she couldn't find her way back. She babbled his name, *Henry*, the one who brought her here, *Henry Henry Henry Henry*, the sound disappearing into the smoke.

"I'm here, Alice."

The singing of a zipper falling, and the haze showed her Henry's dining room as she lay across the table, awaiting that first touch. A quiet grunt. A hand caressing her back. No, that was *now*, not then.

His voice was here, real. "Elegant and strong. Such a flexible beauty. You'll bend, won't you, my sweet? You won't break, not my Alice."

Henry's cock banished the last of her haze, a brand of heat hotter still than the burn that renewed itself as his body slapped against hers on every thrust when he entered her. His hands pinned her hips down, a restraint she welcomed as the bench rocked with their motion.

This was fucking. Hard, fast and demanding. No slow buildup. She was either there with him or she wasn't, and she *was*.

He set a punishing pace testing even his limits, it seemed. He'd be talking otherwise. Honeyed words of praise and appreciation, of encouragement, as she took him deep, her body adjusting to accept his and tightening around him with each thrust. But she heard nothing over the slap of their bodies, his harsh breathing, and, sometimes, a rumbling growl that made her shiver.

He possessed her. In this moment, draped across a velvety bench, nude and blind, thoughts swirling amid the snap of his hips, the flex of powerful thighs, the press of his thumbs on her back and his fingers wrapped around her sides . . . she was *Henry's* Alice. Just that.

Her body hung on the edge of flashover, so hot she might melt if she didn't combust, so eager for it she didn't care which happened so long as one did. He gave her everything she'd been craving. Pure fucking. Hard cock. All she'd thought she wanted.

Yet it wasn't those things that turned the flame white-hot again, that made her squirm and shake and cry out with pleasure. It wasn't the friction or the burn. It wasn't her focus, the blindfold or the knowledge that Jay had to be watching, his breathing harsh and rapid off to her right. It wasn't Henry's powerful thrusts, delightful as they were. Nor even the knowledge that he had to be at the edge of his own control and she the one who'd brought him there with her willing submission.

No. Wrung out as she was after the night's games, her exhausted, shaking body grateful for the supporting bench holding her up . . . no. None of those things alone would've been enough to give her body the energy it needed.

It was Henry, hips still snapping hard against hers, curving his body over her. Possessive. Protective. The fucking was animalistic, but the feeling was indescribable. Outside her sexual experience with anyone but him.

He laid his head atop her back, his skin warm, his hair soft. He pressed his cheek to her spine, his breath hot and fast across her skin. He turned his face. Kissing. Kissing her back. The lightest brush of his mouth, again and again, between puffs of breath, and each kiss a burning brand that ignited under her skin.

Flash point. Combustion. Her body burning to a cinder beneath his, her scream silent. Her victory complete when Henry thrust hard and groaned, the bench lurching beneath them.

Her eyes flooded, and she was grateful beyond words for the silk tie covering them. How could she ever explain why she was crying as she came, what this feeling was that burned through her, when she couldn't understand it herself?

She lay across the bench, trembling, with Henry snug against her back. His right hand caressed her arm from shoulder to wrist and rubbed her fingers.

He whispered in her ear. "It's all right, dearest. A bit of exhaustion, hmm? I've pushed you hard tonight, sweet girl, and you've responded beautifully."

She made a quiet humming moan, a sound of agreement, of happiness at his praise of her, as she tried to blink away the tears.

Henry kissed her cheek below the edge of the blindfold. If he tasted salt, he didn't mention it. "Happy birthday, my lovely Alice."

She mumbled, her voice thick. "Thank you, Henry." She didn't add that it was quite possibly the best birthday celebration she'd ever had, though it was. Or that he was the best sex partner she'd ever had, though he was.

His fingers stroked back up her arm and across her shoulder, danced over her neck, and slid the silk tie from her eyes. She blinked, though his body shielded her from direct light.

Jay knelt beside the end of the bench. She could only hope if he noticed the tears, he thought them a reaction to the light. She blinked faster. Henry's index finger slipped down her nose and tapped the end.

"Much as I enjoy this, I expect we'll all find the bed more comfortable for the rest of the night." His hand dropped from her face and brushed her thighs as he pulled out.

She gave a hitching half sigh. He wrapped his arms around her waist and shoulders, lifting her from the bench and settling her on his lap as he leaned back on his heels. Like Jay. She and Henry were sharing a waiting pose.

She smirked and pressed her head against his shoulder. "I don't know, Henry. Your lap's awfully comfortable."

Jay laughed, and Henry chuckled.

"Yeah, Henry. Your lap's awfully comfortable." Jay's smirk matched hers. He'd come at some point, though she hadn't taken notice. His chest gleamed with it.

"A ringing endorsement from you both." Henry's voice was dry, but his arms squeezed her tight. "Come here, my boy. You've a kiss for me and one for Alice, don't you?"

He did. Jay's kisses were tender, and Henry sent him off to the bathroom to clean up and fetch a washcloth. Henry lifted Alice to the bed, setting her on the edge and tipping her face up toward his own. He swept his thumbs beneath her eyes, from the inner corners to the outer.

His voice dropped to a gentle whisper. "My sweet girl, tell me truly now, are you well?"

He'd sent Jay off to give her privacy. She swallowed hard, nodding. "I am, Henry. I—it was—I don't know how to describe it."

Henry kissed her forehead. "Shhh. That's all right. There's no need, dearest. Such things can be overpowering, hmm? And difficult to understand. You needn't worry yourself, Alice. It'll come to you." His fingers combed through her hair. "It'll come."

He stripped off the condom and discarded it. Bathed her and himself when Jay, his chest clean, returned with the washcloth. Rubbed soothing cream into her backside.

She struggled to keep her eyes open. A comfort and a pleasure, Henry's care further relaxed her. She snuggled into the sheets, the heated handprints on her ass not enough to stave off sleep when she was so exhausted. She didn't bat an eye when Henry and Jay slid under the sheets beside her. Even the shifting movement as Henry pulled her onto his chest couldn't draw more than a muffled grunt of agreement from her.

"Thank you, Henry." Jay's hushed voice flowed past her ear. He had to be tucked into Henry's shoulder.

"You're welcome, dear boy. You performed wonderfully tonight, Jay."

A happy hum. Jay's. "I could thank you more . . . personally."

Her lips twitched in a smile. *Thanks, Jay. I know what I'll see in my dreams tonight.*

"In the morning, my boy. We might enjoy Alice's boneless contentment a while longer, hmm?"

"Do you think she—"

"I think she's not quite asleep yet, Jay. Perhaps we ought to be quiet and allow her that pleasure."

"I think we could be shouting right now and she'd still get there. You wiped her out, and she loved it."

"Mmm." Henry's whisper was the last sound that reached her ears. "One can only hope so."

Chapter 11

When Alice closed her apartment door behind her and checked her messages on a Saturday morning in early December, she found she'd missed one. A text from her sister reading *Noon yr tm.*

Fuck. Less than five minutes away. She'd lingered too long at Henry and Jay's. Or not long enough, because if Henry had demanded she spend the whole day, she wouldn't have been able to say no. Then she wouldn't be facing her sister still keyed up from the morning and unshowered. She booted up her laptop, and the chime alerted her to an incoming call the instant she opened the program.

She sat at the table and accepted the call.

"Allie!" Eating a bowl of cereal, Olivia wore a t-shirt and pajama bottoms, her legs curled up in front of her. Twenty-five now, and aside from the partly completed medical degree, pretty much the same as she'd been at eleven. "I wasn't sure the time would work for you. You didn't answer my text. Something I should know about?"

She'd loaded her voice with insinuation, an impression spoiled by the milk spilling over the side of her spoon. "Damn. I need to work in a laundry day. This intern schedule is killing me."

"Hi, Ollie. They're keeping you busy?" *Yes, good, let's talk about you instead of me, and then you won't ask—*

"What's that you're wearing, Allie? It looks rumpled."

She concealed her moment of panic. She hadn't told her sister about Henry and Jay—and she told Ollie everything.

"You should work in a laundry day, too. We could keep each other company while we do laundry on opposite sides of the country."

Oh thank God. She wasn't about to be called out for wearing last night's clothes.

"I'll need the company if I want to stay awake long enough to do it anyway. Double shift, overnight. But I got to suit up and help on a gallbladder removal."

"Sounds disgusting." Alice wrinkled her nose and stuck out her tongue. "And messy."

"It's pretty clean, actually. We doctors do know what we're doing." Olivia teased with a hint of pride. "You look kind of dirty, though. What's that on your neck? Is that a *hickey*?"

She looked down, though seeing her neck that way was impossible. She'd have been better off looking at her tiny image in the corner of the screen. At least then Olivia wouldn't have crowed about it.

"I knew it. You have a boyfriend!" The cereal bowl tipped toward the camera, milk flirting with freedom, as Olivia leaned forward and stared into the lens. "You've been getting sex on a regular basis. Tell me everything."

"Nothing to tell, Ollie."

"Oh, right, sure, 'nothing to tell' my ass. This from the woman who told me all about her sexual experiences to keep me from sleeping with scruffy-but-totally-hot Jimmy Wiebersick senior year."

She'd known she'd live to regret being so open with her then-seventeen-year-old sister. Getting across the point that masturbating would be safer and better than fooling around with an inexperienced boy in the back of his dad's pickup after homecoming had seemed of vital importance at the time. She'd donned her cloak of college experience, which at the ripe old age of twenty had consisted of two guys in two years, and given her sister a vivid, humorous description of her first time.

"Now, Alice, I want you to know you can come to me with any questions you have."

She closed her eyes and tipped her head back. Her baby sister's revenge. Ollie even had her tone down, the delivery the same as hers had been years ago. How long had she been waiting for this one? And would it ever end?

"You're being careful, aren't you? Because you don't want to end up with a baby while you're still—"

"Oh, for crying out loud, Ollie. Yes, I'm using birth control, and they're—*he's*—using protection. I'm not going to make you an aunt."

Alice looked at the screen and wished she hadn't.

"You just said *they*. As in, more than one."

"I said he."

"Nuh-uh, no way, you aren't backtracking now. How many guys are you dating? Do they know about each other?"

"My God, what kind of person do you think I am? I'm not sleeping around behind some guy's back."

"Hey, five minutes ago I would've said you weren't the kind of person to be sleeping with anyone, based on the lame guys you pick. Unless you're trying to hide that you have a *girl*friend." Olivia crunched down on a bite of cereal. "Is that it? Because it's totally fine if you do."

"So I'm either some conniving bitch with a guy on the side or a secret lesbian? Those are my choices?"

"Unless you're in some kinky three-way arrangement, but—"

Fair skin was a curse. A gods-be-damned curse coloring her face right now.

"Oh. My. God. You are. You're having fabulous sex with two guys. I've got to meet the men who got my sister to relax and enjoy herself in bed."

"Not happening."

"C'mon. You gotta give me something. I'm so dead tired from working so many shifts I don't even have time to look at a hot guy and imagine the possibilities. Tell me about them, at least. Out of bed. How did you meet?"

"They . . . live across the hall."

"Wait. Wait. You're having sex with smoldering art guy and flirty bike boy? When did this happen? Where did they take you?"

On the dining room table was on the tip of her tongue. *Don't say that. Whatever you say, don't say that.*

"Where—uh, what?"

"On your first date."

"Our first . . . umm . . . right. Uh, Henry made us dinner. At their place."

"Sounds romantic. And?"

"And what?"

"What's it like? Dating two guys. Do you go on separate dates? Do you all three go on dates together? Do you like one better? Jeez, it's like pulling teeth here. You're never this closed off about guys."

"It's not . . . we don't . . . look, Ollie, let it go, okay?"

"No way. Not now. Are you all right? Allie? Are they . . . is this re-lationship . . . I mean . . . you're in it because you want to be, right?" Olivia set her cereal bowl aside and pulled her computer into her lap. The screen adjusted. The camera showed her little sister's face dis-turbingly close, as if they sat in the same kitchen instead of three thousand miles apart. "Talk to me, Allie."

Alice sighed. Her fingers rubbed the tabletop. Almost five months. Longer than she'd expected to be able to avoid talking to her sister about this . . . thing.

"It's not a relationship. We don't go out."

"Okaaay . . ." Olivia raised her eyebrows.

"It's a . . . I agreed . . . umm . . . we're sort of trying—"

"Is this some gayboy hetero exploration? Are you a guinea pig?" Olivia made a face. "Sorry, bad image. But you know what I mean."

"No. I don't think so. Maybe. I don't know." She pulled her legs to her chest, feet resting on the edge of the chair, arms curling around her knees. "I think maybe Jay—"

"Bike boy?"

"Yeah. He dates women sometimes. At first I thought he badgered Henry into it or something, because I didn't think Henry was into women. Whatever." She shrugged, forcing herself to smile. "It's not like they're my boyfriends or anything. It's just sex. Really good sex."

"How good could it be if the one isn't even into women? No of-fense, Allie. It's just you don't have a history of stellar picks."

"No, he's into women, I guess. Maybe not totally, okay, I don't know. But he *is* totally into being in control. And it's fantastic. Tie-me-up-and-spank-me fantastic."

"You're being serious." Olivia stared as if Alice were something new and different and not the sister she'd known her entire life. "You let this guy tie you up and hit you."

There was some sort of satisfaction in shocking her little sister.

"Not always," she said, her voice as bland as she could make it. "Sometimes he blindfolds me and does whatever he likes. It's in the contract."

"Contract? Is he paying you for sex? Jesus, Allie, what the hell have you been doing?"

"What he wants me to." Holding back her smile was a challenge. Olivia deserved this. Pushy little sisters needed a reminder sometimes that they were still the *little* sister. "And no, he's not paying for it."

"It sounds like this guy's forcing you to do things—"

"No." Her amusement fled. Torturing her sister was all well and good, but letting her think the worst of Henry was wrong. "That's not true."

Henry hadn't forced her to do anything. He'd enticed her, yes. Excited her. Encouraged her. Explored things she would've never tried on her own. But he'd done it by showing her she wanted to do those things. He'd painted pictures with his words and baited the hook with Jay and himself. She hadn't been coerced, and she sure as shit hadn't been forced.

"You're just letting him do what he wants?

Doing whatever he tells you to? Like a slave or something."

"It's not like that. The things he tells me to do are things I want to do. If I don't, I can say so, and he'll stop." She hadn't tested that, but she believed without proof. Henry hadn't hit her limits. More territory ripe for exploration lay ahead.

"I swear, Ollie, I'm perfectly safe. Probably the safest and happiest I've ever been. I'm just exploring stuff. And so are they. And eventually they'll get tired of it, or I will, and we'll go our separate ways." Not something she wanted to think about.

She let Olivia interrogate her for an hour before her baby sister seemed satisfied she wasn't being used or abused. And then she interrogated Ollie about her internship, whether her surgical rotation

214 • *M.Q. Barber*

was turning out the way she'd hoped, if she still thought it was the specialty she wanted, and if she was eating enough and getting enough sleep.

"This is my punishment for asking you so many questions, isn't it?"

She laughed, and agreed it was, and the conversation wound down with promises to talk again soon. Once her sister's face had faded from the screen, Alice stepped into a long-delayed shower. The steam heightened the mingled scents of Henry and Jay, the leather and citrus and mossy evergreen musk, on her skin until she washed them away.

She wasn't doing anything wrong by putting her sex life in Henry's hands. He was a creative, adventurous lover. Dominant, not lover, she corrected. She enjoyed their time together. She wasn't guilty about finding unconventional sexual fulfillment, and she wasn't worried about her physical safety.

Henry was meticulous about respecting limits and ensuring he didn't hurt her beyond what she wanted and could handle. If she had some emotional pain, it was no worse than any relationship where one partner wanted greater commitment and the other didn't. And that was practically every relationship.

At least she had the benefit of knowing there was no hope. Henry and Jay had each other. No matter how fun she was in bed, she'd never take either's place in the relationship.

But Ollie might be right about the other thing she'd said near the end of their talk. Maybe Alice did need to look for a more permanent relationship, one where she wasn't the third wheel. She could be more open to that.

Ugh. Sitting at a bar for hours? Trying to make a meaningful connection with a stranger when she already had two friends who knew her well and found her compatible in bed?

I'll think about it, Ollie. But no promises.

Alice had almost talked herself into attending the office Christmas party and trying to make a new friend when one of Henry's short notes appeared on her door Thursday. Not Friday. Not even a contract week at all. Something non-sex-related? A friendship thing? If it was, it would be the first since August.

Jay had kept up their Tuesday lunches, but she hadn't spent time with Henry outside of contract nights in months. Not unless she counted running into him on her way out the door in the morning. She missed their casual talks, learning from him, making him laugh. Nothing she *needed*, but something she wanted. If he wanted it too, he'd have said something, wouldn't he?

Asking him to spend time with her now would've been like stealing time from Jay. Jay, who'd already been so sweet about sharing Henry's bed with her.

She curled up in her everything chair. One of Henry's pieces from basement storage, so named because it was the only chair in her apartment aside from the two with the little table she called her kitchen. The chair where she sat to read or listen to music or just relax. Everything.

The dark leather upholstery on a high back supported her head, and the deep seat made ample room for her legs. Broad, flat, wooden arms as dark as the leather proved perfect for stacking books or balancing a laptop. The chair better suited to a den cradled her in warmth and surrounded her with the faint smell of leather. The perfect place to read Henry's note.

She laughed at the contents. He requested the honor of her presence at Sunday brunch, to be served in his apartment promptly at eleven thirty. Responses were to be regrets only, which meant he assumed she'd be attending. He wanted her default answer to be yes. How encouraging. She forgot all about scoping out potential date prospects at the cross-department Christmas party Friday and declined invitations to the various after-parties. Sunday brunch couldn't arrive fast enough to suit her.

Jay threw open the door with a grin. She'd arrived a few minutes early, but he didn't seem to care. Pulling her in by the hand, he shouted over his shoulder as he closed the door. "Hennn-ry! Your brunch date's here."

Date? He meant that casually, didn't he? She stomped on the thrill the word invoked.

A gentle shove earned her a faux-wounded look and a teasing rub at his shoulder. A second got her pouty Jay-lips and dancing fingers threatening to tickle.

The temptation too much, she dove into playing shoving match, though her pushes couldn't budge Jay's wide-legged stance. Dodging his attacks on her ribs, she caught a glimpse of Henry in the dining room, carrying a platter heaped high with what might be crepes or wraps or one of his crazy culinary experiments with some foreign-sounding name.

"Good morning, Alice. Do forgive Jay." Henry set the plate on the overloaded dining room table. "He's been particularly obnoxious thus far today, and he seems to find shouting necessary despite the scant distance between us."

"He's only been obnoxious today?" she teased, wandering over to the table. "Has he been on a vacation from it every other day?"

"I'm afraid I must have forgotten to slip the sedatives into his food today." Henry winked at her.

"Cute, very cute, you guys." Jay snatched a piece of bacon and fit the entire thing in his mouth at once, chewing and swallowing with rapacious hunger. "You should be nicer, what with me getting out of your hair for hours."

"You're leaving?" If brunch was just her and Henry, that explained Jay's warm leggings and long-sleeved thermal top. Biking gear.

"Yup. I got to eat my breakfast before the grown-ups." He stuck out his tongue. "I'm planning a long ride. Really long. A long, hard ride. For hours. You should try it sometime."

Jay's smirk made her wonder if Henry had planned the same for her. Without the bike. Was brunch a prelude to sex? Maybe she wasn't about to have a chance to sit and enjoy his company. Maybe everything between them had to be about sex now.

"Honestly, Jay." Henry's voice. Disapproving. "If you've finished your plate, take it to the sink, please."

"Sorry, Henry." Jay didn't sound contrite, but he cleared his place setting. "I just thought Alice should know she could try out fun activities. After brunch. Or whenever she wanted. It was only a ... um ... helpful suggestion."

"Mind your suggestions don't land you in trouble, my boy." Henry gestured toward the dining room. "Alice, please, have a seat. I recommend the crepes. Fresh fruit and toppings are on the table. Would you care for juice or coffee?"

"Juice, please." She sat and helped herself, more nervous than she'd been when she'd knocked. A sense of expectation rose in her, an uncertainty about the purpose for this meal.

"Okay, I'm going before the boring grown-up talk starts." Jay swooped in and planted a kiss on Alice's cheek, whispering, "Have fun" in her ear before he removed his bike from its wall hooks and headed out the door. "See you in hours. Lots of hours."

She stared at her plate and toyed with her fork when Henry brought the carafe of juice to the table and filled her glass. And while he seated himself and laid his napkin across his lap and made his selections. He cut a piece from his crepe. He'd put blueberries and maple syrup on his. She'd topped hers with strawberries and whipped cream. His fork settled back to his plate with a *clink*, the bite of crepe uneaten.

"Jay's insinuations aside, my dear, I would very much enjoy having a pleasant Sunday brunch with you. There is no obligation or expectation for anything more. I've a matter I wish to discuss with you. Perhaps I ought to broach it now, before your anxiety becomes unmanageable, but I won't do so when you cannot even look at me, Alice."

She remembered Jay's words, wrapped a gag around her nerves and raised her head to meet Henry's gentle smile. She smiled back. "Boring grown-up talk?"

"Precisely that." He picked up his fork and pointed at her plate. "Can I persuade you to relax and at least try your brunch first?"

She tried a bite of crepe with strawberries and whipped cream. Light, fluffy, delicious, with a creamy lemon filling that sharpened the berries' sweetness. As if she'd expected anything less from Henry's kitchen. Cooking was a science for her, and a rare one at that. Follow the recipe, measure twice and add once, get the same result every time. It must be an art for Henry, though. Flavor and color and texture balanced on his whims. She swallowed and sipped her juice. Pineapple-orange, the sweetness cutting the acidity, but tart enough to match the balance of the crepes.

"Well. I'd heard amazing things about the crepes. The server recommended them to me personally." She glanced at Henry. His smile seemed to hold back a chuckle, and his attention stayed fixed on her face. "So of course I expected the praise would be overblown. They couldn't possibly live up to that reputation. But . . ."

She cut another bite and swirled the fork in the whipped cream. "As it turns out, they're even better."

"Indeed? I'll have to verify it for myself, I suppose."

They ate in a much more comfortable silence as she allowed herself to relax. Henry offered her a bite of his blueberry-and-maple concoction, feeding her from his own fork. She agreed the taste mimicked a slice of blueberry pie wrapped in a short stack. He educated her on the blueberries. Organic, handpicked in Maine, frozen for freshness.

She tried not to moon over him like a teenager with a crush.

This was the Henry she'd been missing, the friend who inquired about her work and asked after her sister. The one who confided he was making significant progress on a project he'd started a few months earlier and that he hoped to put together a show in the spring.

He was vague about the subject matter, but then Henry rarely discussed his art. The door to his studio was always closed. Even Jay professed to never have seen works in progress, only the finished pieces at Henry's shows or the ones hanging on the apartment walls.

Eventually the talk came back to Henry's purpose for inviting her. Which, as it turned out, was sex-related, but not in the way she'd thought.

"I do apologize, Alice. We simply won't be able to stay in the city Friday night owing to family obligations for the Christmas holiday."

"No, I get it, that's not a problem." Henry and Jay had family nearby, and they probably juggled schedules to make the holiday work for both of them. It wasn't their fault Christmas would interrupt her contract schedule. She wouldn't expect them to bring her home to meet their families.

God, what would that conversation look like? *Hi Mom, hi Dad, meet Alice, the girl we fuck sometimes. She's staying for Christmas.* Yeah, that would go over great.

"You guys should spend Christmas with your families. Do you split it? Or alternate holidays or something?"

"Split it or alternate holidays, my dear?"

"Christmas Eve with one family and Christmas Day with the other? Or Thanksgiving with Jay's family and Christmas with yours?" It wasn't something she'd done, but childhood friends with divorced parents had been overjoyed to celebrate twice with adults who doled out extra presents to ease their guilt. One of her coworkers had spent the entire company Christmas party complaining that this year they'd spend Christmas with his in-laws.

"Ah. No." Henry's face showed surprise, and he shook his head. "I'm afraid I've given the wrong impression. Jay will be leaving Wednesday. It's a busy season for his family's tree farm, and he'll give them a hand right up through Christmas Eve before they enjoy their own celebrations. I'll be leaving Friday morning for my mother's home. This time of year is difficult for her, and I expect to stay a week or more."

"Oh. I'm sorry. I just assumed. So you don't . . ." If a polite way to ask existed, her tongue couldn't find it. She rubbed the tablecloth with nervous agitation. Henry squeezed her hand.

"Jay's family doesn't know. To them, we're no more than roommates." He said it quite matter of fact, as if it didn't bother him. Maybe Jay had always dated women to hide his relationship with Henry from his relatives. "Although my mother knows and approves, her health can be fragile. Jay's presence might be too boisterous for her to handle at this time of year. My brother's children will be plenty."

Henry paused, squeezing her hand once more before he let her go. "Perhaps next year, if Jay's family can spare him and I'm able to provide him with a steadying influence to keep him suitably entertained."

Well, that was mysterious. And none of her business. It wasn't like she'd shared her family dramas, either. "I'm sorry you can't spend the holidays together this year. And I hope your mother's health improves."

"It's an old pain." Henry half smiled, a resigned flicker that told her his mother's health was unlikely to improve at this late date. "But I asked you to brunch to talk about your needs, my dear, not to tell old and uninteresting tales."

"My needs?" He'd told her their Friday night was off. What else was there to say?

"Of course. My time and attention are yours. If you desire an alternate date, either decided upon in advance or spontaneous when the need arises, I will happily accommodate you. The disruption to our schedule is not your fault, nor should you suffer for it."

All of which was a very polite, very Henry way of saying if she was such a selfish child that she couldn't wait for her next contract night, he'd handle the interruption with grace and never mention whatever he'd had to set aside to deal with her neediness. Henry had probably told Jay to make himself scarce in case she pitched a fit or demanded compensation now.

"We're both adults, Henry. I think I can manage to wait. I was never the kid tiptoeing downstairs at two in the morning to see if Santa had left me a present yet anyway."

"No, I don't expect you were. That would have been Jay, no doubt, if he didn't refuse to go to bed altogether and fall asleep waiting beneath the tree." Henry gathered his silverware on his plate and stood. "Nevertheless, the offer stands. If, at any point between this moment and Friday morning, you change your mind, you will be entirely welcome here."

She followed suit with her own dishes, and the two of them worked together to clear the table and set the kitchen to rights. The comfortable domesticity seemed almost better than sex.

Fuck, she'd lost her mind if wrapping up leftovers was better than sex.

At well past one in the afternoon, with nothing she needed and no excuse to stay, she lingered at the breakfast bar. Henry placed the last dishes in the dishwasher.

"I should probably . . ." She had no ready excuse. She'd done her laundry Friday night, as she did on the Fridays when she wasn't with Henry and Jay, and she had no errands to run. "Let you get back to your . . . uh . . . stuff."

"If you wish, Alice, of course." The mildness of his voice could've hidden anything. Amusement. Irritation. But he was speculative, thoughtful, as he continued. "I don't have particular plans for the day, but perhaps you'd care to join me for an afternoon at the museum? The MFA recently opened an exhibit with architectural pieces that I believe you'd enjoy."

An outing with no strings, no sex, no expectations? Hell yes. She could hardly keep her feet still. "Sounds great."

"Wonderful. Fetch your coat, my dear, and we'll be off."

They spent the better part of three hours exploring halls and sharing thoughts. He never failed to ask her opinion on anything she studied for more than sixty seconds, and he offered insights of his own that sometimes matched hers and other times challenged them. It was a stimulating afternoon, despite, or maybe because, they shared only the briefest of touches. A tap on his arm or a light hand on her back as they called each other's attention to the displays.

When they returned to their building, Henry insisted she come in for dinner. So she found herself enjoying leftover breakfast-for-dinner with Henry and Jay. He'd been waiting for them, full of curiosity and clearly restraining himself from asking how they'd spent the afternoon. She couldn't help herself; she asked about his day.

Jay described the meandering path he'd followed around the city, taking advantage of the unseasonably sunny day. "It was a great workout. Supersatisfying."

"I had a great workout, too. I can't believe how sore my legs are. I guess I was having so much fun that I was too distracted to notice." *Poker face, Alice. Don't crack a smile now.*

Henry chimed in. "Yes, it was quite a stimulating day. An excellent workout."

Jay looked between them, back and forth, his face growing suspicious. "You're putting me on. You weren't here. I was waiting almost an hour for you to get home. And I know you weren't getting a workout in public."

"Oh, no, it was all public." She shrugged. "You know how it is. Sometimes you want something so bad you can't wait."

"It doesn't hurt to occasionally indulge one's desires," Henry added. "And even public spaces may feel private when one is in pleasant company."

"So you really . . ." Jay zeroed in on Alice's face, and she lowered her eyelids, feigning embarrassment. "Really? I want details. Can I have details, Henry, please?"

He sounded so eager, so puppylike, so excited and unenvious, that she almost felt bad laughing.

"We went to the museum, you oversexed goof. And there was no hanky-panky."

"Oh." Jay gave an exaggerated sigh. "I should've known you two would find stimulation in all the wrong places."

They finished dinner together, the three of them, talking about whatever came to mind, and Jay insisted she stay and watch a movie. Because, as he'd put it, it was unfair that Henry had gotten to monopolize her time all afternoon and Jay himself wouldn't have her attention again until after the holidays. An exaggeration, because she knew he'd text her Tuesday to meet for lunch. But she'd stayed anyway.

Sunday had neared perfection. Except, of course, that she slid into bed alone. But there was nothing unusual about that.

The week moved quickly. Jay wished her a merry Christmas at their Tuesday lunch. Henry left a card on her door Thursday wishing the same. Temptation begged her to knock on his door, but . . . no. She wasn't that needy.

She called her parents on Christmas and managed to catch Olivia during a brief break. Her sister had opted to work on the holiday, since neither of them had made it home to South Dakota this year. The day crawled by, and the week, too, and she celebrated New Year's alone in her apartment. She hadn't seen her boys in more than a week. She hadn't seen them naked in more than three weeks.

Four days. It's only four more days.

Henry and Jay weren't even back yet. She could wait until Friday. She could. But God, it felt like forever.

Chapter 12

Henry was trying to kill them. All three of them.

Four weeks since they'd been in bed together. When Alice entered the apartment at seven, even a hard look from Henry would've been enough to make her come.

Jay had opened the door, a familiar occurrence. But after closing the door he enveloped her in a hug, an entirely *un*familiar occurrence.

He was hard against her stomach, his erection unmistakable despite the clothing between them. His hands roamed her back. He turned his face into her hair and inhaled, his body shuddering against hers. She peered over his shoulder.

Henry was watching. "Sixty seconds, Jay."

She'd missed Henry's voice.

Jay dropped his arms and stepped away, breathing hard and watching her with undisguised lust.

"You were very close, weren't you, Jay?"

"Yes, Henry."

"Because your need for Alice after four weeks of waiting is so great." Though Henry moved up behind Jay as he spoke, he didn't touch the younger man. His eyes stayed locked with hers. Something flickered in them before he controlled it. "I understand the impulse, my boy."

He paused a moment, still staring, and touched Jay's arm. "You'll have your reward, Jay. Go to the bedroom, undress and wait for me on the bed. No touching yet."

"Yes, Henry." Jay beamed at Alice and left the room.

She doubted his reward would be an A+ and a sticker to put on the fridge, but his infectiously buoyant and proud attitude made avoiding the mental image impossible. She wanted to share with Henry, to be amused together that Jay deserved praise for not coming in his pants in under a minute.

But Henry's intense stare hadn't wavered. He stepped closer. Jesus. She might fail a similar test before he even touched her.

He leaned in. She swayed toward him, but still his body didn't touch hers. His breath puffed against her ear. She shivered. Her nipples had hardened, and the pulse between her legs reminded her of the emptiness waiting for him to fill it. *If he told me to come, right now, I think I could do it.*

"Go to the bedroom, Alice. Stand at the foot of the bed. Do not undress." He stepped back from her body, his face composed. "Go."

She sucked in a breath and hurried down the hall. Henry was very much in control tonight. On edge, but in control of it. The thought melted her anxiety and heightened her arousal. An amazing night would help her forget all the nights she'd spent alone. He'd make certain she got one.

Entering the bedroom, she positioned herself as Henry had directed. She fixed her gaze on Jay, who'd sprawled naked with his back propped against the pillows. He clutched restlessly at the sheets. His erection stood tall between his hips. Her tongue flicked against her lips, and he groaned.

Their heads turned as one when Henry entered.

"Such perfect attentiveness," he murmured. "Could it be that my lovelies are eager to begin?"

He didn't seem to require an answer. Following Jay's lead, she remained silent.

Henry came to stand behind her. He led her through the familiar questions, ensuring she knew her safeword and understood she could use it at any time.

Sliding his hands around her waist, Henry clasped her in front of him, allowing her to feel his erection. He stroked upward, over her dress, the one she'd chosen to meet the requirement in his note for a button front. A summer dress. In January. Deep blue cotton, calf-length, with wide shoulder straps, no sleeves and buttons from the square neckline down to the hem.

He swept his hands up and over her breasts, pausing to tease her nipples through the fabric with his thumbs.

"Tell me, Jay, in the last two weeks, did you think of Alice while you lay in your childhood bed with your parents down the hall?"

"Yes, Henry." Jay stared, nostrils flaring, chest rising with every breath as Henry slipped open the top button on her dress.

"Yes. Of course you did." Henry slipped a second button free. "And you took yourself in hand, didn't you?"

"Yes, Henry."

Three buttons, and Henry folded the fabric back to reveal her bra. Sky blue. From one of the matching sets he'd given her.

"Because thinking of Alice makes you hard, and being hard makes you ache to be inside her, doesn't it?"

Another affirmative answer. Jay's hands tightened on the sheets in rhythmic motion. Henry loosed another button. His fingers ran along the edge of her bra. He pulled the cups back until her breasts lay exposed and the fabric bunched around them, pushing them together.

"Show me how you touched yourself, Jay."

More buttons, laying her stomach bare, until Henry's hands hovered at the edge of her underwear.

Jay grasped his cock with his right hand and started slow and loose, as though he feared he might come on the spot if he risked a tighter grip.

Henry's right hand, splayed across Alice's stomach, mimicked the movements. His fingers slid beneath her panties and stroked her clitoris. She shivered.

His left hand gave her left nipple the same treatment, and she whimpered. Her hips pushed back, her ass rubbing against Henry's erection.

"I think Alice would prefer a heavier touch, my boy. I don't think she can feel you yet."

Jay tightened his grip, and Henry increased the pressure on Alice's clit. She writhed against his body as Jay watched. She watched him stroke his cock in return, fluid leaking from the tip and sliding down to coat his fist.

"You imagined how wet she would be, didn't you? How easy it would be to sink into her heat, to press her deep into the mattress beneath you and rock against her?"

"Yes." Jay gasped for breath. His hips thrust faster against his fist. "Yes, Henry."

Henry pushed a finger into her, down to the last knuckle, pulling back and adding a second as she pressed forward to meet him.

"She feels you now, Jay. She's soaking through her panties for you. Will you make her come? She wants to come with you."

Henry tweaked her nipple with his left hand, pinching it between forefinger and thumb. He repeated the motion while the thumb of his other hand rubbed against her clit and his fingers worked within her. She couldn't catch her breath. Her legs trembled.

Jay groaned again, a low sound ending on a frustrated whine.

"She's so close, Jay, her body swelling around you. Tight and hot, her hips rolling up to meet you. You have to be quiet, don't you? So quiet, because she's not to be in your room at all. Not to be under you in your bed, making you feel like a god as she whimpers in your ear and begs you to let her come."

Her desire built for the orgasm Henry held perched on the tips of his fingers.

"Please. Please . . ." Her voice mingled with Jay's, both of them desperate to fall.

"Come for me. Both of you. Now."

She shook, her body obedient to the command in Henry's tone. She gave what he demanded of her as Jay's orgasm spilled over his chest and stomach.

Wrapping his left arm around her waist, Henry kept her on her feet as she sagged. He pulled his fingers from her and hummed as he tasted her. His right arm clasped her across her shoulders.

"Well done," he murmured. "The two of you make a lovely duet."

Jay grinned, head lolling against the headboard.

"But we're not nearly done yet." Henry eased his hold on her. "Steady, my dear?"

She nodded, her head bumping his shoulder, though her legs trembled with echoing delight.

He kissed her cheek as he pushed the straps of her dress off her shoulders and allowed the garment to fall. Her bra followed. He pressed a second kiss to the base of her spine when he knelt to remove her underwear and the sandals she'd slipped on her feet to cross the hall. What seemed like hours ago but couldn't have been more than thirty minutes. Or just under fifteen, she amended, with a glance at the bedside clock. Jesus.

The orgasm had taken the edge off her need, but it waited within her, sparking with every touch of his skin against hers. He stood and pulled her hair aside to drop a third kiss on the side of her neck.

"Play with Jay for a moment, Alice." He patted her backside, making her giggle as she climbed onto the bed. "Ahh, there's a sound we've missed."

He stepped out of the room.

Jay smacked his palm against the bed beside him, and she settled next to him, laying her head on his shoulder. "Well, you didn't come in your pants."

"Nope, just all over myself." Jay nuzzled her hair. "Trust me, I've been doing a lot of that."

"And you'll have your reward for it, my boy." Henry returned bearing a washcloth and sat on the bed. Unlike the two of them, he was still fully clothed. His left hand tugged at Alice's right ankle. "Open for me, my dear."

She spread her legs, always happy to obey that command when it came in Henry's voice. He bathed her with tenderness, in long strokes, and performed the same service for Jay before he carried the washcloth out of the room.

"Fresh and clean and ready to go again." Jay waggled his eyebrows.

She flopped on the bed, laughing, and ran her hand along the in-

228 • M.Q. Barber

side of his calf muscle, up his right leg to the back of his knee. He wasn't quite ready to go again, but Henry's patient attention with the cloth had gotten him started.

"You hope."

"I know," Jay corrected. "Henry promised I'd get my reward."

"Maybe it's not what you think." Sexual, she assumed, but she stuck her tongue out at Jay anyway.

He laughed, his eyes fixed on her tongue. "He told me in advance. Incentive to be patient, he calls it. I dunno how or when, but I know what."

Now she was curious. Her fingers teased along Jay's thigh. "You gonna tell me?"

"You'll find out in a moment, Alice." Henry's voice came from the doorway. "As it happens, you'll have an important role to play."

He crossed the room to the special dresser, the one that held the toys for their games, where several items had been laid out on top. She sat up to see better.

Henry's body blocked her view, but the dresser was a brief stop for him. He came to the bed and sat with a fistful of green silk. Scarves. Bondage? They didn't look menacing, not when she'd already tried the wrist and ankle cuffs.

But Henry wasn't holding them out to her. He laid them across his lap, and he took Jay's right foot in his hands, massaging.

"I'm going to tie you, Jay."

Jay flinched despite Henry's soft tone, his foot twitching between Henry's hands.

"You've nothing to fear here, my boy. And you'll have your reward. But I want you to submit to this. I know your capabilities, Jay. Will you trust me?"

"I do trust you, Henry." Jay's voice trembled. "I'm just . . ."

"You've only to say your word and the games will stop. But you're my brave boy, and you'll have Alice here with you. You'll be able to see her. You simply won't be able to touch." Henry smiled, a coaxing, enticing curve of his mouth. "We can't have you rushing your own reward, can we?"

She played silent witness as Henry tied the first scarf around Jay's right ankle and pressed a kiss atop his foot. The floaty fabric wasn't long enough to fasten to anything, not the way he'd tied it. With the ends tucked inside, the scarf fit like nothing so much as a wide bracelet.

"It's not long enough." Jay's voice hovered between confusion and relief.

"It's exactly as long as it needs to be," Henry corrected. "You won't be tied down, my boy. Nothing will hold you but your own belief. Your promise to me that you will treat these scarves as though they restrained you utterly."

Jay nodded, his smile blindingly beautiful. "I can do that. I can do that, Henry."

"I know you can, my boy." He reached for Jay's left foot with the second scarf.

She was missing something, some key piece of information about Jay's past that would tell her why the idea of being tied made him skittish. Why Henry would want to push his limits with such gentleness. The panic on Jay's face the night Henry had first flogged her had been real. The "bad choices" he'd mentioned. He'd been with Henry for years, but what about before?

Because Henry would've never hurt him. Henry was trying to help him, clearly. And now she was, too. Tender affection flooded through her, a warm bath for her arousal.

Once Jay's wrists were tied as symbolically as his ankles, Henry positioned him against the headboard with arms spread wide along the top rail. Legs spread on the mattress. He commanded Jay to stay in place, reminding him the scarves bound him, and kissed him sweetly before rising.

Her gaze followed Henry to the dresser. She recognized the blindfold dangling from his fingers when he turned back, but not the fistful of dark brown leather and silver rings.

"I'm certain Alice won't mind waiting on your pleasure, my boy, as your need is obvious."

She glanced at Jay, who was more than half-hard again already. Whatever his reward, he was eager to receive it if he'd managed such a quick recovery. Henry had taken his time bathing her and Jay, sure, but biology was biology. She hadn't expected Jay would get another turn before Henry had even gotten off.

"Alice is quite a patient girl, isn't she?" Henry sat on the bed, facing her, watching her as he ostensibly spoke to Jay. "I'm sure she knows very well she ought to have come to me if her need was too pressing to wait. But waiting four weeks was no trouble for her, was it? So she won't mind waiting now. Will you, Alice?"

He had to be punishing her. Gently mocking her, because he knew damn well how strongly just his voice had affected her. She'd brought this on herself. Was it a control thing? Was that why Henry wanted her to admit how damn needy she'd been?

She couldn't blame Jay. He'd expected her to spend that Sunday in bed with Henry. He'd all but shoved them into bed himself. She didn't want to delay his reward. So she swallowed hard and shook her head. "No, Henry. I don't mind. I can wait."

"Self-sacrificing," he murmured. "A bit too willing to deny her own needs." His lips quirked in an odd smile.

She was tempted to verbalize her own mental response. *Says the man with the hard-on who brings us to climax but won't even take off his pants yet.* His smile grew. Shit, was he reading her mind?

"She puts you first, Jay. So you'll be allowed to come first. Alice will work very hard to make that happen."

Jay's seated position, his hips forward and his body reclined against the headboard, would make riding him easy. Was that what Henry had in mind?

"Because until it does, she won't be coming either."

A test. A challenge. How hard could it be? She could outlast Jay. A few Kegel contractions and he'd be over the edge in a heartbeat.

"Alice. You're familiar with Jay's waiting pose. Kneel for me, just like that, between his legs, please."

Between? Not straddling? She climbed over Jay's right leg and faced him. Sat on her calves, her legs folded beneath her, feet curved under her ass.

He gripped the headboard railing. His hips shifted. He liked being dominated or he wouldn't be with Henry, she supposed. The idea of her on top would excite him.

"Hold out your arms, Alice, straight in front of you, please."

Henry hadn't brought any more scarves to bed. But the leather . . .

She extended her arms, a tremor of excitement rolling through her. He wrapped the strange cuff around her left first, slipping straps through rings, tightening until leather encased her from wrist to elbow. He followed suit with her right arm.

Aesthetics, maybe? She twisted her arms to look. The lining inside of the cuffs wasn't rough or harsh. The outside was the glossy brown of a freshly oiled saddle. She stifled a giggle. Jay ought to have the leather and she the silks if she was playing jockey tonight.

Henry bent her arms toward her chest, bringing her hands under her chin. Metal closed with a snap. What?

She tried to turn her arms, to see what he'd done, but they wouldn't go far. She tugged harder. Metal clinked. He'd bound the cuffs to each other somehow. Her arms, from wrist to elbow, couldn't move more than two inches apart. She tugged again.

Henry closed his right hand over both of hers in a gentle squeeze.

"You know how to stop the game if you need to, my dear." He let go of her hands. "Do you need to?"

Did she? Jay was watching her almost as closely as Henry. Nothing to panic about. If Jay could play his part, she could play hers.

"No, Henry."

"Good. Wiggle your fingers for me, please."

She wiggled.

"And clap your hands."

She clapped, the sound soft as the cuffs limited her ability to part her hands.

"No numbness, tingling or discomfort, my dear?"

She shook her head. The position was a little awkward, and her balance would suffer for it, but it wasn't painful. "No, Henry."

"Thank you, Alice. If you find you need to stop and cannot say your word, I want you to clap your hands for me. Do you understand?"

"Yes, Henry." Easy enough to remember, although unless she ran out of breath or—oh.

Henry pulled her hair back and lowered the blindfold over her eyes.

She took a deep breath as her heart raced. She wouldn't be able to see, and she wouldn't be able to touch with any precision. Jay wouldn't be allowed to touch her, either. To keep him from trying to control her movements?

"Stay like this for a moment, Alice." Henry kissed her cheek.

The bed shifted. She strained to hear something, anything. Footsteps. The rustle of fabric. Undressing. Henry was undressing and . . . surveying the scene he'd created? Pacing around the bed?

A soft hum of approval came from somewhere behind her.

The bed shifted again, and she flinched as warm skin slid along the outside of her legs. She started to tip left. Couldn't catch herself. Other hands settled on her shoulders and righted her. Heat brushed her spine.

"It's time for Jay's reward, my girl. Make him come for you, and then I'll make you come for me, hmm?" Henry pressed his erection against her back. His thighs squeezed her own. "The nice, hard fucking you weren't missing two weeks ago, because there was nothing you *needed*."

A whimper left her throat. Henry's hands guided her down, until she knelt on her knees and forearms. One hand tipped her chin up. From Jay's gasp, she guessed where the other had gone. His cock touched her lips, all heat and velvety skin and Jay-musk.

"Open, Alice," Henry commanded her. "Taste."

Alice opened her mouth and took him inside. Jay moaned, long and low, as she slid her lips downward until they encountered resistance. Her tongue swiped a knuckle. Henry's hand, holding Jay's cock at the perfect angle for her mouth.

She hadn't done this before. Not given a blowjob, of course; that, she'd done dozens of times. But in the last five months, she'd done only what Henry had asked of her, and not once had he asked this. Not for himself and not for Jay.

She'd expected it months ago. Expected it would be one of the first demands. Blowjobs had always been high on the list of sexual favors demanded by previous lovers, and now she had two cocks to play with instead of one.

Jay must've been waiting patiently—or not so patiently—for months for this reward. So she kept her lips sealed around him, rolled her tongue in sweeping movements and alternated a deep, twisting slide with quick suction around the tip. She sped up with his quiet whimpers.

"Stop, Alice." Henry's voice.

She allowed Jay to slip from her mouth. He'd been close. A bit more and it would've been her turn.

She practically heard the smile on Henry's face. "Our Alice is very good, isn't she, Jay?"

"So good," he agreed, a slight rasp in his throat. "Really, really good."

"But you don't want to come for her that quickly, do you? And end your fun?"

"Don't want it to end."

"No. I didn't think you did." A pause before the tip of Jay's cock swept across her lips again. "Go ahead, Alice. I doubt Jay can manage more calm than this, given the delightful provocation."

Her mouth still met the edge of Henry's grip as she sank down. He must've staved off Jay's approaching orgasm with a quick squeeze. Hardly fair. She'd have to work extra hard to make him come so she could have her turn.

She applied herself to the task with enthusiasm. Got Jay nice and wet with her mouth. Blew air across him to make his hips buck. She teased the tip with her tongue and dropped suddenly, her mouth tugging at him on every return sweep. Her ears filled with the sound of his harsh breathing. The rasp of his inhalations and the soft groaning "uh" of his exhalations became a symphony, and she a musician trying to match the time signature.

Henry's hand moved away, allowing her to slide deeper. Not quite to the base. She wasn't so practiced as that. Maybe Jay would give her tips sometime. No laughing, she chided herself. Choking wouldn't have gone over well at all. But she had more than enough sensations to catalog to keep her from laughing.

Henry pulled her legs apart, disrupting her rhythm as his legs moved from around her own to between them. His hands smoothed over her back and down the outside of her thighs. His cock slid between her legs, bumping her clit.

She sucked in a surprised breath, and Jay's hips bucked under her.

Henry spoke. Casually, as if his hands weren't caressing her ass and his cock wasn't parting her labia. As if his hips weren't moving in slow circles against her, reminding her he was waiting for her to make Jay come.

She strained to hear his voice over her own breathing. Over the wet sounds of her mouth moving and Jay's panting moans.

"You've been waiting a long while for this, haven't you, Jay? To have Alice focused solely on your pleasure? It's all right, my boy. I know you haven't breath to answer just now.

"Alice will receive her own reward when she's finished pleasing you. My cock is ready for her, waiting to drive deep inside her, to fill her with pleasure. You know that pleasure, don't you, Jay? You crave the same fullness she does."

Henry's hands splayed across both sides of her ass, pushing them outward.

"So much potential, my dear boy. Think of all the games we haven't played yet with Alice." A single finger traveled a line down the center of her ass. Her body lunged forward, bunching up as his finger pressed against her, not seeking entry, but rubbing. Circling. Nervous energy made her tremble. Was he going to . . .

"She isn't ready for all of those games yet, Jay, but she will be. And when she is, when she wants it as badly as you want to come right now . . . we'll take her together, my boy. No one waiting. No one finishing alone. Both inside her heat, sharing, showing her how deeply satisfying it can be to feel so full."

Her thighs quaked. She needed Henry *now*. Not later, now. She nudged her elbows forward, a delicate dance of weight and balance well worth the effort. Stretching out her bound hands, she stroked her fingertips across the tightness of Jay's scrotum and down, pressing firmly as her lips dragged upward over his cock.

Jay came with a shout, his hips thrusting even as she pulled back to enclose just the tip of his cock, rapidly swallowing. His climax wasn't unmanageable. Was that why Henry had allowed them the quick orgasm earlier? To make this last longer for Jay and finish more easily for her? It was the sort of thing he'd think of.

Her thoughts scattered as a hand tugged her hair, for once lifting her away rather than trying to force her down. Jay's cock had no sooner fallen from her mouth than Henry plunged into her from behind. She was grateful for the cuffs around her arms keeping her stable when he set a punishing pace.

The hand in her hair moved to her stomach, holding her to him until her hips bucked and she matched his pace. His fingers dipped lower, teasing her clitoris, squeezing and rolling, rubbing and circling.

She startled as his other hand made the same motions against her ass, teasing and circling. The sensations aroused her equally when she shoved aside the voice in her head that said good girls wouldn't like it. *Fuck that. Who said I have to be a good girl?*

"I'll make certain you enjoy it, Alice," Henry whispered, his voice tight, strained. "You'll still be *my* good girl."

She dropped like a stone in a lake, drowning in the waves. Had she spoken, or had he just known? Did it matter?

His fingers still moved, and his cock still moved, and over the buzzing in her ears as her body vibrated against his, clenching around him, she caught stray words. Beautiful, and tight, and *fuck*, uttered low when her pleasure peaked again and she fell on her arms.

Her hips pistoned uncontrollably, driving her onto him until his hands held her hips as he gave three short, sharp thrusts and covered her body with his own, his chest sweaty and warm against her back.

She never wanted to move again. She let her head tip against Jay's thigh and relished the possessiveness and security of Henry's weight on her back.

She'd gossiped with girlfriends before, sharing general details of her sex life and getting theirs in return, and most had agreed being taken from behind lacked the intimacy they wanted. She hadn't spoken up, because sex had all been the same to her. Intimacy wasn't part of the equation. Fucking was fucking, whether they were panting in each other's faces or barely touching at all.

With Henry and Jay, she could define a difference, even if it wasn't the negative one her friends had harped on. Being face-to-face was a good feeling, sure. A little scary and intense the way Henry did it, with his eyes watching hers and so full of something indefinable, but good.

But having him behind her reminded her of their first night together every fucking time. Maybe it was a submissive pose, but it didn't feel submissive. Not even with her hands bound. It just felt right.

The blindfold tonight had heightened the intensity. Made her concentrate on Henry's voice, that low, teasing, intimate rumble. Sex with Henry was intimate no matter how he took her. She couldn't separate herself from the experience while she was having it. She wasn't imagining herself somewhere else with some*one* else.

A kiss to the top of her right shoulder had to be Henry. She whined when his weight left her back.

He rubbed circles over her spine as his cock slipped from her body. "Is this something you've been missing, my sweet girl?"

Was there any point in pretending? Four weeks had been too long. She needed more from them than that. And maybe Henry needed her to admit that.

He'd been the one to set the contract terms. He'd probably had some complex reason for choosing a two-week interval, and she'd gone and tried to wrest control back by not asking for a replacement night when he told her their regular Friday wouldn't work. She hadn't intended to, but she had. She should've trusted his greater knowledge and experience. Instead, she'd tried to show him she could be independent.

"Yes, Henry. I should have . . . four weeks was too long. I missed this."

The hand on her back paused. A soft sound came from Henry, impossible to place and soon swallowed by silence.

"Thank you, Alice." Hands pulled her upright and slipped the blindfold from her face. She blinked in the brightness, catching flashes of Jay watching her. Henry reached past her to stroke Jay's cheek. "I'm very proud of you both for being so brave and trusting tonight."

Henry unhooked the leather sleeves, allowing her to separate her arms. She wiggled her fingers without prompting.

Jay hadn't yet moved. He treated the scarves as if they restrained him in truth.

Henry placed a kiss above her ear. "Would you like to help me untie Jay, my dear?"

She agreed in an instant.

Henry raised Jay's left leg, drawing his foot closer and unwrapping the scarf. Her breasts neared Jay's face as she reached for his right hand along the top of the headboard. Following her motion, he rolled his head to rub his cheek against the side of her breast.

She lifted his arm and sat back on her heels. Held his hand in both of hers. She unwrapped the scarf where he could watch her work, letting it fall to her lap and kissing his wrist afterward. Remembered the sensation on her own skin in nights past. Jay's fingers tickled her chin, and she giggled.

Henry dropped a passing kiss on her back as he shifted behind her, turning to Jay's other side, and she let go of Jay's right hand to release his left. The metal rings on her leather cuffs danced as her arms moved. The scarf on Jay's left wrist was the last to come off. Her eyes closed as she kissed the bare wrist.

"It's all right, my boy. Come here, Jay."

She was crushed against Jay's chest as he launched himself forward, throwing his arms around her and Henry, too. His chin rested on her right shoulder.

"Thank you, Henry." Jay babbled in her ear, repeating his thanks with giddy joy.

She slipped her arms around his back and held on.

"My brave boy." Calm, confident Henry. His arms covered hers, a solid weight, a steadying presence as he hugged them both to him. "You played so well tonight, Jay. It's a joy to have Alice here again, isn't it?"

Jay nodded vigorously. "She's even better at rewards than I am at apologies."

Her laugh came out as a snort. "Don't sell yourself short. Your apologies are beautiful things."

Jay kissed her ear, but it was Henry who replied. "As are your myriad charms, my dear girl. You're quite correct. It's been entirely too long."

Did he just say he missed this, too?

"We'll take a moment to clean up and have a snack, and then we'll see if we can't manage to make the night even more enjoyable for our wayward girl."

"More enjoyable than that?" She wasn't remotely unsatisfied with Henry's performance or Jay's adorable appreciation. Did he think she was?

"Mmm." Henry's fingers interlaced with hers. "You surprised me tonight, Alice." His fingers clenched. "Squeezing me so tightly. Such a beautiful, rippling pull, coming so quickly for me. Jay and I would happily make you climax a dozen times to feel that pull, my dear girl."

She couldn't help the moan that escaped her throat at the thought. She knew why she'd come so easily for Henry tonight. She'd been waiting for it.

Not that she hadn't masturbated with thoughts of them in the last four weeks. She had, and enjoyed herself. But she hadn't reached for her vibe. Hadn't even slipped her fingers inside and thrust. She hadn't wanted her fingers or her vibrator. She'd wanted her boys inside her, their heat and motion, the feel of them so different from any substitute.

"Hold that thought, dearest, the one that makes you moan so prettily. Leisure time first."

She and Jay submitted to Henry's tender attention as he cleaned them both and unfastened the leather sleeves from her forearms.

They fetched the snack tray from the kitchen as he directed. She drooled over the chocolate cheesecake slices, thinking them store-bought until Jay confessed he'd been begging for a piece since the cake had gone in the refrigerator.

"Had to wait, though." Jay pouted, his lower lip drooping in exaggeration as he picked up the drink tray and she took the cheesecake and fruit. "Henry said he made it for all of us, so it wasn't fair to have any until you were here, too."

He sighed. "I offered to drag you out of your apartment last night so you could watch me eat cheesecake, but he said I couldn't bother you on a work night because you needed your sleep."

She laughed. "How selfless of you." Warmth flooded her chest. They'd been thinking of her the night before, anticipating tonight just as she had.

"I would've let you eat some, too. But c'mon. It's cheesecake. And it's *chocolate*." He danced into the bedroom ahead of her. "It's every submissive for themselves."

"And here I thought your mantra was share and share alike."

He grinned at her, walking backward. "Only in Henry's bed. And only with you."

She almost stumbled. He had to be teasing. She returned his goofy grin. "Good thing we're eating the cheesecake in Henry's bed, then."

"Only if the two of you manage to reach the bed, my dears." Henry sat propped against the headboard, the pillows behind him. "And I'm afraid you'll be sharing the cheesecake with me as well."

They set the trays on the nightstands and feasted, playfully feeding each other while Jay told her about his Christmas holiday. A jumble of names she'd never remember, but stories that made her laugh. Henry mentioned visiting his mother and his brother's family.

"And you, Alice? How have you passed the time, sweet girl?"

She finished a bite of chocolate cheesecake with caramel sauce before she answered. "Work. Stuff. The usual."

"You didn't go home for Christmas?" Jay's childish incredulity proved he couldn't understand the concept.

"Nope." It would've been too far, and too expensive, and too awkward, but she wasn't about to get into that discussion. "We talked on the phone. It was fine."

"But you went to some awesome New Year's parties, right?"

She wished she had a fantastic story to tell Jay. "I went to bed early, actually. How did your family celebrate?"

"You spent the holidays entirely alone, Alice?"

Shit. She wouldn't be able to distract Jay with questions about his family if Henry got involved.

"It wasn't a big deal. I'm used to it."

"You told me you had plans."

"I did. I talked to my parents and my sister."

The silence hung for a long moment, and it seemed even Jay knew better than to fill it.

"In the future, two phone calls will not count as 'plans' for a ten-day span of time. Had you better informed me of the situation, I would have made alternate arrangements."

Alternate arrangements? What did that mean? Henry wasn't in charge of her travel plans.

"Are you seriously mad at me? Because I didn't give you an itinerary for my holiday in advance?"

Henry stroked her cheek. "No, Alice. I am not angry with you. I am, however, disappointed in myself for not having more thoroughly interrogated you on the subject. You have an independent streak that occasionally makes it quite difficult for people to help you, my dear."

He slipped his arm behind her and coaxed her forward, until she lay snug against his chest. "I would not have had you spend so much time alone over the holidays. You ought to have been with those who care for you."

Fuck. She felt the tears waiting in her eyes. *Do not fucking cry.*

Henry's voice, soft but brooking no argument. "The dishes, Jay. In the sink, please."

The bed shifted, and dishes rattled on the trays. Silence, then, as Jay presumably left the room. She refused to pull her face from Henry's chest to look.

"Oh, Alice." One hand caressed her back with slow, circular motions. "My dear girl. I understand you are accustomed to handling things on your own. So perhaps it doesn't occur to you that you might simply *ask* for the things you need and have them provided. For tonight, at least, that decision is not yours."

His legs tangled with hers under the sheets, rubbing against her skin. "We'll have to see what we can do to make up for the lack of touch in your life these past few weeks, hmm?"

She nodded against his chest, forcing back the tears with an ungraceful sniffle. He held her closer.

"All will be well, dearest."

Jay crawled back into bed a few minutes later, and Henry thanked him and gave quiet instructions. Two warm bodies cradled her between them. Bodies whose hands stroked and mouths kissed until she found herself on her back with Henry moving slowly inside her, a belated but very welcome Christmas gift.

Alice might be submissive for Henry, but her dominant voice forced M. Q. Barber to tell her story. While writing "Neighborly Affection: Playing the Game," the author discovered two things: her husband boasts an unending store of patience, and her mother is impossible to faze. Ladies, keep this in mind—when your daughter says, "Mom, I wrote a book of erotica and it's getting published," the proper response is, "When can I read it?" (Thanks, Mom.) Keep up with MQB on Twitter @MQBarber. If she's quiet, give her a nudge. She's probably chained to her laptop, trying in vain to get Alice, Henry, and Jay to slow their chatter long enough for her to capture their words.